STAR TREK®
FIRST CONTACT™

STAR TREK®
FIRST CONTACT™

A novel by J.M. Dillard
based on the film
STAR TREK: FIRST CONTACT
Story by Rick Berman & Brannon Braga
& Ronald D. Moore
Screenplay by Brannon Braga & Ronald D. Moore

POCKET BOOKS
New York   London   Toronto   Sydney   Tokyo   Singapore

This book is a work of fiction. Names, characters, places and incidents are products of the author's imagination or are used fictitiously. Any resemblance to actual events or locales or persons, living or dead, is entirely coincidental.

POCKET BOOKS, a division of Simon & Schuster Inc.
1230 Avenue of the Americas, New York, NY 10020

STAR TREK is a Registered Trademark of Paramount Pictures.

A VIACOM COMPANY

This book is published by Pocket Books, a division of Simon & Schuster Inc., under exclusive license from Paramount Pictures.

ISBN: 0-671-00316-X

All photographs by Elliot Marks

Printed in the U.S.A.

For Doc Marcia

Acknowledgments

First and foremost, I am grateful to all those whose efforts went into the creation of both script and film, and to those who gave me the honor of novelizing the former, specifically:

John Ordover, *Star Trek* editor at Pocket Books and all-around cheerful and adorable guy (at least, so far as I can tell over the phone);

Paula Block, Viacom Consumer Products, the licensing division of Paramount Pictures, also a kind soul;

John Eaves, illustrator for *Star Trek: First Contact,* another nice guy, who graciously provided material that helped me flesh out the details;

And to Rick Berman, Brannon Braga, and Ronald D. Moore, who don't know me—but who, if I may say so, wrote a kick-butt movie that was pure pleasure to novelize.

STAR TREK®
FIRST CONTACT™

ONE

─────────── ☆ ───────────

Apathy—that was the greater evil, Picard knew, for an indifferent foe is more to be feared than one whose heart burns with honest hate. Apathy: it stretched out before him in infinite rows of face after flesh-and-metal face, body after motionless body, in a gray metal sea that knew no beauty, no artistry, no appreciation of life— only the singular voice of the collective.

He stood, the only living spot of color in a vast chamber, surrounded by thousands of cells. In each— on the walls, the ceiling, the deck—an upright Borg drone slept dreamlessly. The effect was that of a great hive; yet to compare this chaotic, thoughtless accretion of exposed conduits and circuitry to those handsome structures wrought by instinct and with care by insects seemed wrong. Insects might be mindless but not soulless; the Borg were both.

And it was that fact which made him struggle, helpless

though he was, against the flesh-and-metal arms that propelled him suddenly down surreal corridors, corridors lined with dulled, sleeping faces, their individuality obliterated by black sensor-scopes.

It was that fact which, when they pinned him down and slammed his head against the surgical table, made him cry out in darkest rage and frustration: rage that they should dare so to violate him; frustration that they saw his fury, saw his hatred . . . and simply did not care. *That* was the bitterest part—that his enemy could be so heartless, so cold that his violent hatred of them did not—could not—touch them.

And as he stared up at his approaching fate, in the form of a silvery, needle-sharp probe descending directly toward his eye, he thought, *This is a foe I can never engage, for they will never care enough to return my hate.*

Then followed a time of forgetfulness. He came to himself again back in the center of the hive, surrounded by slumbering drones who never witnessed his frantic struggle against the restraints that held him.

In the midst of his struggle, an image came to him: a mouth, bloodless and Borg.

And yet not Borg, for those pale lips curved in a smile, revealing teeth even whiter. They spoke—and he heard not the thunderous voice of the collective, but that of a woman, low and teasing:

Locutus . . .

A fresh image now: himself as Locutus, half of his face no longer his, no longer living flesh, but thrumming metal and circuitry. Half of his mind no longer his, but consumed by the collective and the detailed report from the blinking sensor-scope. And the half that remained the possession of Jean-Luc Picard was consumed by agony.

He shuddered at the sound of his own voice—the voice of the Borg.

I am Locutus of Borg. Resistance . . . is futile.

He closed his eyes at the horror of it, and when they opened, he found himself impossibly pinned fast to the surgical table at the very instant the probe pierced his eye.

He screamed, not so much with pain as with pure rage at the enemy who did not care enough to hate—and so could never be truly hurt.

Picard woke with a lurch to find himself sitting on his couch in the ready room; he put a hand to his sweat-damped forehead and rose at once, dismayed that he had dozed off while on duty and still alarmed by the intensity of the nightmare. Propelled by adrenaline, he hastened to the small adjacent restroom and leaned low over the sink. Instantly, cold water spilled into his cupped hands; he splashed it onto his face—again, again, again—washing away all traces of panic until his breathing slowed and he at last dared rise to face his mirrored reflection.

His image was, as he had known it would be, reassuringly human and free of the Borg's mechanical taint. Yet the dream itself disturbed him greatly; he had not had one in almost a year, and then it had not left him this shaken. Indeed, he had not had one this terrifying since the first horrific month following his existence as Locutus.

Locutus . . .

Abruptly, he recalled the image of the ghost-pale lips seductively uttering his Borg name. Try though he might, he could not remember the face attached to that mouth; he knew only that he had known her, and that the memory evoked a profound sense of horror, of revulsion . . . of attraction.

As he stared into the mirror, trying to conjure a face other than his own, a muscle just above his jaw spasmed. The event was sharply painful, as though someone had plunged a needle from the inside of his mouth outward through his cheek. More distressingly, it was accompanied by an odd chirping sound—that seemed to emanate from within Picard's own head.

Impossible, of course, that the chirp and the spasm were connected, or that the sound had come from inside his skull . . . yet a mere second afterward, he grimaced at a second surge of pain that left the muscle twitching—and a second chirp.

Tension, he knew; nothing but tension, brought on by the stress of the dream. It would pass, and if it did not, he would consult Beverly, and she would solve the problem with a prescription for more time in the holosuite or more intense exercise or perhaps even a brief shore leave.

It would pass. . . .

But as he stood over the sink, it did not. To his confusion, the pain intensified, and the muscle began to writhe continuously, accompanied by the persistent high-pitched sound; hoping to smooth the spasm away, he ran his hand over his cheek—to no avail.

When the last and sharpest burst of agony came, instinct instructed him to gaze up at the mirror, at his twitching cheek. He watched with dread, but not necessarily surprise; hadn't he always *known,* in the deepest recesses of his brain, which even Beverly's medical probes could not touch?

Hadn't he always known?

So he watched as the flesh of his cheek trembled, then stretched out, as if he were pressing hard from the inside with his tongue. It was not his own tongue, of course, but something much harder and longer, and it pushed until the skin and muscle could expand no more.

At last, the muscle tore and the skin burst; he stared in horrified fascination as darkly gleaming metal, slick with his own blood, emerged from within him.

A Borg servo. It rotated with a series of high-pitched chirps, while Picard descended into mindless panic. . . .

Picard awoke, gasping, on his own couch and thrust himself abruptly into a sitting position. To his fleeting dismay, the chirping continued unabated; he put a hand to his cheek to feel for the servo before realizing that he had awakened again from a nightmare—*truly* awakened now, for the feel of his palms against the couch and his arms beneath him were solid, real.

Yet he wished he were again asleep. As frightening as the dreams had been, they were simply that: dreams.

This was reality; and the horror of it was, he had awakened *knowing.*

The chirping, too, was real. And as he rose from the couch and moved to the terminal, he consciously slowed his breathing and composed himself before tapping a control. A message coalesced on the screen.

INCOMING TRANSMISSION. STARFLEET COMMAND TO CAPT. J. L. PICARD. USS *ENTERPRISE NCC 1701-E.* COMMAND AUTHORIZATION REQUIRED.

He cleared his throat and told the computer: "Authorization: Picard, four-seven-alpha-tango."

The image on the screen shifted fleetingly to the Starfleet chevron, pointing upward like an arrowhead aimed at the stars. It faded at once, replaced by the image of Admiral Hayes. Hayes was not quite so old as most of his peers at Fleet Headquarters; his hair had only recently begun to silver. But his demeanor was august, almost severe, his eyes framed by countless deep furrows, carved by the responsibilities of duty.

A line for each life lost under his command, Picard thought silently, then said aloud, "Admiral."

Hayes paused to study him. "Catch you at a bad time, Jean-Luc?" Under normal circumstances, his voice would have been infused with a casual warmth that his stern appearance belied. But these were not normal circumstances.

"No, of course not," Picard lied, realizing that it was not the residue of nightmare-induced panic Hayes had detected in his expression. Rather, the admiral had seen the dread that came from Picard's already *knowing* what his superior was about to say.

Hayes clearly did not quite believe the captain's reply, but his own apparent turmoil and the urgency of his message kept him from wasting a second pursuing the matter. "I just received a disturbing report from Deep Space Five. . . ."

As Hayes spoke, Picard felt growing pity for him. The imminent future would etch itself into the admiral's features, leaving behind new and deeper lines, more fresh ones added than he had even now. If he survived what was to come.

Picard listened as the admiral continued. "Long-range sensors have picked up—"

"I know," Picard said, interrupting, causing Hayes to subtly recoil and narrow his eyes in surprise. "The Borg."

TWO

Surrounded by his senior crew, Picard sat at the conference table in the observation lounge of the new *Enterprise*. The room was an elegant improvement over its predecessor, beautiful, spacious, and comfortable, but its most striking feature was a multitude of windows opening onto star-littered indigo. At that instant, the ship was passing through a gas cloud, which refracted the starlight into a swirling gossamer display of rainbow colors.

A stunning sight, but Picard could only think: *All those suns . . . and orbiting them, how many habitable planets? And of those planets, how many life-forms assimilated by the Borg? How many cultures forever lost over the millennia, and how soon shall we join them?*

Six months earlier, he had sat in this room and stared up at the bulkhead, where models of all the *Enterprise*'s previous incarnations, A through D, hung in a glass case alongside other mementos of past missions, past glories.

The sight had filled him with optimism and pride that he had the honor of commanding such a worthy vessel with such a noble tradition. He had already worked through his lingering sense of loss at his previous ship's destruction and had begun to feel hope. The *Enterprise*-D was irretrievably gone, but her spirit remained, permeating every atom, every cell of this vessel and her crew.

Now Picard looked at his surroundings and dared not allow himself to feel attachment. This was merely another ship that might be lost.

He drew his attention back to his staff. This sight was also familiar, yet not; Data, Riker, Troi, and Beverly's faces were the same, but they now wore the new uniforms—black, softened only by an inset at shoulder and collarbone of dark gray. The effect was flattering but a bit severe—and perhaps appropriate for the moment, Picard reflected grimly, given the devastating nature of the announcement he had just made.

In the silence that followed his brief, blunt statement that the Borg had reappeared, expressions grew somber and five pairs of anxious eyes focused upon him. The fifth pair of eyes belonged to Geordi La Forge, who, like the *Enterprise*-E, seemed familiar yet changed. La Forge's VISOR had been replaced a short time before by electronic ocular implants, and Picard still felt mildly disconcerted every time he looked into his chief engineer's large eyes, with their dizzyingly intricate geometric designs traced in black upon starkly blue irises.

"How many ships?" Riker asked.

"One," Picard replied. "And it's on a direct course for Earth. It will cross the Federation border in less than an hour." The statement caused another swift round of startled looks to pass among his senior crew members, but they said nothing and immediately refocused their attention on the captain as he continued. "Admiral Hayes has begun mobilizing a fleet in the Typhon Sector. He hopes to stop the Borg before they reach Earth."

Data, whose pale golden face reflected the concern he felt, courtesy of his activated emotion chip, interjected, "At maximum warp, it will take us three hours, twenty-five minutes to reach—"

Picard swiveled in his chair to face the android. "We're not going."

A heartbeat of stunned silence, during which expressions slackened, then grew taut again. Riker leaned forward, his dark eyebrows arching upward. "What do you mean, we're not going?" His tone was just civil enough, but the undercurrent of indignance was unmistakable.

Picard averted his gaze and stared out at the blurring stars. "Our orders are to patrol the Neutral Zone . . . in case the Romulans try to take advantage of the situation."

"The *Romulans?*" Deanna Troi repeated, her expression frankly disbelieving; Picard watched similar emotions play over the faces of all.

"Captain," Data added immediately, "there has been no unusual activity along the Romulan border for the past nine months. It seems highly unlikely that they would choose this moment to start a conflict."

He stated the obvious, of course; the captain drew a breath, meaning to tell him so.

But before he could speak, Beverly rested both elbows on the table and lifted her cupped hand as though it held an excuse she might literally offer up. "Maybe Starfleet feels we haven't had enough shakedown time." Perhaps she believed it; perhaps not, for Picard shot her a glance—and she at once lowered her gaze, as if in admission that there might be another, deeper reason Starfleet had ordered the *Enterprise*-E to stay away, but she was too loyal to utter it.

"We've been in space for nearly a year," La Forge countered, dismissing Crusher's argument with a wave of his hand. "We're ready. The *Enterprise*-E is the most advanced starship in the fleet. We should be on the front line."

If Geordi suspected the same reason Beverly did, he did not show it; neither did Troi or Data. Riker's expression remained inscrutable.

"I've gone through all this with Starfleet Command," Picard said heavily, working to keep his own outrage from showing . . . and not particularly succeeding. "Their orders stand."

This time, the leaden silence that followed lingered a time, remaining unbroken until Picard lowered his gaze from the backdrop of glittering stars and fixed it on Riker. "Number One, set course for the Neutral Zone."

He rose, then exited swiftly, before the others saw his anger and shame.

At the entrance to the ready room, Will Riker paused, padd in hand. He had performed the distasteful task assigned him, as second-in-command; the *Enterprise*-E now sailed a respectful distance from the Neutral Zone's border. The first scan had been completed, and it fell to Riker to present the results to his captain.

Almost a full day had passed since Picard's stunning announcement that the Borg were headed toward Earth. During that time, the captain had spent as little time as possible with his crew, preferring to closet himself away in his quarters or ready room. Riker understood; the crew members, himself included, were undeniably frustrated, restless, even angry at Starfleet's refusal to let them be of real service. And if *they* were offended and furious, how much more so was Picard—who had once been captured by the Borg and used to kill his own people, whom he had sworn to serve?

Now Picard's greatest opportunity for expiation—and the *Enterprise* crew's greatest opportunity to avenge their captain's suffering—had arrived, and Starfleet denied him, and them, that chance.

True, the very thought of confronting the Borg again terrified Riker, as it surely would any sane, sentient being. But the thought of waiting uselessly while fellow Starfleet officers, and perhaps Earth itself, were destroyed or assimilated horrified him even more.

Will drew a breath and stepped forward. The door to the ready room slid open, allowing a blast of dark, thunderous music and anguished voices to assault him. He gritted his teeth and entered. So skull-shatteringly loud was the music that a vein in his forehead began to pulse in time to its beat, while a half-full teacup on the captain's desk rattled in its saucer.

As for Picard, he stood staring out at the stars, his back to the door; the tension coiled in his shoulders and tightly crossed arms telegraphed his mood more eloquently than the agonized opera. Rage seemed to emanate outward from his body into the air, riding upon each blaring, furious note.

Riker neared the desk separating them, but the captain had heard neither the gentle hiss of the door opening and closing nor the sound of his first officer's footfall. Only when Riker's transparent reflection became superimposed over the captain's view of the stars did Picard turn to face his second-in-command.

Without a word or a change in his taut expression, the captain tapped a control on his console; blessedly, the opera dropped in volume. As it did, Riker felt his face relax and realized he had been wincing.

"Wagner?" he asked, with the faintest of smiles. The music played softly on, speaking to Riker of utter loss, destruction, despair—the ironically appropriate *Götterdämmerung,* the twilight of the gods.

Picard did not return the smile but replied curtly and without humor, "Berlioz. What do you have?"

Riker leaned forward and handed him the padd. "We finished our first sensor sweep of the Neutral Zone."

As the captain scanned the readout, his lips thinned to a grim line, one end of which tugged downward. "Fascinating," he said bitterly. "Twenty particles of space dust per cubic meter . . . fifty-two ultraviolet radiation spikes . . . and a class-two comet." He tossed the padd onto his desk. "This is certainly worthy of our time."

"I know how you feel," Riker offered sincerely. He was about to add that the rest of the crew was experiencing the same sense of frustration when Picard interrupted, his voice taut with an undercurrent of bitter emotions.

"Actually . . . I doubt very much that you know how I feel." The captain's hazel eyes narrowed and stared deeply into Riker's with a fury, an intensity that would have made any less loyal or determined friend and officer flinch and turn away in apology.

But Will's stubbornness matched Picard's. He met that gaze firmly with his own and saw that it held not just a challenge, but an invitation. There was something hidden there, something deeper than the insult the rest of the crew felt at being relegated to uselessness. Pain, he decided. Surely, though Picard eyed him squarely, the focus of the captain's gaze seemed beyond him, as if it were fixed fast upon ghosts from another time: the flaming hull of the *Starship Melbourne*. The *Saratoga*. The *Gage*. Thirty-seven more starships and tens of thousands of lives aboard them were lost at Wolf 359 in the battle against the Borg—thanks to the strategic knowledge of Locutus's human half, Captain Jean-Luc Picard.

Will Riker had endured the horror of confronting Locutus face to face, of staring at the *Enterprise*-D's bridge viewscreen and witnessing the Borg's handiwork: his commanding officer and friend rendered chillingly, obscenely inhuman. It would have been easier, Riker thought, to have looked instead upon the captain's mangled corpse.

How much more agonizing must that encounter have been for the human Picard, trapped inside Locutus's flesh-and-metal skull, looking upon his friends, his loyal crew, yet unable to warn them of the coming danger?

Riker saw vestiges of that pain in the captain's eyes now, the same enraged helplessness that had possessed Jean-Luc in the early days after his release from the collective. Starfleet's orders had unwittingly evoked from Picard the very same response as the Borg's mental rape.

"You're right," Will said at last, still studying the captain intently. "I don't. But then . . . I don't know what's really going on here." He took another step forward, his tone pointed. "Captain—why are we out here chasing comets?"

Picard drew himself back into the present and visibly worked to release some of the tension in his face and voice. With a sigh, he glanced down at his desk. "Let's just say that Starfleet has every confidence in the *Enterprise* and her crew"—he looked back up at Riker, his expression faintly rueful—"but they're not so sure about her captain."

He folded his arms tightly across his chest once more, as if to contain the bitterness in his heart, and began to pace. "They believe a man who was once captured by the Borg and assimilated . . . should not be put in a situation where he would face them again. To do so would be to introduce"—here he paused and changed the timbre of his voice to indicate a direct quote—" 'an unstable element into a critical situation.' "

"That's crazy," Riker said, his face taut with fury at Starfleet's attitude toward his old friend. "Your experience with the Borg makes you the perfect man to lead this fight."

Picard's expression darkened. "Admiral Hayes disagrees."

Riker opened his mouth to reply, but closed it when Counselor Troi's voice filtered through the captain's comm badge.

"Bridge to Captain Picard."

There was a tense formality in her tone that immediately caught both Riker's and Picard's attention. "Go ahead," the captain replied.

"We've just received word from Starfleet Command," she said. "They've engaged the Borg."

The bridge was, Picard reflected as he strode from the lift, like everything else aboard the *Enterprise*-E—including the situation that now confronted him and his crew—strange yet familiar. Strange, in that the captain's chair was now elevated above the rest, to provide a better overview of the entire bridge (and, he thought ruefully, to more thoroughly expose him at this most difficult of moments, as he struggled to contain a firestorm of emotions). Familiar, in that once again, the *Enterprise* crew anticipated a nightmarish battle with the Borg—yet so unutterably strange that they should not be permitted to be part of it.

Picard could not help but note the lines of tension etched on each officer's expression, beneath the careful composure. Troi failed to entirely hide a glimmer of edgy frustration as she glanced up at Riker and Picard's entry, while at ops, Data's demeanor was more candidly anxious, courtesy of the emotion chip.

The expression closest to conveying real calm belonged to Lieutenant Hawk at the conn, whose unflappable, direct personality reminded the captain of Will Riker's, although Hawk was younger, clean-shaven, lean to the point of wiriness. Of course, Hawk had not been aboard the *Enterprise*-D when her captain had been captured by the Borg; he had never heard Locutus speak nor witnessed the fiery destruction of forty of Starfleet's finest warships. Impossible to understand the horror of the Borg unless one had met them in battle—or worse, in their own hive. Hawk's confidence sprang from ignorance—and the captain did not look forward to seeing him lose either.

As he reached his chair, Picard spoke. "Commander Data, put Starfleet subspace frequency one-four-eight-six on audio."

As much as he could not bear to watch, he was just as urgently compelled to listen.

"Aye, sir," the android replied, his long, golden fingers moving with an artist's skill over his panel.

Picard gripped the armrests and leaned back against comfortable support without feeling it. He felt only an agonizing degree of helplessness as faint, disembodied voices—occasionally obliterated bursts of subspace static—filled the *Enterprise* bridge.

"Flagship to *Endeavor* . . . stand by to engage at grid A-fifteen."

"Defiant and *Bozeman,* fall back to mobile position one. . . ."

Will Riker, who sat in one of the two chairs slightly below and flanking the captain's, glanced up at Picard; they shared a pointed look at the mention of the *Defiant.* Troi's gaze grew frankly concerned. All of them, Picard knew, shared a single unspoken thought: *Worf.*

A cascade of overlapping voices, some laced with adrenaline, followed.

"Acknowledged, flagship."

"We have it in visual range!"

"We see it—a Borg cube on course zero mark two-one-five—"

"Speed: warp nine point eight."

In the midst of the purely humanoid cacophony, a new sound came—not an individual voice adding a fresh skein to the chorus, but one consisting of a hundred, a thousand, a million whispers hammered into a solitary thought that obliterated all others:

"We are the Borg. Lower your shields and surrender your ships. We will add your biological and technological distinctiveness to our own. Your culture will adapt to service us. Resistance is futile.

"We are the Borg."

Picard felt the flesh on his arms, on the nape of his neck, prickle; the emotion those words evoked within him was too raw, too visceral to neatly label fear or fury or hatred. He stared out at the speechless stars on the main viewscreen and thought, *How many planets . . . ?*

At the same time, an ominous realization came to him. He had *known* they were going to speak just then, hadn't he? Even before they had uttered a sound, he had *known* the precise second they were going to speak. . . .

Static over the subspace channel, followed abruptly by the stern, confident command of a Starfleet admiral: "All units open fire."

A deafening squeal of static made all on the *Enterprise* bridge wince—but not so much as the muted explosions that came after. A jumble of humanoid voices— punctuated by more static and ever closer explosions—followed: some female, some male; some the low, stern orders of experienced captains, others the high-pitched reports of green young officers.

"Remodulate shield nutation."

"We're losing power. . . ."

"Warp core breach!"

"All hands abandon ship!"

One more explosion, this so thunderous and shattering that some of the fresh-from-the-academy officers jumped at their stations; Picard briefly closed his eyes. Tainted by the Borg or not, unsure of himself or not, he was sure of the *Enterprise* and her crew—and knew he could endure the agony of helplessness no longer.

The admiral's voice came again, no longer stern, but laced with panic.

"This is the flagship! They've broken through the defense perimeter. They're heading toward Earth! Pursuit course. Break off the attack and—"

Picard caught Data's gaze and sliced a hand through the air; blessedly, the transmission ceased at once. There followed an instant of pregnant silence on the *Enterprise-*E bridge, during which the captain became keenly aware that all eyes were focused on him, waiting.

In any other situation, he would have asked the senior bridge crew to accompany him to the ready room, where he would have sought opinions and advice. After all, at the moment, he was on the verge of making a critical decision based entirely on emotion, one possibly colored by a personal desire for revenge. The wisest course was to consult cooler heads than his own.

But at the moment, he didn't give a damn. The emotion that fueled him was too pure, too primal to deny. This was the right decision, the only one possible to him in this instance. No, more than that: this was his destiny and that of the *Enterprise*-E and her crew. He leaned toward the conn.

"Lieutenant Hawk. Set course for Earth. Maximum warp."

Hawk's blue eyes widened with surprise—and something very like admiration. He said not a word—not even, in his surprise, remembering to acknowledge his captain's orders—but immediately set to the task.

Picard shot a brief glance at an approving Will Riker before turning to address his crew. Even if Riker had protested vehemently at that instant, it would not have changed a single word Picard was about to say.

"I am about to commit a direct violation of our orders. Any of you who wish to object, do so now and I'll note it in my log."

A ripple seemed to pass over the bridge crew in the form of shared, determined looks. After a heartbeat of silence, Data swiveled to face the captain and said, "I think I speak for everyone here, sir, when I say . . . to hell with our orders."

Picard permitted himself a small, bitter smile, one that faded at once as he spoke. "Red alert. All hands to battle stations."

As the klaxon sounded and crew members scrambled to their stations, he told himself: *You are probably taking all of these people to their deaths, and you to your own— if all of you are lucky. And if you are not . . .*

It was a reasonable fear, a responsible fear. But he would rather live with it for the time being than surrender without a fight to the evil of mindless apathy. And so it was with an uncanny degree of satisfaction that he settled back into his chair and ordered Hawk: "Engage."

THREE

☆

Aboard the *Defiant*'s bridge, Lieutenant Commander Worf sat staring at the viewscreen's display of the monstrous and ungainly Borg cube surrounded by a dozen tiny starships—a leaden, lumbering beast attacked by a pale, shining swarm of insects, insects that packed an impressive sting. Dazzling bursts of phaserfire lit up the surrounding blackness, leaving scorch marks on the Borg cube's dully gleaming pewter hull.

The *Defiant* was among the ranks of those ships that had left their mark; Worf watched the effects of recently ordered photon blasts with a grim warrior's smile of satisfaction, while Weapons Officer Tutu raised his dark, clenched fist to pierce the air in a gesture of victory. The hull of the massive Borg vessel was as pockmarked as an unsheltered moon.

But Worf's satisfaction was, as the Klingon had known it would be, short-lived. The cube—an unappealing conglomeration of external metal tubing, wiring, and conduits that looked as if its builders had decided to simply turn the vessel inside out, exposing its bowels to space—shuddered briefly at the blast, then immediately struck back.

A burst of fire-bright torpedoes—one, then two, three, four, five—slipped from it and sailed with unerring aim toward the flagship, which had had the honor of first opening fire on the cube. But after several volleys with the Borg, her defenses were weakening, as were the *Defiant*'s. After the last exchange of fire, Worf was informed that the *Defiant*'s shields could not withstand further pummeling.

"Evasive maneuver," he shouted, glancing over his shoulder at the conn as Lieutenant Kizilbash, a lean human female with a sculpted, angular face and Klingon-intense eyes, complied. As a moving target, the *Starship Defiant* was less likely to be hit and thus had more chance of disabling the enemy.

But Worf harbored no false hopes about his chances of surviving the battle. Such a death would be supremely honorable, and he did not fear it; indeed, he would embrace such a fate, for he had long ago decided—upon his first look at Picard as the Borg drone Locutus—that he would indeed die rather than submit to the crime against freedom called assimilation.

Thus he fought today with special fervor, remembering. The Borg had taken Captain Picard, one of the strongest-willed humans Worf knew, and drained from him all life, all honor, all volition, until nothing but a mindlessly obedient shell remained.

Worf would fight to his last breath against such an evil; but his secret fear was that he would die and the Borg would be undefeated—and assimilate all beings in the galaxy, including those Klingon warriors too unfortunate to die.

Picard, he thought; it was unfair that Picard was not here, to redress the wrong done him. And unfair not only to him, but to all those asked to risk their lives to fight the Borg, for the *Enterprise*-E was Starfleet's newest, finest vessel, equipped with the latest improvements in shields and weapons. When the *Defiant* had first arrived at the battlefront, Worf had asked Starfleet Command why the new *Enterprise* had not appeared and was informed curtly that she was patrolling the Romulan border. No further explanation was given. It seemed to him an outrage to keep Picard from an act of redemption and the *Enterprise*-E from providing aid to those who desperately needed her now.

All this Worf considered as the *Defiant* sailed in a swift arc, causing the sight on the viewscreen to shift. The Borg vessel lay dead ahead, while at two o'clock, the flagship shuddered, its forward hull and one nacelle illumined by a flood of eye-searing, deadly light.

One, then two, of the blasts had already struck home.

Abruptly, that brightness dimmed, leaving behind the section of hull nearest the bridge and half a nacelle scorched, pitted. Fire is immediately extinguished in the vacuum of space, Worf knew; but beneath that blackened hull were dull glimmers of swift-moving redness— the oxygen-laden decks, where people were being burned alive.

Three, four. The next two blasts followed in less than a Vulcan heartbeat. The third sliced into the already-weakened hull; the fourth hammered the crippled nacelle, whose surface crumbled and emitted the shocking orange flare that heralded a warp-core breach.

Five. The final blast limned the wounded starship with a writhing corona of light whose brightness was only increased by the sudden, nova-intense eruption from the warp-core nacelle. The flagship erupted in a glorious but fleeting blaze that sent quickly extinguished, darkening bits of shrapnel hurtling into the breathless void.

For those aboard her, it was the most honorable and noble of deaths—most importantly, a free one, untainted by their enemy's peculiar brand of slavery. But Worf had little time to contemplate it, as the entire exchange between the Borg cube and the flagship had taken only a few seconds.

And even as the starship's debris went hurtling past the *Defiant,* Worf kept his gaze fixed on the viewscreen for another curiously timeless instant. A fresh barrage of torpedoes birthed from the Borg ship's underbelly was now streaking directly toward his vessel, his crew.

One—then two, three, four, five.

The sight made him bare his teeth and roar, "Fire phasers!" in the second before the blasts found their mark; astoundingly, Tutu had anticipated his commander's order and at once unleashed a retaliatory burst from the *Defiant*'s phaser banks.

Worf did not have the pleasure of seeing the toll his response took on the pewter-colored cube. The instant

Tutu's ebony fingers touched his controls, the first blast hit.

One. The *Defiant* pitched hard astern, throwing Worf back against his chair and tossing the communications officer to the deck. He tried to shout orders for evasive maneuvers and more phaserfire, but the sound was swallowed by the thunder of impact.

Two. The second blast followed almost instantly, rendering all hope of communication with his bridge crew impossible. Impact came now from the ship's right flank, hurling him from his chair; all about him, officers were flung from their stations onto the deck. He fought to right himself, then scrabbled toward the weapons console. Nearby, Tutu was now part of a jumble of bodies working to free themselves and return to their stations.

Three. The conn erupted in multicolored fireworks; sharp bits of debris flew past Worf's face and eyes, stung his skin as he pitched forward against the deck. The ship was beginning to come apart, the Klingon realized grimly—but this was the *Defiant,* one of the finest, strongest warships in the fleet, designed to hold up against the deadliest onslaughts. If she could bear two more blows . . .

He managed another shaky step and flung himself toward Tutu's console. Once there, he leaned face and chest against the control panel and hugged it tightly. The air surrounding him became acrid with smoke.

Four, five.

The *Defiant* lurched upward and back, like a boxer struck hard in the jaw. The impact lifted the Klingon off his feet on a back-and-up diagonal, then, as the ship righted itself with a jerk, slammed his cheek against the console again, tearing the skin. The rebound from the collision lifted him again—and at that instant, the final shock came, dashing him headfirst against the floor.

The blow to his head and chest left him momentarily stunned and breathless, and the fall had turned the cut on his cheek into a gash—or so he assumed from the warm, damp feel of blood trickling down his face. But the warrior's fury in his heart obliterated all pain, all fear, and bade him rise to his feet.

So he did—slowly, one hand clutching the nearest console, which still rained sparks. To his relief, he did not hear the computer's urgent voice warning of an imminent warp-core breach; but neither did he hear the expected drone of voices reporting the extent of the damage. The bridge itself seemed ominously silent, veiled in thick smoke that rendered the other bodies on the bridge—some lying still as death (and indeed, probably dead), some writhing in pain, others crawling back to their stations—unrecognizable. So it was that he growled at the nearest body, moving slowly on hands and knees: "Report!"

The voice that filtered through the haze belonged to Kizilbash; as she spoke, she neared, her cropped, dark hair and features becoming gradually more visible, and pulled herself up into her chair. "Main power is offline!" she exclaimed, clearly struggling not to cough. "We've lost shields and our weapons are gone!"

Worf paused the length of a single breath, no more. "Then perhaps today . . . is a good day to die." He sought Kizilbash's gaze through the stinging smoke and found an unflinching determination there that filled him with pride. *"Ramming speed!"*

Kizilbash moved toward Tutu's console, prepared to comply, but something she saw there made her instead glance up at her commander. "Sir," she said, her voice sharp with surprise, "there's another starship coming in. It's the *Enterprise!"*

In the flashing crimson glow of the red alert, Picard sat in his new captain's chair and watched as the *Enterprise*-E's powerful phasers found their target: the scarred, blackened surface of the Borg cube. Its lifeless, featureless gray metal was briefly illumined before instantly darkening again, as the phasers gouged a great smoldering ravine in its hull.

Against the sinister backdrop of the monstrous vessel, the battered *Defiant* drifted, clearly helpless. Another onslaught would surely destroy her and all aboard. The remaining Federation ships hovered about the cube, clearly contemplating their strategies.

But as Picard had known it would, the *Enterprise*'s attack immediately drew the enemy's fire away from the crippled warship. The Borg in turn unleashed a retaliatory barrage—one that, the captain noted with pride, the new ship absorbed with the faintest of shudders. She had not yet been tested in an actual battle; but thus far, Picard was already impressed.

Riker glanced up from his station, slightly lower than and flanking the captain's. "The *Defiant*'s losing life support."

Without pause, Picard spoke to the comm, returning his gaze to the viewscreen. "Bridge to transporter room three. Beam the *Defiant* survivors aboard."

Riker's voice again, this time pitched ever so slightly higher: "Captain, the flagship's been destroyed."

Picard did not look at his second-in-command as another blast caused the chair under him to vibrate, but instead kept his eyes focused on the screen. "What's the status on the Borg cube?"

The question was addressed to Data, whose voice relayed an undercurrent of excitement. "It has sustained heavy damage on its outer hull. I am reading fluctuations in their power grid."

In the millisecond before the android replied, Picard realized that he inexplicably knew—*knew*—the information he had requested, for his question had already been answered by a whisper in his own head—a voice that was one, yet many; a voice that evoked the ghost of a half-remembered feminine face.

Without thinking, he rose, entranced, and moved toward the viewscreen where the image of the massive and unlovely vessel hung. They were there; he could sense them, hear them speak. For an instant, he felt as though he had only to reach toward the screen, and he would touch them.

The whisper of the one and the multitude grew briefly louder.

. . . critical damage to shields at power sector one-one-one. All drones coordinate repair immediately. . . .

The mental whisper died abruptly, as if the speakers had realized he was listening. But it was too late; he had already experienced a revelation beyond the mere words he had detected.

They were wounded. They were *vulnerable,* and he knew beyond all reason the precise spot.

He wheeled toward Riker. "Number One, open a channel to the other Starfleet vessels."

Riker complied, but Picard caught the fleeting expression of curiosity on his first officer's face and on the faces of those surrounding him. The awe he felt at his revelation must have been clear, but he did not, could not, take the time to explain. The window of the Borg's vulnerability would soon close.

He moved swiftly to Data's console and fingered the weapons control while the android watched in frank amazement.

By then, the channel to the remaining warships was open, and he spoke without delay. "This is Captain Picard of the *Enterprise.* I'm taking command of the fleet. Target every weapon you have on the following coordinates . . . and fire on my command."

Data stared down at the coordinates Picard had just entered, then looked up at him with a worried frown. "Captain, the coordinates you have indicated do not appear to be a vital system."

"Trust me, Data." He stared straight ahead at the viewscreen, already seeing in his mind's eye the Borg's dazzling fate and experiencing a decidedly unaltruistic sensation at the image.

"The fleet's ready," Riker reported behind him, and as he uttered the last word, Picard was already giving the order to the remaining starships.

"Fire."

Picard would not turn away from the screen, though the light was of such magnitude that he was forced to close his eyes. Even then, the brightness was painful—and when he opened them again, the yellow afterimage left him partially blinded for a few seconds.

But he could see enough to know that the Borg cube had dissolved into hurtling debris beneath the combined firepower of the Federation vessels. The explosion caused the deck beneath his feet to shudder.

Oddly, the sight brought little comfort—a mystifying reaction until he saw, emerging from the flying dust and shrapnel, a smaller vessel. Not a cube but a sphere, with the same Borg disregard for aesthetics as its predecessor, the same peculiarly unappealing leaden color, the same honeycomb design with exposed circuitry and tubing.

The sphere flew past the assembled starships directly toward Earth.

"Pursuit course. Engage," Picard said as he returned to his chair. As he settled into it, the reality of what had just happened struck home; he let go a silent, troubled sigh.

So he *was* still tied, to some degree, to the Borg. Had Starfleet been right? Would this—at some point—make him a danger to those he wished to protect?

Yet in this instance, he had been quite the opposite; he had saved the *Defiant* survivors, and his intuitive knowledge had permitted him to win at least this one battle. The connection had not been two-way; the Borg had clearly not known he was about to destroy their ship.

Or had they?

Deanna Troi clearly sensed his turmoil. She moved toward him and asked softly, "What?"

I heard them, Picard thought in reply; but the notion was too unsettling, too horrific to give voice to, and so he answered not at all.

Troi's black eyes narrowed with concern; she parted her lips to speak, but before the words could come, the turbolift doors opened to reveal Beverly Crusher.

She stepped onto the bridge, her expression business-like, yet edged with a faint mirth Picard could not understand—until he saw who stood beside her. "I have a patient here who insisted on coming to the bridge," she said, with feigned disapproval.

And she turned to smile at her companion: Worf. The Klingon's uniform was torn and bloodied, his deep brown face further darkened by soot, save for a patch Crusher had no doubt cleaned and bandaged. But his stance was straight and strong as it had been the last time Picard saw him, and his eyes as clear and fierce.

Picard did not smile at him; the situation was too grim for that. But he did not suppress the honest affection in his voice. "Welcome to the *Enterprise*-E, Mr. Worf."

"Thank you, sir," Worf said sincerely. His tone became abruptly concerned. "The *Defiant* . . . ?"

Picard understood the question very well; he knew the grief of losing a ship. So it was with pleasure that he told the Klingon, "Adrift . . . but salvageable."

"Tough little ship," Riker interjected. Worf snarled, revealing a glimpse of particularly fearsome-looking, yellowed teeth.

"Little?"

Will smiled, rightly interpreting the display as good humored.

"We could use some help at tactical, Worf," Picard said, noting how much they had all missed the Klingon; Troi and Data were both grinning broadly at Worf, and the captain himself was on the verge of doing so. But he could not—not yet.

Not even when Riker followed the Klingon over to tactical. When Worf relieved the young ensign there and immediately began familiarizing himself with the new console, Will leaned over him and asked, sotto voce, "You *do* remember how to fire phasers?"

Worf glanced up, his expression one of perfect innocence. "It is the *green* button, right?"

Riker snickered. It seemed, Picard reflected, that the Klingon's interaction with those on Deep Space 9 had definitely honed his sense of humor.

Still, the captain could not smile; not yet. Though he no longer heard the voice of the Borg, he could sense them, and knew: defeat was too near. As near as the planet Earth.

And all too soon, the *Enterprise* viewscreen revealed the marbled blue-white sphere of Earth—and a second smaller, more sinister sphere that dove swiftly toward her.

"Captain," Data said sharply, scowling down at his monitor, "sensors show high concentrations of tachyons . . . and chronometric particles emanating from the sphere. . . ."

He looked at Picard, who now stood beside him,

studying the monitor. The captain glanced at the information for the space of a second, no more, then stared up in wonder at the viewscreen, where the Borg vessel began to glow scarlet in the upper reaches of Earth's atmosphere.

With the same sudden certainty that had seized him earlier, Picard *knew,* and had no need to consult readouts. In a whisper, he said, "They're creating a temporal vortex."

"Time travel," Riker echoed, his tone laced with horror.

Picard did not reply, but merely stared along with his stunned crew as, ahead of the Borg sphere, a tunnel of blazing, writhing energy and light opened.

The sphere flew directly into the heart of the brilliant maelstrom, displacing a wave of crackling energy that surged outward, enveloping the *Enterprise.*

The deck beneath Picard's feet convulsed; this time he looked away from the blinding splendor on the viewscreen. Thunder roared in his ears, muffling Riker's shout: "We're caught in some kind of temporal wake!"

The worst of it swept over them; and then, gradually, the light and the ship's trembling subsided.

He permitted himself a sigh at the realization that the wake had not killed them, but he knew the worst had not yet begun.

Nearby, Worf called, his tone stricken: "Captain! The Earth . . ."

On the screen, the energy wake had begun to dissipate, revealing the Earth. Or rather, the Earth *changed,* for any trace of blue or white or any other lush, rich color that Jean-Luc Picard associated with his native planet was entirely gone. The atmosphere was now storm-swirled, turbulent, dark.

A darkness that was colorless, lifeless, beautyless.

Leaden, Picard thought—and then could scarcely draw the next breath. He gazed again at the glowing vortex, still open—and within, the sapphire jewel of the true Earth.

"The atmosphere contains high concentrations of methane, carbon monoxide, and fluorine," Data announced.

With dread, the captain asked, "Life signs?"

Data again consulted his console. "Population . . . approximately nine billion." He looked up at his superior, his pale, iridescent face perfectly slack, apparently calm; yet in his amber eyes shone depthless horror. "All Borg."

Through an act of pure will, Picard managed to continue breathing, to force his dazed mind to think. But several seconds passed before anyone could speak.

"But how?" Troi demanded at last. Her question served to galvanize the others.

"They must have done it in the past," Picard reasoned. "They went back and assimilated Earth. Changed history . . ."

"But if they changed history, why are we still here?" Crusher challenged.

Picard was on the verge of replying when Data answered instead. "The temporal wake must have protected us from changes in the timeline."

As the android spoke, an alarm on his console beeped. He glanced down, then said, "The vortex is collapsing."

Picard hesitated not a heartbeat; any other decision

would have been violently unacceptable. "Data, hold your course. We have to follow them back, repair whatever damage they've done."

Data immediately began working his console. No one on the bridge spoke or even stirred; the loss of one's present and future, Picard realized, was far too stunning to permit reaction. So stunning, indeed, that he had lost all sense of connection to the Borg. Where they were headed, what they planned, he could not say.

In silence, the *Enterprise*-E hurtled straight ahead, into the blinding brilliance, into the past.

FOUR

☆

The air was close in the old Crash & Burn, stale and unpleasant, filled with the scent of sour sweat, moonshine, and smoke. It was the smell, Lily decided, that had caused her headache. That and the two shots of brain-numbing, vile-tasting swill that passed for the local liquor . . . and the fact that Zef had himself had ten shots and was beginning to slur again.

Or maybe it was simply the fear.

Whatever it was, she had grown suddenly furious, seized Zef's arm, and pulled him off his barstool and out of the tattered olive-drab tent into the freezing night. He'd been just drunk enough to go with her (fortunately, not so drunk as to be combative), and she paused a few steps away from the bar and filled her lungs with fresh air. The first breath was bracing; the second, bitterly cold.

She swore softly. It was April, all right, but this sure as hell wasn't Paris.

"Lily, c'mon," Zef pleaded. He was in one of his manic moods tonight, a rather charming one, his cheeks flushed bright pink from liquor and cold, his eyes bright. Combined with his nicely silvering hair, they made him look younger, more handsome, than she'd ever seen him; for a moment, he looked like a boy instead of a worn, fifty-year-old man. It wasn't just the booze, Lily knew; it was the excitement, the anticipation of tomorrow. "We're *celebrating,* remember?"

"We can celebrate when it's over," she said curtly, making her way cautiously around the larger mud puddles, which were capped by a layer of frosted ice. Zef followed alongside, arms out, pleading.

"Lily . . ."

"You're going to regret this." She kept her expression hard and began walking faster.

He tried to keep up with her, but between the booze and the icy patches, he caught the edge of a mud puddle with his heel and almost slipped. She slowed, grabbed him, and wound an arm firmly around his waist.

He grinned. "If there's one thing you should've learned about me by now, young lady, it's that I have no regrets."

Right, she thought bitterly. *Like I have none. Everyone, everything we ever loved is dead and the world's a mess, but we don't care, do we?*

Zef stopped suddenly and gave her a conspiratorial wink. "Come on, Lily. One more round." He moved to turn back, but she forged straight ahead, jaw set.

"You've had enough," she told him. "I'm not riding in that thing tomorrow with a drunken pilot." As she

37

spoke, she wondered why she was so angry about the upcoming launch.

Because it might not work, that's why. Because after all the tears and sweat he and I have put into it, it might just be a miserable flop.

Because, for the first time in ten years, something came along that made me dare hope . . . and if it fails . . . If it fails, there really won't *be any reason left to feel optimistic about anything.*

And I don't think I can go back to living that way again.

It was hard, after ten years—a whole third of her existence—to remember much about life before the war. Or maybe it was just that remembering hurt too much, so she did her best to forget the details. But she couldn't forget the university; it seemed now like a dream, a beautiful place that couldn't really have existed because it was simply too wonderful. If she'd only known, when she was there, that it was an ephemeral phenomenon, impermanent, she would have treasured it more. All the math and physics classes that she secretly adored while complaining vocally about them . . .

After three years, they simply went away, ended in a moment of political insanity. She was twenty then, eager for a future. Suddenly, there was no more university, no more friends and teachers. No more dream of being an engineer.

No point in even being smart anymore. Academic knowledge no longer mattered; being tough and cautious did.

She learned about the tough part when she went home to her parents—except that home was lost, too. When it became clear that war was imminent, the university president sent them all home, and she stepped through the old doorway, luggage in hand, just in time to hear Dad's voice coming from the family room: "That's it. It's started. . . ."

As for the mom and dad, they packed up their emotional tents and mentally stole away during that first terrible night, sometime after the television went dead. Their eldest, Lionel, had been foolish enough not to flee the draft the year before and was presumed dead. Their middle child, Denise, had been living with her husband and kids in D.C.—ground zero. Ma had kept going to the comm and punching up Denise's number, staring into the blank screen and muttering to herself, even after all the news reports early that evening confirmed that Washington and three surrounding states had been blown off the map.

But the three of them—Ma, Dad, Lily—lived, and for a long time, she wished they hadn't. They didn't live in one of the directly nuked cities; they should have been so lucky. The house was left standing . . . but the growing radiation levels, carried on the wind, forced them to leave most everything behind. So they packed up the groundcar and roamed like nomads, with Dad's old camping gear, looking for clean ground.

What they took with them was stolen, of course, by road thieves with guns. She wound up stealing a gun—something she had never, ever believed herself capable of—in order to protect her parents. She'd even shot a total of five men and one woman in that first awful year, wounding four and killing two—she, Lily, genteel college student, almost-engineer, who had wept upon learning from her biology professor that she would have to kill a mouse before dissecting it. The roads were deadly then, back before new communities started forming and learning how to protect themselves.

Just when she thought things couldn't get worse, all the charging stations shut down, and the car ran out of juice within a month's time. They'd had to abandon it and head out on foot, finally winding up at a horrifically crowded KOA campground. The latrines were vile beyond description—who had the heart to clean them anymore?—but there were good people there who helped look after her parents and provided protection against the road gangs.

The first night at the KOA, Ma'd laid down in the borrowed tent and said, *Lily, I think I have cancer.* And she'd showed her the lump.

Don't worry, Ma, she'd said, and meant it. After all, it was only cancer, a disease they'd cured a half-century ago. No big deal. You go to the doctor, you get your shot, you come home. Checkup in a month.

Or so she'd thought. But the doctors who came through the KOA couldn't carry with them every medicine ever invented, and what they did have ran out pretty fast. Find the medicine? All the pharmaceutical companies were in the big cities, which were now dust. The drug Ma needed should be available *somewhere,* but none of the doctors knew where, and so the next six months were a constant battle to get from town to town where supposedly a hospital was still in business . . .

But none of them ever were.

So Ma died of cancer, a disease you weren't supposed to have to fear anymore; but now, you had to be afraid of *everything* again, even illnesses from medieval times. In the California deserts—all that was left of the state—people were *dying* from bubonic and pneumonic plague. Hell, you could die these days from an infected cut.

Soon after, her dad took to drink. No more pills to take the pain or the craving away, and Lily was too stunned herself to stop him. She let it go until the night he used her pistol to kill himself.

Life was numb for a long time after. For some odd reason, she kept existing—it certainly couldn't be called living. And she kept moving from place to place, teaching herself along the way to scavenge and steal until she became expert at it.

Why she kept going, she couldn't say—except that maybe she was looking for something. And she found it the night she met Zef.

She had finally headed far north, to Montana. It was safe, one of the cleanest places around, air- and water-wise, and she tried to tell herself the cold wouldn't be *that* bad. (Hah!) All the warm places were either still sizzling from the nukes, stricken by plague or dysentery or typhoid or rabies (all diseases long forgotten before the war), or controlled by the new drug lords. She was tired of wandering and just wanted to rest.

She'd wandered into the local bar, the Crash & Burn— an old army tent, really, set with a few tables, a rickety bar, and an honest-to-God jukebox. Her intention was to make her need for shelter and her particular skill known to the locals, in hopes of working out a trade.

And she'd sat right down beside Zefram Cochrane. He was holding court in the bar, in one of his life-of-the-party moods, not yet drunk because it was still early. To say he charmed the socks off her was putting it mildly . . . but she was hardened after too many years on the road and not about to let *him* know how she felt. Within five minutes, he'd learned her name and trade and history—and propositioned her.

Not exactly in the way she'd expected. He had a get-rich-quick scheme, he'd told her, and she could be a part of it.

Yeah, right. Find another sucker, white boy.

No, no, he'd said; he had come here to Montana because of the old missile silos. There really was a use for them after all. If she really was as talented a . . . provider as she claimed, she could help. He was a physicist, working on a project. But he couldn't talk about it there in the bar. Would she come to his place? There was something there he wanted to show her.

She'd laughed aloud at his blatant, clichéd attempt; he'd flushed crimson, as if suddenly realizing how it all sounded, but he had recovered his poise enough to turn to the bartender: *Hey, Charlie, tell her I'm okay.*

He was okay, Charlie had said, as had a couple of other people there who'd overheard, including a sweet-faced older woman. Against her better judgment, she had gone with him, but she'd kept one hand on the gun in her jacket. And before she knew it, she was sitting cross-legged across from him on the cold dirt floor of his hut, listening to him explain that he needed certain mechanical parts.

42

To build something, she interjected. It wasn't a question; after all, from where she sat she could see a large section of what looked like an air shuttle console propped against a short, rusting metal cabinet, atop which lay a pile of roughly sketched blueprints.

Yes, he admitted. *A spaceship.*

She leapt up. And she would have walked right out and never looked back except that Zef jumped up, too, and gently caught her hand.

Damn it, Lily, help me, he said. *I can't do this alone. Here, let me show you.*

Those words could never have stopped her, but his eyes did. There was something breath-taking, fiery in them—something she hadn't seen in so many years that at first she didn't recognize it, but it caught and mesmerized her all the same.

Hope.

He'd named his ship the *Phoenix.*

Let me show you, he repeated, then grabbed a handful of blueprints off the cabinet, spread them out on the ground, and knelt before them. He spoke swiftly, happily, of how the nuclear core contained in an old warhead could be harnessed for something he called a "warp engine," and he traced in the dirt some mathematical equations to prove it. She knew then that he really was what he claimed to be—a physicist. One, because he rattled on with blithe confidence that she would understand everything he said; after all, it was simple and obvious to *him.* Two, because she actually *did* understand much of what he told her, and it made frighteningly good sense.

Warp drive. Back at the university, they had called it hyperspace, and it was only a hypothesis, an intangible dream: light-years reduced to a day's travel, the stars no longer impossibly distant. But even then, there were rumors that a breakthrough was coming soon, that a handful of elite scientists had devoted themselves to finding a practical way to implement it.

And if there were other beings out there . . .

Please, God, don't let them be bad guys. Let them bring help.

I have a deal with some Indonesians, Zef finally said. *They see the potential and know it'll take some time. But they're willing to pay millions.*

Indonesia, huh? She had paused and rubbed her freezing arms. *Is it warm there?*

So for the next few years, they played a little game with each other: he pretended to be nothing more than a hard-bitten entrepreneur desperate to strike it rich, while she pretended to be nothing more than a hard-bitten thief hungry for a piece of the action. They were in it strictly for the money, because the war and its subsequent hell had taught them that dreams and futures were made to be shattered. Idealism was for fools, as were feelings. Or so she reminded herself everytime she dragged him from the Crash & Burn and tucked him into his own bed when he was too drunk to find his way home, or kept watch over him everytime a minor setback on the project plunged him into a depression so deep he threatened suicide.

Affection had nothing to do with it, she told herself. She was merely taking care of her investment.

In the future . . .

* * *

Beside her, Zef grunted, bringing her back into the present—to the frozen mud and biting air. She shivered and rubbed her arms as she had done so long ago, then stared up at the star-littered night sky, wondering. Would it really happen? Would they be up there making history tomorrow as the first two people to travel using warp drive?

And would the Indonesians really pay them all that money? She stared dreamily up at the glittering darkness, allowing herself for the first time to consider success. What would it be like, to have a solidly constructed house with real running water and her own charging station and car? To pay a farmer to grow anything she wanted? To indulge in the shameless luxury of feeding a pet dog?

Her gaze grew unfocused—but not enough to miss a fantastically swift-moving disc of light amid the stars, one that seemed to grow nearer as she watched. She touched Zef's arm. "What the hell is *that?*"

He glanced up, squinting hard to keep from seeing double. "That, my dear, is the Constellation Leo."

"No, *that,*" Lily insisted, pointing. She tried to calm herself, to keep her breathing steady so that her heart would not race, but this was no falling star, and all satellites had long ago been blown back to Earth.

Take it easy, girl. You're being childish. Maybe somebody in Indonesia launched a new satellite. Or maybe that's just one weird freaking meteor.

Then Zef lifted his face toward the sky and finally saw

it. She glanced sideways at him, praying he would shake his head, smile, and dismiss her fear with a scientific explanation.

Instead, his faint, inebriated grin vanished; his face hardened, then slackened into that disbelieving, stunned expression Ma had worn when the newscaster announced the total destruction of Washington, D.C. The sight had instantly sobered him, and as she glanced back up at the sky, she saw two bright streaks emerge from the shining disc—and a half-second later, heard the distant thunder.

For half a heartbeat's pause, both of them stood frozen with fearful puzzlement, trying to understand. . . .

The drab world around Lily vanished, replaced by a yellow-white burst of blinding brilliance, as if she had stepped inside a star. A screaming roar accompanied the light, rattling her teeth, her bones, searing her ears with such pristine agony that she knew the drums had ruptured; her skin pricked and tingled as if reacting to a nearby lightning bolt.

She jumped—or was she hurled?—toward a small berm at the path's edge. For a second or two, she knew nothing but blindness, deafness. Slowly, her vision began to return, each blink clearing away a bit more afterimage; her ears still rang shrilly, but she could hear the sound of other nearby blasts ripping through the settlement. Beneath her belly, the cold, muddy ground shuddered continuously.

Some yards distant, Zef scrambled on his hands and knees away from a great smoking crater—all that remained of several nearby Quonset huts and tents. There had been people in them, a couple of families—maybe twenty-five, thirty victims inside; some of those glowing cinders, Lily realized, sickened, were bits of bone. This wasn't a nuke; this was something newer, deadlier.

She pushed herself up, dashed out into the street, and pulled Zef to his feet; the two of them dove again for cover while more dazzling streaks of light rained down from the heavens. In a fleeting millisecond of quiet, Zef sighed beside her. "After all these years . . ." He rolled his eyes skyward—and in them, Lily saw reflected the blazing bolts . . . and the death of all dreams.

"You think it's the ECON?" she shouted in his ear, her own voice sounding distant, muffled. It was the only thing that made sense: the Eastern Coalition must have somehow recovered, rebuilt, and were determined to wipe out what small pieces of North-, Central-, and South-Am remained. She almost sobbed with pure rage at the cruelty of it all.

"They couldn't have waited another day . . . ?" Zef said, his expression one of irony and defeat. Abruptly, he jerked to his feet and pulled her up with him, then ran, dragging her into the exposed street.

Toward the Crash & Burn.

Lily pulled free. "We've gotta get to the *Phoenix!*"

She ran toward the silo at top speed, without a glance back at him. At first, he followed—one step, then two— then abruptly stopped, and in the growing distance between them, she heard his voice, both sorrowful and hard. "To *hell* with the *Phoenix.*"

For an instant, she was tempted to join him—to go get blindingly drunk and die numbed—but another thought occurred. What did it matter if she was doing something risky, unsafe? The whole freaking *world* had gone insane again, and there was no point in postponing death. Better to die trying . . .

Even so, the *Phoenix* was probably ashes again, and would never rise. . . .

The *Enterprise* had finally stopped shaking as if trying to tear herself apart; Jean-Luc Picard leaned forward in his chair and saw, with unutterable relief, that the Earth on the viewscreen was most definitely blue, beneath a slight grayish haze. He turned toward his second-in-command, who gazed at the viewscreen, then the bridge itself and let out a small but audible sigh.

"Report," Picard requested of him.

Riker glanced down at his console. "Shields are down. Long-range sensors are offline. . . . Main power's holding."

Despite his operative emotion chip, Data had already reoriented himself and offered, in a composed voice: "According to our astrometric readings, we are in the mid-twenty-first century. From the radioactive isotopes in the atmosphere, I would estimate we have arrived approximately ten years after the Third World War."

"Makes sense," Riker said quietly, with a grim upward glance at the captain. "Most of the major cities were destroyed; only a few governments left. Six hundred million dead. No resistance."

"Captain!" Worf interrupted, in an alarmed baritone.

Picard looked up at the screen to see the Borg sphere firing a rapid volley of photon blasts down at one particular target on the unprotected planet. "Quantum torpedoes! Fire!"

The Klingon complied at once. Within two seconds, a burst of five torpedoes struck the small sphere, each penetrating its bland gray surface. The craft had been unshielded, Picard realized, since the Borg had anticipated no spaceborne enemies in this era. As he watched, the sphere's interior began to glow, to flash, from a series of internal explosions.

In a blessed beat, the metal hull glowed white and seemed to expand slightly, then burst into a million whirling fragments.

The deck beneath Picard rocked briefly from the shockwave that followed. He permitted himself a single exhalation of relief before demanding, "They were firing at the surface. Where?"

Riker rose and moved to a distant console. After fingering a combination of controls, he consulted the brightly colored image on his screen. "Western hemisphere, North American continent." The image shifted, and he frowned at it in fleeting puzzlement before adding, "Looks like some sort of missile complex in central Montana."

"Missile complex," Picard half whispered. The location triggered a mental alarm. Something of crucial import had occurred at a missile complex in Montana in this century, something submerged in his memory that was struggling to rise. . . .

He wheeled toward the android. "The date. Data, I need to know the exact date."

A brief pause as Data consulted his readout. "The date is April sixth, 2063."

Picard and Riker exchanged a swift look that spoke of mutual horror and triumph.

"April sixth," Will said. "That's one day before *first contact.*"

"That's what they came here to do," Picard said, rising. "Stop first contact."

"If that's true," Crusher stated grimly, "then the missile complex must be where *Zefram Cochrane* is building his warp ship."

Picard addressed Riker again. "How much damage did they do?"

"Can't tell." Riker shook his head at the console. "Long-range sensors are still offline."

Picard wasted no time in making his decision. "We have to go down there, find out what happened," he told his crew. "Data, Beverly, you're with me. Number One, have a security team meet me in transporter room three. Twenty-first-century civilian clothes. You have the bridge."

The blasts had stopped by the time Lily made it to the stairs leading down to the silo. The entire area surrounding it was gouged with smoking craters that smelled of ozone. There had to be *some* damage down there, Lily decided, but thank God, it wasn't a direct hit.

But an eerie realization, not the electrical static lingering in the air, lifted the hair on her arms: this particular area had been hit harder than any other she'd passed on her run through the encampment—almost as if someone'd aimed at it intentionally.

No *direct* hits, but so many peripheral ones that there *had* to be damage down below, and if the *Phoenix* had been spared, it would be the most major of miracles.

And if there had been any harm done to the blast door

and the metal shielding on any one of a dozen components that were radioactively hot—

Damned if she was going to die from a nuke.

Lily squared her small shoulders, walked through the slowly opening door, and at the sight of what lay within the outer control room, sighed.

"Aww, God . . ."

FIVE

Freshly materialized, Picard drew in a breath and savored the stinging cold of a spring Montana night upon his face, feeling as though he had stepped inside a history text, one both thrilling and horrific. For there in front of him—and the away team of Data, Crusher, and four guards—was Zefram Cochrane's famous missile silo, situated at the foot of the grim, poverty-stricken mountainside settlement that was so commonplace in the first decade after the Third World War.

That was the thrilling part; but the horror came from the sight of the great smoldering craters the Borg's weapons had left surrounding the silo itself. At least part of the underground structure had collapsed, or was in danger of doing so.

There, beneath the scarred and muddy earth, Cochrane might already be dead.

For an instant, the seven of them hesitated at the

massive concrete door covering the actual shaft where the original missile had lain. No obvious means of entry there; Picard scanned the broken, uneven, sometimes smoking ground, and at last spied beneath a dirt mound a metal staircase leading downward.

He signaled to his team, which was already drawing phasers and tricorders, and pointed. "There." The word emerged as white mist and hung in the starkly cold air.

So they proceeded underground, the guards leading the way. The staircase, rickety and half rusted, led directly to what had been the original control room, where bored soldiers had sat awaiting a launch order that never came, because their superiors died in the first swift nuclear attack. Had they yielded to the madness infecting the rest of the world, they might have chosen to retaliate on their own; because they hadn't, the missile had remained intact . . . until Zefram Cochrane discovered it and beat it into a plowshare that would change not only Earth but thousands of other planets for the better.

Now the control-room ceiling was partially collapsed, most of the equipment crushed beneath chunks of concrete and fallen beams. Three of the consoles were illumined and active, but several others were dark. The lighting, too, was dimmed, and it, along with the wisp-like haze of dust, gave the chamber an unsettlingly eerie air. In the ghostly shadows, crushed to death beneath one of the dully gleaming beams, lay the sprawled corpse of a dark-haired man.

His face was turned away, half hidden by the beam, which lay on a diagonal across his back, from his left ear to his right hip. He lay atop the corpse of a woman; apparently his last act had been to shelter her.

53

In another corner of the room, another man had apparently been sitting in a chair at the console and had been thrown backward when the ceiling caved in on him. His face was covered by a mountain of rocks and silt, but his legs were visible.

The sights chilled Picard to the bone. He stood quietly while Crusher scanned them all, then looked askance when she approached him to report.

"They're all dead."

He nodded, grim. "See if any of them's Cochrane. Data—let's check on the warp ship."

The silo was of such historical significance that calling up a detailed map of it on the *Enterprise*-E's computers presented no problem; yet Picard could not get over how different it seemed now, in the twenty-first century. He had visited it in the twenty-third, and it had been a clean, well-lit, cheerful shrine, filled with the voices of cheerful tour guides and dotted with commemorative plaques bearing Cochrane's likeness.

Seeing it now, covered with dust and smoking soot and bloodied corpses, brought the reality home. *This* was where Cochrane had existed, in a violent, hostile past. No one hailed him then as the genius he was; no one helped him, no one believed, in those hard, embittered times, that the very thing that had destroyed the Earth would become her salvation, or that her greatest artistic and technological renaissance would come about because of Cochrane's work in these grim, rusting rooms.

Silently, Picard made a solemn promise to Zefram Cochrane, be he living or dead: The *Phoenix* had risen from the ashes of such horror, and he, Picard, would not permit her descendants to perish in another holocaust or to live without hope.

With Data beside him, he headed out into the corridor that led directly to the warp ship.

Moments before, Lily had staggered through the same control room, wiping angry tears away with the back of her hand. She had known the three people killed—John and Grace Weir-Quintana and Marcus Lee—in this little community, everyone knew everyone else. As best she could figure, her neighbors had been out strolling that night and had ducked into the nearby silo when the bombs came, figuring that it offered the best protection. They were right; it was far safer than a tent.

Who could have known this spot would have been hit hardest?

Almost as bad as the deaths was the damage done. The minute she saw the collapsed ceiling and the crushed consoles, any hope she'd had for the warp ship's launch died. The prewar computer that constantly monitored the silo's radiation levels lay buried beneath a mound of rubble; Zef's rebuilt console that normally displayed a schematic of the ship and warned of leakage or malfunction had gone distressingly dark.

At best, it meant that the sensors aboard the ship had been damaged or that there had been a jolt to the electrical systems; at worst . . .

She could not bring herself to finish the thought. Instead, she carefully made her way through the control room—being forced once to squeeze through a narrow opening between the wall and the largest pile of concrete chunks and steel beams that buried Grace and her husband. John lay face down, his boots extending out beyond the hillock of rubble, their patched, worn soles a mere foot from the wall; Lily moaned softly as she was forced to brush against them.

Ironically, the corridor that led toward the missile chamber itself was less damaged and thus more easily navigable. Lily made her way quickly to the lead blast door—still sealed, still protecting her from whatever might lie inside.

She let go a long exhalation of pure relief. The blast door, at least, had not given way—a sign that the *Phoenix* might be basically intact and that she hadn't absorbed a fatal amount of radiation already without knowing it.

Even so, she hesitated. There was simply no way to know whether the inner chamber was hot, with the computer destroyed. A few old Geiger counters—antiques used by a miserly army just before the war—had been stashed in a cabinet under the buried computer console, but they were now impossible to retrieve. Zef kept a couple of the Geiger counters in the missile chamber, just in case the main alarm system failed.

To know whether the chamber was hot, she would have to enter it. Lily drew a breath and stepped forward; the great leaden door rumbled as it slid slowly over the smooth concrete floor.

When it was open, she released all the air in her lungs with a single gusting sigh. If there was a leak, she was already a dead woman. Nothing to be done about it; she didn't care, she told herself, didn't care. Hadn't cared about anything after Dad died.

And yet, stepping over the threshold onto the catwalk, she felt fear seize her imagination. Her skin began to tingle and crawl—was she sensing the radiation?—and her breathing grew shallow, as if her lungs rebelled at the notion of taking in tainted air.

Lily stood on the highest catwalk, the one that led to the ship's cockpit in the vast chamber's heart. Beneath, two more floors of metal scaffolding led to the engineering and reactor levels on the *Phoenix*. The ground level was scattered with Zef's tools and equipment, partially buried beneath chunks of fallen ceiling; all, including the catwalks, were sprinkled with rubble and the same pulverized-concrete dust that had coated the outer control room.

When Zef had first brought her here, she had protested each step of the way—first because the very thought of walking into such a place evoked the blind panic that had so often seized her during the war, and then because she was outright terrified of heights, and the sweeping, vertiginous view from the entry sickened her as much as the sight of the slumbering death missile.

Now, she saw only the *Phoenix*.

To Lily, the warp vessel remained a thing of beauty, though it looked to be little more than an ICBM missile whose warhead had been replaced by a cockpit. She had carefully painted *Phoenix* across its shining flank, and had smiled when Zef had christened it with a bottle of stinking moonshine; now, the sight of ugly gashes on the ship's hull pained her more than if they had been etched upon her own flesh. Worse, some of them were scorched, as if the mysterious and blinding blasts had simply reached through the layers of earth and lead and fingered the warp ship, leaving the silent message: *Do not dare hope in* this. . . . *See how easily it is crushed?*

There was damage, yes, but perhaps not fatal; much of the fuselage seemed intact. A week's repair work, maybe, unless there was more damage inside . . .

Boots ringing against the metal grating, Lily ran across the trembling catwalk to the cockpit. It lay open, the way she and Zef had left it late the night before, and she immediately slipped into the pilot's chair.

The previous midnight, she had sat in one of the copilot/passenger seats, her stomach fluttering with excitement, and tried to imagine what it would look and feel like to sit beside Zef and stare out at the stars—at warp drive. Her one condition, when she first had agreed to become his "supplier," was that he had to take her with him on the test flight, had to teach her enough about the ship so she could assist him in piloting it.

Now, her stomach in knots from a very different kind of excitement, Lily glanced down at the control panel: dark. Electrical systems all down, and the cockpit stank of scorched metal and fabric. She tried to flick on the overhead lighting, but only the dim running lights came on. She swore softly, then opened a compartment and retrieved a flashlight. Next to it rested one of the old Geiger counters—a safety backup, Zef had said, in case the ship's sensors failed. Lily had never quite understood the point. If they were either working in the silo or up in space and the *Phoenix*'s metal shielding suddenly ruptured, what possible good would it do them to know how much radiation they'd absorbed? Dead was dead, whether the dose was six hundred or three thousand rads. They'd know soon enough, when the vomiting started.

And if that ever happened, she'd vowed darkly, she would put a bullet through her brain.

Still, she stared at the Geiger counter a good ten seconds before reluctantly picking it up—but she could not yet bring herself to turn it on.

Don't want to know. Not yet.

Not yet . . .

She put an arm through the counter's long strap and slung the instrument over her shoulder, then aimed the flashlight at the cockpit ceiling and examined it for damage.

What she saw made her gasp: directly over the right passenger seat, the fuselage had completely buckled, leaving a great smoldering wound that had spilled a mound of blackened cinders and pulverized concrete into the chair, which had collapsed. Worse, a jagged scorch mark indicated the trail of the blast, which had seared the back of the copilot seat, then split open the small hatch leading down to the engine room.

Her pulse quickened at the sight, but she wasted no time following the path of the damage. She hooked the light to her belt, pushed the splintered hatch aside, then grabbed the first metal rung and began the tedious climb down.

It was hard work: the air was surprisingly warm and smelled of ozone, dust, and burned wiring; the lingering smoke made her cough. Ominously, the walls of the shaft itself bore the dark, powdery scars of the blast, as if a nuclear lightning bolt had descended its entire length. After a few feet down, she realized the ladder had become molten and sagged like a Dali clock, then rehardened. Some of the rungs were welded fast to the bulkhead, making purchase impossible. Halfway down, it was clear that she'd either have to climb back up or else get down without the ladder.

Lily was not a tall woman, but the shaft was sufficiently narrow. She finally managed to wedge her shoulders against one wall, her feet against the other, and "walked" down—a terrifying experience, as the bulkheads were uneven, pitted; twice, she slipped and nearly went hurtling downward.

By the time she arrived at the entrance to the claustrophobically small engine room, she was simultaneously shivering, sweating, and feeling queasy. *Nerves, Lily, just nerves. Keep worrying about a leak and you'll make yourself puke.*

As she hopped from the shaft down into engineering, water splashed beneath her boots: a good two inches of water covered the deck. A sweep of the flashlight revealed that a conduit in the coolant system had ruptured—an easy fix and no big deal, but she had no idea how they were going to get all the water out. In a way, the mundaneness of the problem was comforting: one of her repetitive nightmares involved being trapped aboard the ship during a fire.

Abruptly, a wave of dizziness swept over her, and she caught the bridge of her nose with her thumb and forefinger and closed her eyes until it passed.

It was just anxiety and the rotten air, she told herself; the circulation system was probably malfunctioning, and the burned-ozone smell was even stronger here. A sweep of the flashlight revealed that the powerful bolt had slashed its way across the engine room, skittering over the equipment and leaving spots of damage before ending in a deep gouge in the lead deck, which just happened to serve as the major shield that protected the rest of the ship from the core reactors in the nacelles. Had it been pierced, the reactors would have been exposed, and the entire silo—and most of Montana—would have gone to kingdom come in a white-hot blaze of glory.

It was as though someone had—impossibly—*known* what Zef was doing down here and had intentionally targeted the *Phoenix*.

Easy, Lil; you're starting to sound paranoid.

She moved carefully over the slick deck, checking out each system—not just those along the jagged scar left by the blast, since ricochets were entirely possible. From time to time, she touched a piece of equipment and could feel its emanating heat even through her thick gloves. Luckily, the engines themselves were untouched, as was the lead casing, thick as an elephant's leg, surrounding the fuel line—both sights that made her smile. There would be repairs and a delay, but the *Phoenix* would launch after all.

Lily stripped off a glove and lowered herself to a squat, using flashlight, fingertips, and eyes to examine the encased tubing down to the throttle complex. The square, lead-clad complex sat directly atop the thick leaden deck that shielded the entire ship from the core reactor one level below. The throttle's purpose was to regulate the flow of fuel from the core to the engines via a system of valves; hence, it was crucial to the project's success.

She examined the front of the assembly first. It was unmarked, but the wavering elliptical glow of the flashlight revealed a dark ash butterfly painted on the bulkhead behind the throttle. Instinctively, she reached around the casing until her hand rested between the bulkhead and the throttle complex, then ran her fingertips over the startlingly hot metal surface.

Within two seconds after she began the tactile scan, the metal gave way to nothingness; her fingers, then entire hand, reached through all the way until they touched the sizzling-hot throttle itself.

"Shit!" Startled, she dropped the flashlight and snatched her hand away, falling onto her rump against the Geiger counter hanging at her hip; her already-blistering fingers were coated with fine gray ash. Both the casing and the throttle should have been cold, stone cold—so they must have been directly struck by a ricochet from the blast.

Or so Lily told herself . . . until she stared up from her burned hand at the black powder butterfly on the bulkhead.

It was captured now in a brilliant circle of white light—not the pale stream from the fallen flashlight, but a painfully intense glow, as if the casing instead housed a small sun.

"The valve," she said calmly, as though explaining something to Zef. "The valve to the warp cores must have somehow been displaced. There's a leak."

She stared at her blistered fingers, which had touched the superheated throttle assembly, and watched as the dark-brown skin of her hand turned slowly to scarlet. A burn, caused by direct exposure to the radiation streaming from the core. Strangely, there was little pain.

Maybe it wasn't that bad. Maybe it wasn't that bad— *You're dead meat, Lil. Be honest.*

No, maybe it wasn't that bad. Somehow. *Somehow . . .*

Her hands trembled violently as she pulled the Geiger counter out from under her left hip and fiddled with the controls. She *knew* how to use the embarrassingly simple device, but her fingers refused to cooperate. Worse, the counter's readout panel became suddenly blurred as an intense wave of nausea swept over her.

You're not going to puke. You're just terrified, the air in here is awful, and it's all giving you a terrific headache. Calm down, calm down . . .

She closed her eyes for several seconds; when she opened them again, the nausea had eased, and she somehow managed to turn on the counter and calibrate it. No point in exposing herself again to the direct stream coming from the damaged throttle; instead, she remained sitting on the deck and sampled the air there. Within a few seconds, the readout began to flash—in red—a number: three-one-two-nine.

Three thousand, one hundred twenty-nine rads, five times the minimum lethal dose.

She pitched forward onto her hands and knees and vomited.

The spell lasted a full fifteen seconds. When it was over, she was weak, rubber-legged—but rage pushed her to her feet.

"Goddamn bastards," she croaked. "Goddam *bastards!"* The ECON hadn't been satisfied with simply rebuilding the whole freaking world that they'd destroyed—no, they had to use what pathetic few resources remained and make sure every single remaining, ragged bit of the planet was blown to hell, too.

Impossible to climb back up the crawl space to exit through the cockpit; instead, Lily pushed open the emergency hatch and staggered out onto the engine room–level catwalk. She was a walking dead woman, but she had a bit of agonizingly nauseated time before she passed out and/or started convulsing, and she intended to use it to accomplish two things: she would seal off the blast door so no one else—especially not Zef— could get in, then she would go down to the ground floor (ground zero, they called it, she remembered with irony) and retrieve his gun. She would die by her own hand rather than succumb to a nuke. It was a matter of honor, a statement against the war.

She had meant to go up rather than down in order to seal off the door first, but before she realized what she was doing in her blurry, feverish haze, she was crawling on the gently swaying first-level catwalk, pausing twice to stop and retch—so violently it left her gasping and her back and abdominal muscles torn. The ground was only one level beneath her, and she could not spare the energy to turn around and head back up.

The nausea was so fierce, so disabling, so outright painful that it displaced all fear. She moved toward the ground level—and the gun—with a singular purpose: the relief of suffering.

And when at last she arrived at the silo's concrete base, she staggered, reeling over the scattered debris and equipment until she reached the metal cabinet built into the stone-gray wall.

Inside, hidden beneath thick coils of electrical wiring, lay Zef's gun. She had taken it from him almost a year ago, when he had sunk into one of his depressions and threatened to kill himself; he had asked after it only once, then forgotten. She clawed through the neatly arranged coils, letting them fall to the floor and roll away; it no longer mattered now. She lifted the gun in her hand. It seemed astonishingly heavy, and she was forced to grip it with both hands, lest she drop it.

For a moment, blinded by nausea and a skull-splitting headache, groaning from the dizziness and freezing-hot feverish aches, she sagged against the cool wall and lifted the gun muzzle to her skull, just above the right ear. It was cold, solid, comforting against her warm flesh. She closed her eyes and put a finger on the trigger. . . .

No, no, Zef—remember? The door . . .

By then, the world seemed to be swimming, submerged in a blurry, ever-changing ocean. She took the gun and slung it over her shoulder as she had the abandoned Geiger counter, then stumbled back toward the ladder. The climb up to the first-level catwalk was so exhausting she wept when it was over and lay belly down against the metal.

Reality began to dissolve, leaving nothing but the physical anguish. In her mind's eye, she saw her father standing before her on the swaying scaffolding, saying sternly: *I tried to tell you, Lil, tried to set an example. They won. They took our cities, our sons, our daughters, our homes, our properties, our doctors—they took every-thing from us, including our hearts. What's the point? Why did you keep punishing yourself? The only thing of worth you've had for the past ten years was Cochrane's ship, and now they've taken that, too.*

Pick up the gun, baby. Pick up the gun.

She fumbled, sweating, for the weapon, then remembered again: Zef. The blast door. If it wasn't sealed off, he'd come in here and die—after he found her bloodied corpse.

Dying didn't matter, nausea didn't matter, the increasingly blurred vision that made negotiating the catwalk a terrifying experience didn't matter.

Close the door for Zef. He was all the world had. . . .

Impossibly, she rose to her feet, clutching the railing with all that remained of her strength. The world spun dizzyingly again, but she gritted her teeth and took one step, then another.

Two levels above her, the blast door rumbled open. She stared myopically up at the entrance with pure horror; it had to be Zef, which meant she had failed at the one good thing she wanted to accomplish before death.

She almost sobbed his name aloud, but at the last second, instinct held her back, and she sank down behind the railing and peered over the top.

Two blurred figures, not one, stepped onto the upper catwalk. Both were dressed like North-Amers and pale-faced—one ghostly so. They entered and moved over toward the *Phoenix*'s cockpit. Lily could not see their faces clearly, but their posture and movements were unmistakably *not* Zef's.

The paler, taller one lifted a small, dark device and pointed it at the warp ship, then consulted its readout and said, in a masculine voice, "There is significant damage to the fuselage and primary intercooler system."

She squinted up at the two, struggling to focus, to decide in her confusion what should be done. The intruder had a distinctly North-Am accent. Was he enemy or friend? And if he was a friend, then how did he know so much about the *Phoenix,* and where had he gotten that amazing device?

If he was an enemy, it didn't matter. If they stayed long enough or got close enough to the engine, they were both dead.

Quietly, she lifted the gun with shaking hands, aimed it upward, and listened.

"We should have the original blueprints in the *Enterprise* comp—"

She did not wait for him to finish. She pulled back the bolt and began to fire. Bullets zinged off the metal scaffolding; the men at once dove for cover behind the railings.

"Hold your fire!" the other called, in a British accent. "We're here to help you!"

By then, all the pain and rage had surfaced in her and she did not care whether they were friend or foe; she cared only that she might avenge herself, her mother, her father, the *Phoenix,* on anyone, anyone at all. *"Bullshit!"* she screamed, and fired another round.

Silence followed.

She peered over the railing to see if they were dead, and instead watched the paler man *step over the railing off the catwalk,* and drop forty feet to the scaffolding below.

You're hallucinating now, Lil. Hallucinating. This isn't happening; maybe these guys aren't even here. . . .

As she watched, the man did it again—crawled over the railing on the second-level catwalk and plummeted downward.

Hallucination or not, she lifted Zef's gun and pumped

him full of a good dozen bullets. She'd hit him—even with her blurry vision, she *saw* the bullets tear into his torso, saw him recoil from the impact.

All the same, he landed with a loud metal clank on his feet . . . right in front of her on the catwalk.

She gaped at him, stunned, and pressed the trigger again. Once again, the bullets pierced him; once again, he rocked backward from the impact. Yet he *would not fall,* even when she continued to blast away at him, the bullets chewing a large hole in his jacket's breast.

At last, the gun clicked empty. Lily lowered it and blinked, thunderstruck, at the creature standing before her.

He wasn't human, wasn't human at all; his face was the color of shimmering moongold, his eyes amber. He stared down at the bloodless, gaping hole in his chest with perfect impassivity, then looked up at Lily.

"Greetings," he said.

It's a hallucination. You're dying; you can't trust anything you see or hear. Don't be frightened, Lil; it's almost over, almost over. . . .

The creature began to walk toward her. She drew back, then wheeled about to run away, but the dizziness overwhelmed her. The silo dimmed abruptly, and she tripped, then fell forward. In the timeless instant before her head struck the metal grating, she thought: *This is it. This is it. It's all over, and there's no hope for anyone anymore. I'm sorry, Zef. . . .*

Silence then, and blessed darkness.

SIX

☆

As he stepped back into the vast chamber housing the *Phoenix,* Beverly Crusher at his side, Picard heard Data's urgent call: "Captain! This woman requires medical attention!"

Urgent, yes, but somehow detached; before entering the missile silo, the android had chosen to deactivate his emotion chip. It was a wise choice: had Data not done so, he might not so easily have come up with a quick solution, nor faced the desperate and rather violent young woman with such fearlessness.

It was a choice Picard rather envied.

However, at the sound of the android's voice, neither he nor Crusher wasted a second's time hurrying across the scaffolding to the place where the dark-skinned young woman lay unconscious, a twenty-first-century automatic weapon nestled against her cheek.

Beverly knelt down over her patient, tucked an errant

strand of strawberry blond hair behind her ear, and magically produced a medical scanner. The woman had no visible injuries, but Picard noted the subtle change in Crusher's intense expression as she checked the scanner's readout; the condition was grave, very grave indeed.

She glanced up at Picard, her tone somber. "Severe theta-radiation poisoning."

"The radiation is coming from the damaged throttle assembly," Data said; he had been scanning the ship with his tricorder.

Beverly's blue eyes narrowed; she squared her shoulders, a little gesture that said (a) she had made her decision concerning what was best for her patient, (b) Picard would not like it, and (c) his chief medical officer did not, in this case, give a damn about his opinion. "We're all going to have to be inoculated . . . and I need to get *her*"—she nodded at the unconscious woman— "to sickbay."

Picard could not repress an immediate scowl. He opened his mouth to begin a stern speech, one that Crusher ought to have memorized by now, but she stopped him with a look.

"Jean-Luc, no lectures about the Prime Directive. I'll keep her unconscious."

He sighed. "Very well. Tell Commander Riker to beam down with a search party. We need to find Cochrane."

"Right," Beverly said, and pressed her comm badge. "Crusher to *Enterprise*. Two to beam directly to sickbay."

He turned and heard, rather than watched, the women dematerialize; his gaze was already drawn back to the wounded *Phoenix.*

"We have less than fourteen hours before this ship has to be launched," he told Data grimly, then tapped his comm badge. "Picard to engineering."

"La Forge here, Captain," Geordi replied, lifting his gaze from his padd and looking out across the multi-leveled cavern that was engineering. He had finally gotten used to the startling size of the area and all its new bells and whistles, but the sight of the newly designed, more powerful warp core still awed him.

He drew the back of a hand across his forehead and thoughtlessly wiped away the perspiration there as he listened to what Picard had to say.

"Geordi . . . Cochrane's ship was damaged in the attack. I want you to assemble an engineering detail and get down here. We have some work to do."

"Aye, sir," he replied, but his professional tone belied his true reaction, which was embarrassingly similar to that of a kid set loose in a candy shop. A chance to work on the *Phoenix*—Zefram Cochrane's ship, the mother of all warp drives!

He repressed a grin—the situation was, after all, too somber—as he turned to face the others working. "Alpha shift, assemble in transporter room three. We're heading down to the surface."

On his way out, he paused to speak to Ensign Paul Porter, a recent addition to the *Enterprise*-E, but a levelheaded man and a fine technician. "Porter, you're in command here until I get back."

The brown-haired, pink-skinned human nodded smartly. "Aye, sir."

La Forge sighed and ran a finger under his collar; it came away dripping with perspiration. "And take a look at the environmental controls. It's getting a little warm in here."

"Amazing, isn't it?" Picard asked softly of Data, as the two stood watching the engineering team set to work on the *Phoenix*. "This ship used to be a nuclear missile. . . ."

The android raised his iridescent face upward, toward the ship's scarred silver nose, but his eyes betrayed no emotion, only detached intellectual curiosity. "It is an historical irony that Dr. Cochrane would choose an instrument of mass destruction to inaugurate an era of peace."

The captain sighed. Until Data reactivated his emotion chip, it would be impossible to explain to him what "a sense of wonder" meant. Rather than try, Picard reached out and rested a palm against the vessel's now cool, radiation-free hull. Unbelievable, to touch her, to actually feel a piece of the most historically significant hunk of metal ever pressed to his own skin. The *Phoenix* had truly changed history, not just of North America or the world or the solar system, but of the entire galaxy.

The awe must have shown on his face; he glanced up to find Data studying him, and he gave a slight smile.

"Boyhood fantasy," he explained. "I've seen this ship a hundred times in the Smithsonian, but I was never able to touch it."

Data frowned slightly. "Does tactile contact alter your perception of the *Phoenix?*"

"Oh, yes," Picard murmured, his smile widening. "For human beings, the sense of touch is sometimes more important than sight or sound. It *connects* you to an object, makes it more real."

The android cocked his head inquisitively, then stretched forth an arm and pressed it stiffly against the ship's hull. Picard worked to maintain a serious expression as Data absorbed this new concept.

"I can detect imperfections in the titanium casing," Data reported at last, "temperature variations in the fuel manifold . . . but it is no more 'real' to me now than it was a moment ago."

As he spoke, Deanna Troi emerged from around a corner and stopped abruptly at the sight of the two officers lovingly stroking the *Phoenix.*

"Would you three like to be alone?" Her tone was wry, but the vaguely troubled look in her black eyes boded ill. Data continued to pat the ship absently, but Picard immediately pulled his hand away and turned to face her.

"What have you found?"

All humor fled her demeanor. "There's no sign of Cochrane anywhere in the complex."

"He must be nearby," Picard insisted. "This experiment meant everything to him." He paused. "Start searching the . . . 'community' out there. And be careful; the people of this time are desperate and frightened. They're not going to welcome strangers."

"Understood," she said, then paused and lowered her

voice. "Captain . . . we should consider the possibility that Dr. Cochrane was killed in the attack."

Picard stared up at the *Phoenix*'s scorched surface and felt his face harden. "If that's true . . . then the future may die with him."

Back on the *Enterprise*-E, Ensign Paul Porter stood on an upper-level engineering deck and scowled at the exposed circuitry on the environmental panel. Both the temperature and humidity had risen alarmingly over the past half-hour, and his new black Starfleet uniform was definitely not designed for comfort in swamplike conditions; both its front and back were soaked with perspiration that would not evaporate because of the damp air.

At his side, Ensign Inge Eiger followed his gaze. She hailed from one of the ice planets and was appropriately tall, flaxen-haired, with a plain face and crystalline blue eyes. Porter liked Eiger for her easy humor and quicksilver brain; most of all, he liked her because she had made sure from his very first day here that, as the newest assignee to the *Enterprise,* he never had to eat alone. In the officers' mess, he had taken to calling her Inge, and she to calling him Paul, though both avoided such familiarity while on duty. At work, he forced himself to think of her as Eiger.

He hoped their friendship would deepen into something more, though he had no idea how Inge—that is, Eiger—felt.

"What do you think?" Eiger asked, her faint frown echoing Porter's. Her translucent skin was flushed coral, ashine with sweat; a dark hourglass of perspiration stained the front of her uniform from neck to abdomen. "What's going on?"

"I have no idea," Porter replied honestly, reading the hieroglyphic circuitry and finding no answers there. "It's like the entire environmental system's gone crazy. And it's not just engineering—it's the entire *deck.*" He gave a small sigh and stared at the panel in frustration. No sign of malfunction here; it was as if someone had *programmed* in a different set of parameters and the system was merely doing its job. "Maybe it's a problem with the EPS conduits," he said at last, though he had little faith that it was; but La Forge had given the order, and Porter was determined to solve the problem before the away team returned.

Porter moved over to an access ladder and climbed up to the hatch on the ceiling. While Eiger watched from below, he opened the hatch and wormed into the maintenance crawl space.

Inside, the tunnel—too low to allow even a child to stand—was silent and shadowy. Most crew members complained that the crawl spaces were too claustrophobic, but Porter had always found the quiet darkness soothing.

Now, in the damp heat, the tube seemed oppressive, moody . . . even strangely intimidating. Ridiculous, of course; he dismissed it sternly and started scanning the conduits for any sign of malfunction. The dim auxiliary lighting, combined with the scanner's glow, was just sufficient to permit him to see clearly.

He had barely begun when an odd noise emanated

from somewhere down the crawl space—a skittering sound, like swift human footsteps, and yet not. But someone—or some*thing*—was moving toward him.

He stopped scanning at once and glanced down the tunnel—just in time to see a dark shape the size of an adult human suddenly disappear around a corner.

"Hello?" he called, then louder: "Hey!"

Eiger's voice filtered up from below. "Who are you talking to?"

He paused. "Is there anyone else doing maintenance in this section?"

"Not that I know of."

Adamant instinct told him the answer to the environmental problem lay in the direction the shadowy form had appeared. Without explanation to Eiger, he crawled further down the tube until at last he arrived at a four-way intersection.

No sign of anyone straight ahead or to the right. But a glance to the left revealed a stunningly bizarre sight.

The orderly, logical arrangement of conduits that Porter expected to see had been altered in a particularly ghastly manner: alien power-packs had been randomly, almost carelessly, attached using both mechanical cables and those fashioned from flesh, tissue, bone. From all of it emerged free-form tubing that pulsed with radiant-colored fluids and pure energy.

For an instant, Porter could do nothing but gape at the horrific display—and that instant was all that was left him. His amazement was so total that he did not hear the renewed soft skittering, did not see the dark shapes looming until the very millisecond they were upon him.

It was all very swift: swift recognition, swift terror, swift pain.

Swift nothing at all.

Abysmally hot and faintly anxious, Inge Eiger was waiting beside the ladder that led up to the maintenance hatch when the horrible sounds came: a resounding thump, a faint moan, a sickeningly liquid crunch.

The moan had been Porter's; Eiger knew his voice well enough to be certain of it. In the instant she heard the not-quite-simultaneous sounds, she became convinced that something in the crawlway had collapsed on him, that he was badly injured.

"Paul?"

No response.

"You okay in there?"

Silence. She climbed the ladder at top speed and opened the hatch. As she did, another conviction seized her, this one overwhelming and indisputable. There was *someone else* in the Jefferies tube, the person or persons that Paul had seen, persons of ill will who had hurt him. She slowly poked head and shoulders into the crawl space and squinted into the dim distance, trying to see Paul.

She never saw him. Instead, against the ominously charcoal backdrop, she saw a blacker shape—no, shapes—hovering only meters away, waiting.

Waiting for *her*, Eiger realized, and she made a move to pull back, shut the hatch, scramble down the ladder, call security—but there was no time for any of it, no time. In less than a heartbeat, the blackness was upon her, and there was no time to press her comm badge, no time to run, to think, to breathe, even to scream.

Inside the missile silo, Picard stood beside Troi, Data, and Will Riker as the four of them admiringly examined the almost-repaired *Phoenix*. The captain had been thinking of little else except the vessel itself and the chances of finding Zefram Cochrane alive when at once a sense of foreboding seized him.

Whispers in his head, separate yet unified: the collective. And it spoke of the *Enterprise*-E.

Picard turned away from the others and froze, listening, trying to understand . . . but the whispers faded as quickly as they had come.

Troi saw and perhaps sensed his sudden overwhelming concern. She sidled over to him and asked softly, "Captain, what is it?"

"I'm not sure," he confessed, as he tapped his comm badge. "Picard to *Enterprise*. Is everything all right up there, Mr. Worf?"

"Yes, sir." But the Klingon's resonant baritone was faintly hesitant. "We are experiencing some environmental difficulties on deck sixteen . . . but that is all."

The comment served to focus Picard's vague anxiety. "What kind of difficulties?"

"Humidity levels have risen by seventy-two percent . . . and the temperature has jumped ten degrees in the last hour."

Humidity and heat. Something about the combination triggered a mental alarm, but the memory associated with it remained submerged. "Data and I are returning to the ship."

"Understood," Worf said, and Picard terminated the communication, then turned to Riker, who had been listening with half his attention, while the other half was still busy adoring the *Phoenix.*

"Number One, take charge down here."

Riker finally tore his gaze from Cochrane's ship and looked at the captain with a puzzled expression. "Aye, sir."

Picard did not face him long; no point in letting the others see his fear, though Troi no doubt sensed it. The sight of the rebuilt *Phoenix* had made him hopeful, but his optimism was short-lived. For if the Borg somehow managed to seize control of the *Enterprise*-E, there would be hope for none of them: the *Enterprise* crew, Cochrane, the injured woman, the Earth of the past and the Earth of the future.

Dr. Beverly Crusher drew a damp hand across her forehead, trying to smooth back the sweat-darkened strawberry-blond strands that clung there, then gently lifted the surgical stimulator from her still-unconscious patient's torso. The twenty-first-century woman would be a bit woozy when she woke, but otherwise fine— assuming she managed to survive the Borg invasion. Crusher would have to administer a sedative in the next half-hour to be sure the Prime Directive was upheld and the patient remained sleeping; in the meantime, the doctor paused to study the slightly rounded oval of the unconscious woman's face.

It revealed a woman still young but hardened by the ravages of that terrible twenty-first-century decade: loss, deprivation, and exposure; her dark chestnut skin, which should have aged more slowly than paler flesh, bore shallow creases at the corners of the mouth and eye, the delicate spot between the eyebrows. She had seen too many people die in the Third World War, and she had spent too many winters in Montana without proper shelter. Hardened, yes, but she was still delicately pretty, her hair trained in black tendrils that fell onto a high forehead, her lips full and blooming, her taupe lids squeezed tightly over huge eyes that Crusher had yet to see. Beneath the fringes of long, tightly curled lashes were aubergine shadows; she had not had much sleep, lately, either.

She must have known that she was dying; inhabitants of that era were all too familiar with the symptoms of radiation sickness. Why, then, had she been so desperate to kill Picard and Data? For all she knew, they, too, had been lethally exposed and would soon follow her in death.

Delirium? Crusher could not believe it. Instinct told her that the woman had been protecting something: the *Phoenix.*

Crusher ran the back of her hand over her face again and sighed, then glanced up at Nurse Ogawa, who was assisting. Alyssa looked like Beverly felt: sweat-drenched, flushed, and frankly irritable.

"I've repaired the damage to her cell membranes," Crusher said. "But I'd like to run some tests on her spinal tissues." She fanned herself with a hand. "And would you find out why it's so hot in here?"

Ogawa never got a chance to reply; the words were not quite out of Crusher's mouth when every light in the room flickered, then went dark—including every active monitor.

"Now what?" Alyssa said bitterly.

Beverly tapped her comm badge. "Crusher to engineering."

Static.

Her tone rose slightly as she said, "Crusher to bridge."

Static. She drew in a breath, unsettled. Losing power on the decks was not necessarily an indication that something ominous was occurring, but a power failure should have absolutely no effect on communications. For them both to go out at the same instant was simply too much of a coincidence for comfort.

Alyssa started and looked up at the walls; Beverly followed her gaze, hearing the noise, too: an eerie skittering movement inside the bulkheads themselves.

Another skitter above, in the ceiling. She glanced up, unable to suppress a shudder of surprise, then caught Alyssa's gaze; the two of them stared wide-eyed at each other in silent recognition of the other's fear.

Something was outside . . . and trying to get in.

"Report," Picard commanded, as he and Data stepped onto the bridge. Worf immediately rose from the captain's chair and returned to his console.

"We have just lost contact with deck sixteen," the Klingon said, settling into his own station. "Communications, internal sensors, everything. I was about to send a security team to investigate."

"No." Picard ignored Worf's reaction of mild surprise; there was no time to explain how he *knew* what he knew. "Seal off deck sixteen and post security teams at every access point."

"Aye, sir." The Klingon leaned over his console and

set to work at once, though he did not try to mask the confusion in his eyes.

Picard took a step toward the newest lieutenant on the bridge. "Mr. Hawk. Before we lost internal sensors, what were the exact environmental conditions in Main Engineering?"

Hawk fingered his board skillfully, then furrowed his dark brow as he read the results. "Atmospheric pressure was ten kilopasquals above normal . . . ninety-two percent humidity . . ."

"Thirty-nine point one degrees Celsius," Picard chorused with him, and the younger officer glanced up at him in amazement. "Like a Borg ship."

The bridge fell resoundingly silent for the space of several seconds.

Worf spoke first, his tone indignant. "Borg . . . on the *Enterprise?*"

"They must have realized their ship was doomed," Picard said, once again utterly unsure *how* he knew this, and just as unshakably certain that it was true. "So they beamed here while our shields were down. After they assimilate the *Enterprise* . . . Earth."

Another heartbeat of silence. And then the lights began to flicker. Picard whirled about and watched the monitors behind him begin to fritz, then darken, one by one.

"Sir!" Hawk started in his chair, his voice high-pitched with alarm. "Command control is being rerouted to Main Engineering! Weapons, shields, propulsion . . . !"

"Data, quickly!" the captain shouted. "Lock out the main computer!"

The android sped to the nearest console and worked the controls with inhuman swiftness, his hands a blur that dizzied Picard to watch. Instead, the captain watched encryption codes scroll across the monitor. In a matter of seconds, Data turned back to him and said, "I have isolated the main computer with a fractal encryption code. It is highly unlikely the Borg will be able to break it."

Picard permitted himself the merest of sighs, but knew any relief he might feel would be appallingly temporary. As he did, the lights gave their last flicker, then went out, leaving only the emergency lighting. Only a few consoles remained functional; one of them was Worf's.

"The Borg have cut power to all decks . . . except sixteen," the Klingon said, raising his bronzed face to share an ominously meaningful look with Picard.

Hawk's eyes were wide, his tone still taut with tension; even so, he seemed determined to find some comfort in the midst of the horrifying situation. "But without the computer," he countered, "they won't be able to control the ship."

Picard silenced him with a grim look. "The Borg won't stay on deck sixteen."

And the dreadful thing was, he *knew* it.

SEVEN

Sweet, soothing darkness, from which she was reluctant to rise; the first true rest since the war. And so deliciously warm. Yet they wouldn't let her sleep.

Voices, murmuring, fragmented, at times indistinct.

". . . got to take her; can't worry about the damned Prime Directive."

"*They're* the ones changing history. If we let her die, how do we know . . ."

". . . get her up."

". . . take her. Go, go, move—"

Strange noises: the sound of rapidly moving metal against metal, like a hundred mechanical mice scurrying inside a wall.

". . . coming. They're almost *here* . . ."

Lily swore silently at them: *Quiet! Quiet, damn it. It feels too good to wake up. And you're waking me up.*

"Wake up!"

"Let's go. C'mon, *move* it!"

The world began to shake. Earthquake? Lily wondered. Or another blast? She didn't care, didn't care, so long as she didn't have to . . .

"Wake up!" a feminine voice demanded, and Lily grudgingly fluttered her eyelids to see a woman with red-gold hair staring down at her.

She moaned, shut her eyes, and tried to turn away; more skittering noises, growing ever closer. The world began to tremble again, and she peered out at it once again to find the same woman shaking her by the shoulders. "Come on, wake up!"

"Where . . . what?" Lily blinked and lifted her head; as her dimly lit surrounding came into sharp focus, she could better see the woman's expression: wide-eyed, urgent, determined.

"There's no time to explain," the woman told her. "I need you to sit up." No weapons in sight—only a bunch of weird-looking equipment hanging from the ceiling, but Lily got the definite impression that she'd better do exactly as the woman said.

Besides, Lily had had a lot of experience over the last ten years at reading people—who would help her, and who was out to do her harm. She could trust this one.

She pushed herself and staggered off the bed, with the woman's help. She tried to linger a second, because the room was so astonishingly different from anything she'd ever seen that she longed to inspect it. But now was apparently not the time. Other people were rising from beds and being rushed by other people into a hole in the wall—all of them wearing the same black-and-gray jumpsuit; the strawberry blonde, likewise clad, took Lily's arm and began to pull her in the same direction.

They passed by another woman, a plumper, dark-haired one who was pointing a little black instrument at a door. She, too, wore the black uniform.

"Alyssa!" The strawberry blonde pushed Lily toward her. "Take her and go!"

At once, Alyssa grabbed Lily's arm with no-nonsense firmness and began to steer her toward the people crawling into the wall tunnel. It was Alyssa's face— open, honest, taut with fear—that made Lily come to herself and realize: these people were all terrified . . . and fleeing from the source of the ominous metal-on-metal screeching that had grown thunderous.

Something was trying to push its way in, something so horrible these people didn't want to be around for it.

And for some reason, they were protecting her as if she were part of the group. She glanced down and was for some reason relieved to see that she still wore her old leather vest and brown jeans.

This was one damned strange dream. And unsettlingly detailed.

"Those doors won't hold much longer," Alyssa shouted over her shoulder. "They're going to be right behind us!"

The woman who had handed her off to Alyssa was last to follow, and thus clearly in charge; she obviously agreed. She lingered, casting a worried glance at the door, then her surroundings. "We need a diversion. Is the EMH still online?"

Alyssa glanced at a console. "It should be. The holo-buffers are still functioning."

So, Lily thought. *This* is *what it looks like—some kind of hospital. And it has a secret weapon, this EMH. . . .*

The one in charge quirked her lip in disgust, but her worried gaze remained on the door, which had begun to creak as if something was pushing against it. "God, I hate those things."

As she spoke, the door let out a screech and began to buckle inward; she wasted no more time, but looked upward and said, "Computer—activate the EMH program."

At that precise instant, it was Lily's turn to enter the crowded tunnel; Alyssa gestured for her to hurry along, but she lingered—and watched as, out of thin air, a man appeared. He was slender, Caucasian, with dark, thinning hair, thick eyebrows, and a vaguely smug attitude.

Even more amazing, he *spoke.* His voice was calm, measured; he had to have noticed the loud battering sound and the collapsing door, but he seemed absolutely unconcerned about the matter as he addressed the woman who had caused him to appear. "Please state the nature of the medical emergency."

"Twenty Borg are about to break down that door, and we need time to get out of here," she shouted in one urgent breath. *"Create a diversion!"* And she began to run toward Alyssa and toward Lily, who had crawled into the tube but listened to the conversation behind her.

The man's tone grew irritated. "This isn't part of my program. I'm a doctor, not a doorstop."

By then, the woman had climbed into the tunnel, and as she prepared to pull down the hatch, she called back with equal irritation, "Dance for them; tell them a

87

story—I don't care. Just give us a few extra seconds!"

With a loud clank, the hatch shut. Lily waited for both women to crawl past her before at last allowing herself to be pulled along.

Outside, in sickbay, there came a sound like thunder as the door finally crashed inward. Silence for a time, followed by the sounds of whirring, metal clanking.

And the man's unctuous voice: "According to Starfleet medical research, Borg implants cause severe skin irritations. Perhaps you'd like an . . . analgesic cream?"

One wild dream, Lily thought. *One wild dream . . .*

Yet by the time she had crawled on hands and knees a good quarter-mile down the tunnel, listening to the breathing and soft comments of the others, feeling the cool metal against her now-ungloved hands, Lily had come to realize that this was no dream. Her mind was exceptionally clear now, enough to know that certain aspects of this were simply *too* real: the physical effort it took to keep up with the others, for one thing. She was strong, used to lifting and running and walking miles, but she had never crawled as fast as she possibly could before, and new muscles were aching.

For another thing, the thrill of being really warm had worn off; she was *hot,* sweating like a glass of ice on a July afternoon.

And then there was a third thing, one that puzzled her beyond all understanding. She remembered now: the ECON attack had come, and she had gone to the silo and been exposed to an unbelievably fatal dose of radiation from the damaged throttle valve. She hadn't dreamed *that;* she was capable of dreaming only what she could imagine—and nausea that intense, that unrelenting, that unspeakably unbearable was beyond all imagination.

She had been dying, and two men had come, one of them British. She had shot at them and tried to kill the one that looked like a robot . . . but the bullets hadn't stopped him. She'd been so sick, so dizzy that she'd simply passed out in front of him; she remembered that final glance up at his quizzical and pale, golden face.

Then she'd awakened somewhere totally different, in terrible danger and was now following a group of uniformed people she didn't know.

And she felt perfectly fine.

Just in front of her, the strawberry blonde spoke up. "Follow me," she told the group, and scurried toward the front in order to lead them. "We need to get off this deck."

The distraction gave Lily an opportunity. She paused in the semidarkness—there was no one behind her or too close in front of her to notice—and held her injured hand in front of her face.

No blisters, no pain, no radiation burn. The skin was perfect again; in fact, a small scar left on her thumb from the time it'd been smashed by a piece of dropped equipment was entirely *gone,* erased.

So just where the hell *was* she?

Inside some sort of organization, maybe; these people were all wearing uniforms. But were they the ECON, or were they fleeing it? The evidence was contradictory.

The British man and his robot must have picked her up when she passed out . . .

And brought her here? If these people were ECON and wanted to destroy the *Phoenix*, why were they trying to take care of her now?

Too weird. Just all too weird to be true.

Don't forget, Lil. You were dying. Three thousand one hundred twenty-nine rads, remember? Sorry, but even the ECON couldn't have come up with a total cure for a superlethal dose of radiation. Not even in ten years' time . . .

So what are you—dead? This is one sorry excuse for an afterlife.

Are you sure you aren't still hallucinating?

Stop. Stop. Stop.

Whatever this is, it's such a complicated mess there's no point in trying to understand it right now. Just follow your instincts and take care of yourself.

Their leader rounded a corner, and the rest of the group obediently followed—except for Lily, who sat back on her haunches and watched silently as the group headed off in one direction.

And when they were out of sight, she struck off in another.

In the *Enterprise*-E's security bay, as ten officers worked swiftly in the background to charge and test phaser rifles, Worf and Data listened intently to their commanding officer.

"The first thing they'll do in engineering," Picard said quietly, with a conviction that unsettled him but seemed to distress his listeners not at all, "is establish a collective—a central point from where they'll control the hive."

He moved over to a large display padd, activated it, and called up a schematic diagram of Main Engineering. "The problem is, if we begin firing particle weapons inside engineering, we risk hitting the warp core. So I believe our goal should be to puncture one of the plasma coolant tanks." He tapped another control; the schematic rotated and zoomed in on a diagram of the warp core with two flanking coolant tanks, each marked with a flashing biohazard symbol. "Data?"

The android had apparently changed into more than just his uniform; the detachment in his amber eyes had vanished, replaced by warmth, enthusiasm, and more than a little nervous anticipation. "An excellent idea," he replied. "Plasma coolant will liquefy any organic material on contact."

Worf turned, thick red-brown eyebrows rushing together beneath his skull ridges, and regarded Data with a mixture of disdain and concern. "But the Borg aren't entirely organic."

"No," Picard said. "But like any true cybernetic life-form, they can't survive without their organic components."

The Klingon gave one of his abrupt nods of approval, accompanied by a stern grunt, then turned and reached into one of the lockers and began to prepare his own phaser rifle. "I have ordered all weapons to be set on a rotating modulation. But the Borg will adapt quickly." He paused and shot a meaningful look at Picard. "We will have a dozen shots at most."

The captain acknowledged with a glance, then hesitated a heartbeat before speaking again. "One other thing. Warn your teams they may encounter *Enterprise* crewmembers who have already been assimilated. They mustn't hesitate to fire." The memory of Locutus rose unbidden, and with it the agonizing moment when he had stared at the Borg's viewscreen and seen the horrified faces of his own crew there—and been unable to cry out, to warn them, to do anything except parrot the words forced upon him by the collective. He fought to keep the pain from his voice; it came out sounding grim, hollow. "Believe me . . . you'll be doing them a favor."

And he himself reached for one of the phaser rifles, trying to ignore the surprised reactions of his two friends and fellow officers, refusing to meet their eyes and see the concern that was, perhaps rightly, there. Even so, in the periphery of his vision, he saw a glance pass between them.

The Klingon cleared his throat. "Captain . . . I do not believe you should accompany us on this mission. Your place is on the bridge."

Picard had already had this same argument with himself, but reason had lost. He could not let his own people face the Borg without his help, his newfound ability to sense what they were doing; nor could he pass up a test that would prove, beyond a doubt, that he was no longer theirs to control.

He would not sit alone on the bridge and wait for word from others. If anyone had earned the right to fight them, to destroy them, face to face, he had.

Startlingly, a muscle in his jaw began to twitch, one

that did so only during moments of great rage. He was not angry, he assured himself, not angry at all. He was *justified.*

"Objection noted, Mr. Worf," he said easily, though he never took his gaze from the rifle in his hands. As he watched, it began to hum with power. "Let's go."

Will Riker picked his way carefully over the mud-and-ice walkway that served as the ramshackle community's main thoroughfare, taking care to give the faintly smoldering craters wide berth. People had already emerged from their hiding places and swiftly put out the fires; now, they were cleaning up the debris, assessing the damage, and casting worried glances up at the smoke-veiled night sky. One particular image struck him: that of a frail, silver-haired woman who stood staring expressionlessly at the pile of ashes that had been her tent.

The poor woman was stunned, Riker thought; but before he passed by her, she suddenly gave a small, disgusted sigh, then moved to a particular area and began sifting through the ashes with her boot. She found something, too; she lifted it up, blew it off, stuck it in her pocket . . . then turned her back on the ashes and walked away without another sign of regret.

Survivors, he realized, his pity turning to honest admiration; these people were true survivors who had lost everything, everyone, yet still did not surrender.

Riker could only hope that Zefram Cochrane was a survivor, too. He had not been among the dead in the silo's outer control chamber, nor had they found any sign of him in or near the *Phoenix.* Deanna had gone in search of him; after all, in the twenty-fourth century, *everyone* who had ever been to Earth knew the warp-drive pioneer's famous face. Identifying him by sight was not a problem.

Now, the *Phoenix* was almost ready for launch, and Troi had not returned to report on the search for Cochrane. The away team's need to blend in with the locals had precluded the use of comm badges, but invisible transponders had been used in case an emergency required a quick beam-up. Riker had used Deanna's to locate her—but wherever she was, she wasn't moving very fast.

He could only hope she was all right.

As he'd left the silo, he could hear the faint sound of hard-driving music—"rock and roll," they had called it. And the closer he moved toward Troi's coordinates, the louder the music became, until at last he stood wincing at the vibratory effect of the percussion on his eardrums, in front of an olive-drab tent bearing the hand-lettered sign CRASH & BURN.

Riker entered. The place was clearly a local bar, with a twenty-first-century jukebox blaring away in the corner; to his surprise, there wasn't a soul inside . . . save for Deanna Troi, who sat alone at the rickety bar, staring disconsolately down at a glass of amber liquid in front of her. Beside it rested another glass—empty. Elbows resting on the counter, she rubbed her temples, frowning, as if trying to ease a monstrous headache.

And little wonder, Riker thought, what with the music so damned loud his teeth rattled.

"Deanna!" he called.

She did not turn, did not see or hear him.

"Deanna!" he shouted at full volume, and this time when she did not hear, he found the jukebox's old-fashioned power cord and yanked it out of the wall.

Blessedly, the music stopped. Troi immediately turned around at once, her expression dismayed. "Will, no! Don't turn off the—"

The last word was lost in the bright, high tinkle of exploding glass. Riker instinctively shielded his face, then felt the sting of tiny shards, the splash of burning liquid upon the outside of one arm. The volatile fragrance of crudely made alcohol filled the air.

When no second explosion was forthcoming, he lowered his arm and found himself staring at a man, stubbled chin thrust indignantly upward, graying tendrils emerging from beneath a brimless cap onto a heavily lined forehead, blue eyes narrowed and bloodshot. Those eyes regarded Riker with hostility, suspicion, anger—and a brilliance so intense it was painful to behold.

"Who told this jerk he could turn off my music?" he demanded thickly of Troi.

Riker did not move; he had also noticed that the older man held another liquor bottle in his hand and was certainly drunk enough to overreact at the slightest provocation.

Troi ran a hand over her hair, a gesture that she reserved for the most harrying of times. Without smiling or looking at either of the men, she said, "Will Riker . . . Zefram Cochrane."

Of course, Riker realized with awe; *this* was the great

hero, standing right before him. Dissolute, unshaven, drunken, argumentative—not exactly what he had expected.

Cochrane walked on wobbly legs to the bar and sat himself down beside Troi. "Friend of yours?" he asked.

"Yes."

"Husband?"

"No," she said, frosting up as his reason for asking became clear.

Cochrane blithely ignored her defensiveness. "Good." And he picked up her glass and poured the contents onto the dirt floor, then refilled her glass and his. "Now *this,* Deena—"

"Deanna," she corrected him, with such exasperation that Riker grinned faintly. Obviously, she'd found the famous scientist to be quite a handful.

"This is the good stuff," he said, so cheerfully that Will took advantage of the shift in his mood.

"Dr. Cochrane . . ." he began warmly, stepping up to the bar beside the scientist.

Ignoring him, Cochrane lifted his glass and studied it, as if inspecting it for imperfections. "Here's to the *Phoenix* . . . may she rest in peace."

He emptied his glass with a single gulp, swallowed, then grimaced and pounded the bar with his fist. Troi followed suit—without the pounding, though her expression was even ghastlier than her host's.

Disgusted, Cochrane peered at the label, then hurled the bottle to the ground, where it broke. "Okay. That was bad." He rose, and went back around the bar to a secluded storage area.

Troi put her elbows on the wooden surface again and

rubbed her temples. "Will, I think we're going to have to tell him the truth."

Riker glanced warily in the direction Cochrane had gone. "But if we tell him, the timeline could—"

Troi raised her head and faced him; for the first time, Will noticed that her words were slightly slurred. "This is no time to argue about time . . . we don't have the time." She frowned suddenly, as if trying to make sense of her own comment. *"What* was I saying?"

"You're drunk," Riker said in amazement.

She straightened with wounded—and noticeably wobbly—dignity. "I am not."

"Yes, you are."

"Look," she countered, using her elbows as support and leaning unsteadily toward him—a little *too* close, really, and he fought the impulse to recoil from her pungent breath. "He wouldn't even *talk* to me unless I had a drink with him, and then it took three shots of something called 'tequila' just to find out *he* was the one we're looking for. And I've spent the last twenty minutes trying to keep his hands off me, so don't start criticizing my counseling technique!"

"Sorry." He could not entirely repress a grin.

She recoiled stiffly at that. "It's a primitive culture and I'm just trying to blend in. . . ."

"You've blended, all right."

She seemed not to hear but continued, slumping forward on her elbows and growing steadily closer to the wooden counter. "I already tried telling him our cover story. He didn't believe me."

Will grew utterly serious; drunk or not, Deanna had a point. They *didn't* have much time now, and Cochrane's cooperation was essential. The Borg had already altered this timeline with their attack, and there was always the paradox: how could the *Enterprise* crew know that they were not *destined* to interfere? "We *are* getting short on time," he said. "If we *do* tell him the truth, you think he'll be able to handle it?"

The two of them swiveled their heads to look at Cochrane, who emerged from the storage area with a silver disc half the size of his palm, flipping it like a coin into the air with his thumb. He made a beeline for the antique jukebox.

"If you're looking for my professional opinion as ship's counselor," Deanna murmured, "he's *nuts.*"

"I'll note that in my log," Riker said dryly, and winced again as his eardrums reacted to the skull-shattering blare of rock and roll. Cochrane beat his fists in the air and stamped his feet drunkenly in time to the music, then gave a little leap and began to play an invisible guitar.

Beside Riker came a faint thump, one he would not have heard at all had it not been so close. He whirled about to see Troi face down against the counter, passed out.

EIGHT

To Picard, it seemed a long, long way down the emergen-cy shaft ladder and an even longer jump from the last rung to deck sixteen. In truth, he had climbed only one level, and the distance between the ladder's end and the deck was less than the length of his body.

But the mental distance was great, for when his boot soles struck the hard metal deck, the sound had the ring of finality. This, he realized, with that inexplicable way of knowing, would lead to the end of the ongoing struggle against the Borg: either he would see them utterly destroyed, or they would have to destroy him. There could no longer be any partial resolutions, no retreats, no escapes.

And nothing—not the *Enterprise*-E, the bridge, or even duty—would keep him from being at the battle's conclusion. He, more than any of his peers, had suffered at their hands; he, more than all else, *deserved* to be in the thick of it.

This deck, too, was powerless, dimly lit—and stiflingly hot. He activated the light beam on his phaser rifle and peered about him: a corridor, nothing more. Silently, he raised an arm upward and motioned for the others to follow; Data immediately dropped down beside him, followed soon after by five security officers.

Together, weapons at the alert, they moved stealthily toward their destination, as yet out of sight. At the opposite end of the deck, Picard knew, Worf and his team of five should also be heading toward Main Engineering, where the two groups would converge.

It did not take long for signs of the enemy to appear. Data forged into the lead as they approached an intersection and shone his light beam around the corner; he stopped, raising his free hand for others to do the same. Even from the back, his posture telegraphed his fear as elegantly as voice or expression could; Picard hurried silently to his side, then followed the android's troubled gaze.

Beyond, the corridor—bulkheads, decks, ceiling— were entwined by the leaden flesh-and-metal kudzu of Borg technology.

Picard drew in a sharp breath, not so much in fear but outrage at the obscenity. Beside him, Data audibly swallowed.

"Captain," he whispered, "I believe I am feeling . . . anxiety. It is an intriguing sensation. I can see how it would be distracting for—"

"I'm sure it's a fascinating experience," Picard said

brusquely. "But perhaps you should deactivate your emotion chip for now."

"Good idea, sir." The android tilted his head; for a millisecond, no more, his eyes grew vacant . . . then, abruptly, all traces of tension vanished from his face. "Done."

Picard looked at him and sighed. "Data . . . there are times I envy you."

At the same moment, Worf and his team were stealing down their own section of Borgified corridor. Worf's five companions were well trained, experienced enough to remain levelheaded in the direst emergency, but now they were visibly tense, eyes wide and hyperalert, movements taut and nervously quick, lips grimly compressed.

And they had good reason to be. Few starships were able to survive a confrontation with the Borg; how much more dangerous would direct, hand-to-hand combat with them be?

Worf's wish, if he did not survive that day's battle, was to take more than a few of the Borg with him into death. His one regret was that the enemy he faced was indeed powerful but utterly lacking in honor.

He was glad Captain Picard had chosen to ignore Starfleet's orders and fight; the war would be difficult, and only with the help of the most courageous and determined warriors could it be won.

Picard was indeed both courageous and determined; but there was something more Worf had seen in his eyes, something darker than a mere desire for justice or revenge—something bordering suspiciously on obsession. And if the captain allowed it to interfere with his judgment . . .

Worf immediately reigned in his thoughts, forcing his mind to clear and renew its intent focus on every sight, every sound as he led his team forward into a large intersection; in all four directions, Borg machinery coiled, a devouring serpent, around Federation technology.

To the right, a noise.

The Klingon whirled, rifle in hand, and aimed it at the sound's source, a hatch in the bulkhead. The others fell into position in a half-circle beside Worf, all training their rifles at the hatch, which slowly opened.

Something began to emerge from the shadows; Worf caught a glimpse of a pale face, a black sleeve. The six warriors leaned in and fingered their weapons, ready for the kill.

The face finally came out into the arc of light cast by the rifles' beams and became recognizable as Dr. Crusher, hair dark and face shining with sweat. She looked up, blue eyes wide, at the rifle barrels circling her head, and said in a small voice, "It's only me."

Worf relaxed with a disappointed grunt and stepped forward to offer a hand, but the doctor had already crawled out and was extending an arm to Nurse Ogawa, who stared curiously at the assembly of weapons. "Doctor, are you all right?"

Crusher nodded. "Yes—but we have wounded here."

Worf turned to the nearest guard. "Lopez—get these people back to deck fourteen."

Lopez moved forward to the opening and proferred a hand to Nurse Ogawa, who was already climbing out; the

two flanked the opening and assisted the others while
Crusher continued speaking, her pale brow furrowed
with worry. "There was a civilian with us—a woman
from the twenty-first century. We got separated."

The Klingon gave a swift nod. "We'll watch for her."

The urgency in the doctor's tone increased. "She has
no idea what's going on, Worf. You've got to find her."
Then she turned and headed off with her patients, leaving
the Klingon to wonder just how unsettling it would be for
someone born three centuries ago to step from a war-
ravaged Earth onto a Borg-beseiged *Enterprise.*

He gave the thought no longer than it took to draw in a
single breath, then motioned his guards to follow him,
onward to the inevitable encounter with the enemy.

Picard led the way down the assimilated corridor,
with Data a close second and the five guards following
just behind. Impossible to look at what had been the
pale, shining halls of the *Enterprise*-E (a new ship, yes,
but *his* ship, and the *Enterprise* all the same), to see
them darkened, reduced to a chaotic jumble by the Borg
taint, and not feel the same rage, the same sense of
violation as when they had filled his skull with metal
and circuits and taken away his name.

As he rounded a blind corner, he slowed; the others
readied their weapons for quick aim. Yet he did not slow
quite fast enough. Before he or any of the others could
react, two Borg drones walked past them.

Behind him, all but Data jumped and raised their
weapons.

Picard stretched out an arm in front of them as if to
literally hold them back. "Wait—hold your fire."

Once again, he knew the inexplicable; the collective had sensed them yet felt no fear, sounded no alarm. The guards watched in frank amazement as the Borg pair did precisely what Picard expected: continued past the group without the slightest reaction.

"They'll ignore us," Picard explained, secure in his knowledge, yet feeling a thrill of adrenaline course down his spine all the same, "until they consider us a threat."

He began to walk slowly behind the two, motioning for the others to follow. After a brief time, they came to another intersection and turned the corner Picard knew would lead them straight to the heart of the collective.

The instant he rounded it himself, Picard held up a hand again for the others to stop: some fifteen yards directly in front of them stood the tall double doors marked MAIN ENGINEERING . . . the one recognizable landmark.

All else had been corrupted by the same insidious, creeping tangle of tubing, wires, power packs, and circuitry, all jammed together without thought for convenience or design. And between it all—just as he had dreamed—Borg drones stood slumbering in their specialized alcoves, each face bloodless, emotionless, stripped of any sign of individuality, of life.

Close enough to touch.

The two walking Borg slipped into their alcoves and closed their eyes to sleep the dreamless sleep of the collective.

"Captain," Data said beside him, and Picard looked up to see Worf and his contingent arriving from an adjacent corridor. With a flick of his hand, the captain motioned for the two teams to merge. United, the group moved cautiously past the sleeping drones, Picard and Data in the lead, Worf and his officers fanned out in a semicircle toward the motionless Borg, ready to provide cover should any wake.

The distance to engineering's double doors was short, but never, Picard decided, had he ever taken so long a walk. The temperature in the corridor was stifling, yet beneath his sweat-soaked uniform, he felt oddly chilled, for the sight of those doors evoked again the mysterious image of a woman's upcurved lips, pale yet seductive, and the low, beckoning whisper: *Locutus* . . .

Again he tried to summon her face, yet the memory stayed maddeningly elusive; like the Cheshire cat, only the smile remained.

At last, the goal was reached. Picard stood beside Data, rifle at the ready, and watched the android push away the invasive vines of Borg technology to reach an access panel on the bulkhead beside the doors. This, Data opened; inside, amid the circuitry, lay the emergency release handle. The android coiled a white-gold hand around it, then looked to his captain.

Picard glanced back at the security team. Ready, each of them; he tightened his grip on the rifle, then gave Data a nod.

The android pulled.

The captain drew in a breath. Fear gave way abruptly to obsession: he was nothing more than human, but they had violated him, hurt him. And somehow he would find a way to kill them all, destroy their race, make them pay for what they had done to him and every other assimilated soul.

And for what they had done to the *Enterprise.* The

ship had become a symbol of their crime against him, and he would die before he let them have her.

He would not let them hurt him again, even if it meant his own death.

Data pulled harder, then harder still. With a loud snap, the handle broke off in his hand. The doors remained closed.

Picard let go the breath and felt the group tension just as abruptly deflate; for an instant, he felt like laughing, and shared a whimsical look with Data.

"Perhaps we should just knock," he told the android, but before he finished speaking, a chorus of hums came from behind them, then a series of whirs and clicks.

He turned to see a dozen Borg emerge from their alcoves and begin to advance toward the team with implacable, deadly calm.

"Ready phasers," Worf ordered, his voice steady but impassioned, warrior-fierce. His officers obeyed, standing motionless as the drones drew nearer, nearer, until at last the Klingon said, his voice lethally determined, *"Fire."*

Eleven eye-dazzling streaks of light radiated outward from Worf's group; four found their targets, tearing into black-clad Borg torsos with whines and sizzles as the beams encountered metal and flesh. Four Borg fell backward, killed—or rather, Picard decided, freed. Freed so that the original owners of the flesh bodies and helplessly trapped minds could escape the special hell that was assimilation, the special hell he had known as Locutus. Had death been an option then, he would have met it gladly.

Beside the captain, Data whirled about, lifted his rifle,

and fired at a drone who was on the verge of making it past the protective semicircle of guards. Picard repressed the urge to join the battle, instead reattaching his rifle to his belt and hurrying to another access panel on the other side of the doors. Within a few seconds, he had opened the panel, and he began pulling out the circuitry and rearranging it; if the others managed to cover him long enough, he would be able to override the lock. . . .

He worked furiously, trying to concentrate, to ignore the sounds behind him: the whine of the phasers, the steadily approaching army of metallic footsteps, the thud and clank of Borg bodies falling. Body after body after body, yet the sound of more and more footsteps still came. . . .

But he worked—and was near success when Worf gave the warning cry, "Captain—they've adapted!"

The phasers went silent, leaving only the steady clank of metal footfall. . . .

Picard pulled the final adulterated bit of circuitry free and jammed it into the proper socket.

Immediately, the panel sparked, then went dull; the doors jerked open a thumb's span to reveal darkness. Picard rushed to the doors and tried to pull them apart.

It worked. The doors gave a slight groan, then began to slide slowly apart, until they were open almost enough for Picard to slip inside. If he could just make it to the plasma coolant tanks . . .

Out of the darkness, a phosphorescent white face, white hands surged toward him.

Instinctively, Picard recoiled, but behind him lay bulkhead, an empty alcove; the battling security guards and Borg drones blocked all avenues of escape. The drone closed in, its blank chalk face indistinguishable from the others, its androgynous hands reaching out for Picard's neck.

Picard stared at those hands and saw something black, sharp, metal unsheath itself from under each of the white fingernails, something that sought to reclaim Locutus. The collective's knowledge seized him once again: these talons, once inserted beneath the skin, would entwine their swift, evil tendrils about his spine, his nerves, his brain, and give birth to a Borg.

He would not have it, he swore silently, *would not have it.* He was willing to fight to the death—not to the assimilation—but hand-to-hand combat was out of the question. One touch, and he would be theirs to control.

He lifted the butt of his phaser rifle, ready to strike despite the impossibility of victory.

The drone's fingers came within centimeters of grazing his neck—then sailed up high overhead; in an instant of utter confusion, Picard watched as the cyborg's torso, then legs, swung upward into the air, as a different black-uniformed body stepped into its place.

Data, he realized gratefully. The android lifted the drone high overhead, then hurled it across the corridor. With a loud metallic crash, it struck an empty alcove.

Yet even as the Borg went flying through the air, three more swarmed forth from the shadows inside engineering. One seized Data's neck, the other two his arms and shoulders; he struggled to break free, but his attackers were stronger and pinned him fast.

Picard moved to run toward his friend, but more

drones stepped between them and began to stalk the captain with hands extended, talons extruding from beneath their fingernails. His choice was agonizingly clear: rush the Borg who blocked the path to Data and be seized by them as well, or abandon his friend, get the team out, and survive to fight another battle.

"Captain," Data said softly, plaintively, and despite the confusion, Picard heard and met his friend's gaze. Data's eyes were wide, stricken, yet strangely calm, and in that single word Picard heard many things: a plea for help, a statement of friendship, an admission of fear. Yet there could not have been time for Data to have triggered the emotion chip. . . .

In a single instant, the Borg drew their prey back into the shadows of engineering. The doors rumbled shut.

Please, Picard begged silently of both captors and victim, *don't activate the emotion chip. . . .*

At once he whirled, returning mentally to the battle, and saw the security contingent firing uselessly at the Borg, who moved safely now behind invisible shielding. The skirmish line was collapsing; no time for foolish bravery.

"Regroup on deck fifteen!" he shouted, his voice near breaking. "Don't let them touch you!"

And he ran, weaving around his pursuers with a grace and speed born of mortal desperation. As he did, his peripheral vision detected Worf and a few of the guards scrambling up an access ladder; others leaped for one of the many Jefferies tubes in the engineering corridor. Picard headed first after Worf's group, but a group of Borg had already moved there to cut him off.

Oddly, the drones made no attempt to pursue Worf and the others; Picard turned and sped in the opposite direction toward a second access ladder.

Again a pair of Borg stepped into his way, blocking him. *They don't care about the others,* he thought, with a fresh, wild surge of horror. *It's Locutus they're after.* . . .

He spun about to see the first group of drones closing in.

I will not *be assimilated. I will* NOT. . . .

He crouched low and hurled himself along the ground like a projectile toward the nearest Jefferies tube and pulled open the hatch. He was about to climb in when a strangled voice came from the deck beside him:

"Help . . ."

Picard turned. On the deck lay one of the young security guards, hands clawing at his collar, face contorted in frank agony. Beneath the tender skin of his neck, the assimilation device gave birth to a hundred tiny black serpents that lengthened rapidly, branching out like a fine, dark network of veins. Simultaneously, his temples began to pulse, then stretch taut as something metal pushed against the skin, then tore it and emerged with a soft whirr.

A sensorscope.

All this occurred in the fleeting millisecond Picard glanced down; and for another millisecond, he hesitated, staring down at the anguish of this young man.

This distinguished and intelligent Starfleet officer. This Borg.

"Please," the guard begged. "Help . . ."

Picard's chest heaved in a silent sob; he reached for

his phaser, and before the horror of what he had to do could stop him, he fired.

It brought no consolation whatsoever to think that he had done what the young man requested.

Before the Borg caught up with him, he scrambled into the tube and slid the hatch shut.

The tunnel was dark, overheated, close, but desperation and adrenaline spurred him until he crawled at phenomenal speed, gasping from the heat and exertion. Only one thing could be worse than encountering the Borg on his own ship's engineering deck—and that would be to encounter them here, in a claustrophobic Jefferies tube. Certainly, if they *were* in here, his gasps would give away his location. Yet he could not bring himself to really slow down—only enough to glance over his shoulder from time to time at the unrevealing darkness behind him.

At last he neared the first intersection, and he forced both breath and pace to ease before he dared take the turn that led eventually to an access ladder and deck fifteen. It was only then that he permitted himself to think of Data and the obscene existence that awaited his friend. The thought provoked a shudder; with Data's already-incredible strength and brilliant android brain added to the collective, the Borg might become truly undefeatable. . . .

A sharp pain across the skin of his throat made him gasp, pulled him backward; he tried to draw in a breath and could not. The image of the young security officer's neck and the insidious, unfurling tendrils beneath the skin flashed before him in the darkness.

I will NOT *be assimilated*—

He dropped his phaser and clawed briefly at the cable strangling him—then wedged his boots against the tube wall and slammed with all his strength backward, *away* from the pressure.

A body behind him—smaller than expected— groaned as he smashed it back against the opposite wall. The cable loosened at once; he took advantage of his position and plunged an elbow backward.

To his astonishment, he felt nothing but ribs and soft flesh. As his attacker emitted a high-pitched yelp, he whirled about.

And in the dimness saw a dark, sweat-slicked face: the woman from the missile silo, the one who had tried to shoot them down with bullets.

Her eyes were wild, her scorched and torn clothing even more disheveled than when he had last seen her, unconscious and dying on the metal catwalk. Only now, instead of a gun, she held *his* phaser in her hands.

"You," Picard whispered, moving toward her. "How did you—"

"Back off!" she shrieked; the phaser in her grasp remained steady, but a spasm of pure rage and terror coursed through her body as she cried out, leaving her trembling in its wake.

She was teetering on the edge of hysteria, Picard realized, and could very easily kill him; all depended upon his response. He drew a slow, settling breath and forcibly relaxed his own features; in a voice both reassuring and authoritative, he said, "Calm down."

"Shut *up,"* she spat, then immediately contradicted her own words. "Who are you?"

"My name is Jean—"

"No!" Her expression grew even deadlier; she took a step closer and pointed the phaser squarely at his forehead. "What *faction?"*

Picard stared at her blankly for a full second before he understood. Of course: she was from the mid-twenty-first century and had interpreted the Borg attack as coming from the infamous ECON. The people of her era were too focused on their own planetary strife to consider that the attack might have come from beyond Earth.

"I'm not part of the Eastern Coalition," he answered evenly. "Look, this is difficult to explain, but—"

"I said *shut up.* I don't care *who* you're with," she countered irrationally. "Just get me out of this— whatever the hell this place is."

"That's not going to be easy."

She waved the phaser threateningly. "Well, you'd better *find* a way to *make* it easy . . . or *I'm* going to start pressing buttons."

He studied her, thinking. This woman had come alarmingly close to killing him once (and would most certainly have killed Data if she could have). He was trained in the art of hand-to-hand combat, but then so was she—in a harsher arena where losers did not live long enough to learn from their mistakes. If he bolted now, she *would* fire, most definitely killing him—and probably herself—with the ricochet off the tunnel walls.

And as long as she stayed with him, he could keep her out of the Borg's hands.

"Very well," he said finally, and brushed himself off, then rose to a crouched position and began moving again. "Follow me."

NINE

Data woke to abrupt, full consciousness, to the sight of a pale gray bulkhead less than an arm's length from his face, and to a detached sense of mild amazement.

Amazement, because he could not recall the moment the Borg had deactivated him. He reached to touch the wall and discovered the metal clamps and restraints that held him fast to something resembling a surgical bed. An optical scan of the area revealed nothing but smooth gray bulkhead, for as far as his peripheral vision extended; surely, then, he was no longer in Main Engineering—although the gurgles, hums, and odd hissing sounded precisely the same as they had in the instant the Borg dragged him inside. . . .

Captain Picard had been most wise in suggesting that he deactivate the emotion chip. As much as he wanted to experience abject fear, he felt that the lack of it now would permit him to deal more efficiently with such a

114

difficult and most likely fatal—at least for his personality, if not his android body—situation.

He shifted against the restraints. Something about his
perspective was not right, nor was the sensation of his
body pushing hard against his fetters. There should have
been *some* resistance if he were in a vertical position, of
course, but—

Beneath him, the table began to move. And as it
slowly began to rotate, Data came to understand: he had
been staring at the *deck,* not the bulkhead.

As he revolved, he studied his transformed surroundings: the great cavern that had been engineering was now
dimly lit and swirling with mist, beads of moisture
glittering upon the black cables and conduits that made
up the cybernetic jungle. The bulkheads, ceiling, and
decks had been honeycombed with thousands of alcoves
where drones slept, organic tubing connecting them to
more dark machinery. Other drones moved about, intent on various tasks designed to further adapt the room
to their use.

Behind them, Data noted with interest, were the
plasma coolant tanks—fortunately unadulterated, but
nestled within a Borg-modified bulkhead and well out of
reach.

As the table continued to rotate, a curious new sight
caught the android's attention: four Borg standing together, each one's face connected by an elaborate series
of tubing to the ceiling. The tubes, which appeared to be
made from organic matter, pulsated with energy and a
glowing, viscous liquid.

As best he could tell, the Borg appeared to be feeding,
but from what?

Abruptly, the table arrived at precisely one hundred eighty degrees from its starting point and clicked into place. Nearby—and invisible to Data until the table had come half-circle—two drones worked steadily at a console. The android lifted his head and saw upon the monitor the encryption graphics with which he had protected the main bridge computer.

"Your efforts to break the encryption codes will not be successful," he informed them matter-of-factly. "Nor will your attempts to assimilate me into your collective."

"Brave words," came a voice overhead, one that made him glance up sharply at the ceiling; it was not the thundering, multilayered masculine whisper of the collective but a singular voice, one that betrayed passion, intelligence, a personality capable of emotion and thought.

The low voice of a woman.

"I've heard them before," she said, "from thousands of species across thousands of worlds, since long before you were created."

Data gazed up at the thick, dark tangle of tubing and circuitry that hung from the ceiling, swaying like weeds in a gentle sea. His eye caught a rustle of movement amid them, shining beads of moisture trembling, falling as something both raven and white slithered through the jumble.

And a woman's face: chalk-pale but hauntingly beautiful, with ancient, piercing eyes of silver.

Data frowned as the image vanished as swiftly as it had appeared, though the voice still spoke.

"But now . . . they are all Borg."

"I am unlike any life-form you have encountered before," he countered, peering up at the cybertangle but unable to find any trace of the strange female creature. "The codes stored in my neural net cannot be forcibly removed."

"You are an imperfect being, created by an imperfect being. Finding your weakness is only a matter of time."

As she spoke, three drones stepped forward to stand beside the table, forming a semicircle around Data's head; one of them lifted a forearm completely encased by black metal and held it above the android's skull. In place of hand and fingers, long, stiletto-sharp spikes extruded from the casing—and, as Data watched curiously, began to spin.

And as the whining drill descended and bit into his scalp, the android reflected once again that it was a very good thing the emotion chip had been disabled—a very good thing.

Some few hours past midnight, the encampment had grown quiet at last, and the air piercing cold. There was only one good thing about the war, Zefram Cochrane thought, and that was the night sky; without the once-omnipresent glow cast by civilization, the stars shone dazzlingly bright.

Nearby, the man named La Forge—he of the Lily-dark skin and amazing pale blue eyes—paused in his adjustment of Cochrane's telescope, aimed now at a specific point in the clear, glittering sky. La Forge produced a small black box and pointed it at the telescope, then apparently read something on the screen that prompted him to lean forward and adjust the telescope ever so slightly.

Meanwhile, Cochrane tried to focus his attention on Deanna Troi and the man who'd introduced himself as Commander William Riker.

It was enormously difficult. Cochrane was no longer quite as drunk as he'd been when Deanna entered the Crash & Burn, and that frightened him. It would have been easier to write off what was happening now as an ethanol-induced hallucination, but this was far too real, too rational, too consistent to be anything but real . . . or a paranoid delusion, a product of the madness he'd been fleeing since the war.

Before the war, life had been simple. Mood disorder? Bouts of depression alternating with sky-rocketing mania? No problem; have your DNA toyed with a bit so that you'd never pass on the disease, wear an implant and have it changed once a decade, and you'll never experience a single symptom.

He hadn't until after the war. He'd gotten the implant as an adolescent, before the disease—a particularly severe type, according to the geneticist—had made itself known. To him, it had been a medical curiosity, like having a gene for a sixth finger or diabetes—just something the doctor told you about, something that could be fixed in one treatment, something noted in your medical records that would never affect your life. Soon, his physician had promised, medical science would reach a level where a single alteration of the errant gene would permanently cure the affliction.

Beaten by the holocaust, *soon* never came.

Cochrane hadn't even thought about it until after the war—two years after, to be precise, eleven years after he'd received his last implant. He'd already been here, up in Montana, contemplating warp-drive theory; the one thing he'd salvaged, the only thing that mattered, were his mathematical notes. His plan had been to simply pursue his research, and when the ravaged planet began to recover, share it with the remnants of the scientific community in hopes that someone would have the necessary money and equipment to actually implement it—perhaps even someday build a warp drive.

That was when his acquaintance with mania began. A night came when he was sitting outside the silo—very near to where he sat now—staring up at the silent stars. Most people never went near that far end of the encampment, because they feared the still-viable missile inside. They'd gone to Cochrane, knowing of his work as a physicist, and asked him whether there might be some way to disarm the damned thing. After all, the silo had equipment, robots, for dealing with radioactive waste.

He had little hope it could be accomplished, actually, but he was curious to see it. And so he took a neighbor's Geiger counter along and made local history as the first person to brave the silo since the war.

A visit to the silo's inner sanctum in the afternoon proved fascinating, if disappointing for the community; there was no way to neutralize the nuclear material in the bomb. About the best Cochrane could recommend was to seal the whole place off with a thick layer of lead and concrete.

It was later that day, a few hours after sunset when he was staring up at the stars, that the revelation came.

The nuclear core in the missile: it was the same fuel his theoretical warp engine required, was it not? Why not beat that damned sword into a plowshare and use the bomb to make an actual ship that he could test?

He'd been feeling exceptionally energetic and optimistic the past few days, sleeping little and working feverishly on a design for the warp engine. But at the moment the revelation struck him, followed by the joyful realization that it was, in fact, doable, his optimism turned to euphoria, his energy to outright obsession.

He worked ten days and nights in the silo without sleep, without food, with only the water in his canteen. He would stay there working, he vowed, until he got the ship—the *Phoenix*—ready for launch.

At the time, it never occurred to him that he was looking at a good decade's worth of work. It all seemed so easy, so utterly accomplishable that he did not stop until forced to literally crawl out of the silo, a day after his canteen ran dry. Fatigue overtook him then, and he spent the next day sleeping in his tent and forcing himself to eat and drink—not the occasional beer he was accustomed to, but hard liquor, and quite a lot of it. It was the only available substance that reined in the wildly galloping obsession (the psychoactive drugs that provided some with escape from unhappiness left him raving, delusional) and let him sleep at least a fraction of the night.

Over two weeks' time, the euphoria gradually faded, until one day he found himself racked by such despair and doubt that he couldn't find a reason to get out of bed. He'd been insane, deluded the past few weeks—

frighteningly so—and the whole warp-drive project was impossible, the ravings of a madman. It would take long, painful years to accomplish. . . .

And clearly, his madness had caught up to him, seized him at last and made its presence known. How could this be possible, in a century where cognitive and emotional disorders were unknown, a part of the dim past associated with strait jackets, chains, moldering dungeons where the "insane" howled in despair?

It was a few weeks later, when he emerged enough from the depths of hopelessness to climb down into the silo once more, that he saw all the work he'd done in his speeding, three-brainstorms-a-minute phase. He'd expected to find it useless, poorly wrought, incomprehensible.

Instead, he found it perfect, brilliant, startlingly insightful—in fact, his best work. And the notions that had come to him during his "revelation" indicated genius. In ten days, he had accomplished two months' work.

Yet it did not ease his fear of the madness.

When manic, he drank because it eased the attendant and at times unbearable racing of his thoughts and the insomnia; when depressed, he drank because it eased the pain. And conveniently, his neighbors blamed his erratic behavior on the alcohol; shame prevented him from sharing the truth.

Because of the shame, he drank when he was lucid, too.

There were no implants available anymore for the disorder. He knew; he had checked, had scoured all the surrounding states in search of the cure. He was destined to live the rest of his life at the mercy of the emotional rollercoaster. A week ago, when both he and Lily realized that the *Phoenix* was finally going to be ready for launch, he'd felt himself catapulted from blessed normalcy into manic euphoria.

And he'd spent the whole week bargaining with the universe: *Please, just let this last long enough; don't let me plunge into a depression until* after *she launches.* . . . As long as he didn't become *too* manic, *too* excitable, he'd make an excellent pilot.

Now, Cochrane stared hard and skeptically at William Riker's neatly bearded pink face. If this *was* a full-blown hallucination courtesy of the madness, it certainly possessed the unmistakable smell, sight, sound, touch of reality, right down to Riker's cornflower blue eyes.

And if it was real—

If it was real, he had no damned idea what to think. Certainly, the beautiful and exotic Deanna seemed honest enough, and so did this Riker character. La Forge, too. They all seemed on the up-and-up, but the story they told was simply . . . unbelievable.

"Let me make sure I understand you correctly, 'Commander,'" Cochrane said in his most cynical tone, afraid to show these strangers anything but mistrust. "A group of cybernetic life-forms from the future have traveled back through time to enslave the human race . . . and you're here to stop them."

Riker's open, cheerful face wore a faint smile. "That's right."

"God, you're heroic," Cochrane spat. "Can you fly, too?"

"We're going to prove it to you." The tall, bearded man turned toward La Forge. "Geordi, how are you doing?"

La Forge's admiring and faintly exasperated gaze remained fixed on the telescope. "These old refractors are tricky to align, but I think I've got it." He bent down to peer through the glass. "Yeah. Come take a look."

The last invitation was directed at Cochrane, who sighed and moved over to the scope, then stooped down and looked into the eyepiece. "What do we have here?" he said cockily. "I love a good peep"—his voice went abruptly flat with shock—"show. . . ."

Against the glittering, velvet background of stars and indigo sky, a great ship hung, her sleek hull crafted of shining, pale gray metal. The damned thing had to have been as big as the entire campgrounds.

Cochrane jerked his head up at once and glared at the others. "It's a trick. How'd you do that?"

Beside him, La Forge folded his arms and said smugly, "It's *your* telescope."

Cochrane frowned down at the scope controls, then peered back through the eyepiece up at the impossible, magnificent vessel. After an extended look, he slowly rose, then regarded Riker with cautious amazement.

"I don't believe it. . . ."

"Believe it," Riker said, his smile one of smug pride. "That's our ship, the *Enterprise.*"

"And . . . Lily's up there right now?" After the attack, he had been so ravingly psychotic that he had run to the Crash & Burn and begun gulping down every bottle of booze in sight, so agitated and then later so drunk that he'd completely forgotten about poor Lily, alone in the silo. Once again, the madness caused him shame.

She could have been killed—had in fact been dying—while he was sitting around getting drunk with Deanna in hopes of seducing her.

"That's right," Riker affirmed.

Worried, Cochrane gazed up with his naked eyes at the place the spaceship supposedly hovered. "Can I talk to her?"

Riker's cheerfulness deflated slightly. "We've lost contact with the *Enterprise*. We don't know why."

A convenient lie if ever Cochrane had heard one; yet Riker's direct, vaguely troubled gaze was mightily convincing. Cochrane bent down one more time to peer at the handsome vessel in infinite amazement. "So . . . what is it you want me to do?"

Riker grinned. "Simple. Conduct your warp flight, just as you planned."

Cochrane paused, calculating. They had already taken him down into the silo's belly and showed him the rubble and where Lily had fallen, unconscious from the radiation poisoning. And the *Phoenix,* where unfamiliar women and men were working to repair damage.

Whether this was all a hallucination or not, whether these people who claimed to be from the future were telling the truth or not, what possible harm could it do to try to accomplish his dream? If they wanted to hurt him or his ship, they could easily do it now; they didn't have to wait until he was airborne.

The frightening thing was, their story was starting to make sense.

"Well . . ." He hesitated. "All right—but it'll take a couple of weeks to build a new field generator."

"We have the technology to repair your ship tonight," the one named La Forge said, his dark face ashine with inner excitement. *A true engineer, that one,* Cochrane thought. *He can see beyond the equations, the damaged equipment—to see the real possibilities. He's looking at me right now, but he's seeing the* Phoenix *in flight.*

Hell, if they're telling the truth, he already knows *what she's capable of.*

Riker glanced at both men, clearly pleased at each one's reaction; even so, his expression turned somber as he told the physicist sternly: "It's imperative that you make the flight tomorrow morning by eleven-fifteen at the latest."

"Why?"

"Because at eleven o'clock, an alien ship will be passing through this solar system."

Cochrane sat down hard on the ice-cold concrete. When he could speak, he said, "More bad guys . . ."

For the first time in several minutes, Deanna Troi spoke. Apparently, large quantities of liquor didn't agree with her, for her eyes were narrowed from a headache and her expression was distinctly queasy; but the thought of what was to happen the following morning apparently fired her interest.

"Good guys. They're on a survey mission," she said—matter-of-factly, as if aliens buzzing about in spaceships were so commonplace, so expected, that his question didn't deserve a direct answer. "They have no interest in Earth—too primitive."

With a smile, she glanced up at Riker, who continued the explanation. "But tomorrow morning, when they detect the warp signature from your ship and realize that humans have discovered how to travel faster than the speed of light, they'll decide to alter course and make first contact with Earth—*right here.*" He gestured at the frozen ground beneath his feet.

Cochrane gave up all effort to hide his amazement and gaped openly at them. *"Here?"*

With scientific accuracy, La Forge pointed to a spot just east of the concrete where Cochrane sat; his voice, too, was laced with admiration and pride. *Pride in* me, Cochrane realized wonderingly. "Over there, actually. I think that's where the monument's going to be." He glanced back at Riker for verification. "Commander?"

Riker nodded with satisfaction. "Right over there." Smiling, he moved over to where Cochrane sat stunned and squatted beside him before continuing in a warm tone obviously calculated to inspire; even so, Riker's own sincere enthusiasm shone through. "It's one of the most pivotal moments in human history, Doctor. You get to make first contact with an alien race. And after you do—*everything* begins to change."

Deanna's strikingly beautiful face also lit up with joy at a long-past memory Cochrane had yet to live through. "It unites humanity in a way that no one thought possible, once they realize they're not alone in the universe."

La Forge joined in, grinning like the other two. "Your theories on warp drive allow *fleets* of starships to be built . . . and humankind to start exploring the galaxy."

"Eventually," Riker added, "Earth and a handful of

other worlds form an interstellar government called the United Federation of Planets."

Deanna now: "And before long, Earth becomes a paradise. Poverty . . . disease . . . war—they'll all be gone from this planet in the next fifty years."

Implants, Cochrane thought desperately at the mention of disease. *Will I be able to find a damned implant? And it had better be a helluva lot sooner than fifty years. . . .*

Riker finished up the stirring story. "But unless you make that warp flight tomorrow—before eleven-fifteen—*none* of it will happen."

Cochrane stared mutely at them for a long, long time. At last, he asked, "And *you* people . . . you're all astronauts on some kind of . . . star trek?"

La Forge smiled warmly at him. "I know this has been a lot for you to take in, Doc. But we're running out of time. We need your help. Are you with us?"

He could refuse, Cochrane knew. Could refuse outright and walk away from these people, and instinct said they wouldn't hurt him, wouldn't stop him, would merely watch him go.

But if . . . *if* they were actually telling the truth . . .

Easy, Zef. Stay calm, he urged himself silently as the mind-shattering excitement seized his already-manic brain and sent it reeling. *Stay calm and breathe, and don't think too hard about all this, because if you do, you'll become so damned manic you won't be able to pilot but'll go spiraling up into space* without *the* Phoenix. . . .

He let go a deep sigh, then forced a weak smile. "Why not?"

The others grinned in visible relief; as for Cochrane, he rose and squinted again through the telescope at the sight of the sleek and shining ship.

If he could just hold on . . .

Perspiration dripped from Lily's temples and the nape of her neck and trickled down her chest and back as she trained the futuristic-looking raygun on her captive, Jean Whoever-He-Was. They had crawled from one of the cramped tunnels out into one more brightly lit that permitted Lily the luxury of standing. As Lily watched mistrustfully, the man crouched down and reached for a hatch cover.

Despite his bald, sweat-shined scalp with its fringe of silvering hair at the nape of the neck, he was a handsome man: lean and graceful, but muscular in build, with strongly sculpted features and penetrating eyes beneath still-black brows. It was the eyes, Lily decided, that attracted and frightened her, for they emanated a breath-taking intensity, a fierce singularity of purpose both admirable and fearsome . . . and pain, the victim's pain she had seen too many times in the eyes of those who had survived the worst indignities of the war.

Throughout her strange adventure in the convoluted tunnels inside this strange, sleek metal building, Lily could not stop her mind from racing toward an explanation of where she was, why she was no longer sick, and precisely *what* chased her and this compelling man. She had come up with three possible explanations:

One, this was a no-holds barred intense, intense hallucination in her final dying moments. Not a bad conclusion, but if so, why did she feel no pain, no nausea, no headache—while at the same time keenly feeling the humidity and heat in this . . . place?

Two, this was a long and peculiarly vivid dream—but she almost immediately ruled out that possibility. For one thing, characters in her dreams constantly changed identity or disappeared abruptly or exhibited curious and inappropriate, inconsistent behavior; this Picard was behaving most consistently, continuing to try to escape from these bizarre bogeymen—and consistently annoyed with her defensive behavior. For another, she was experiencing bodily sensations that were distinctly undreamlike; she was actually hungry, a sensation that, like the one of heat, would not go away.

Three—the explanation she liked least but one that was becoming more viable with each passing moment—this was no dream or hallucination, but reality.

And that was the scariest thought of all.

Lily gripped the weapon tightly, its surface slippery with sweat, radiant with her own body heat—and all too solid in her hand. As she watched, the man lifted the hatch cover the merest slit, revealing on the level beneath them endless rows of the silent, standing cyborg men, each sporting the same white face with nondescript features, each clothed in black metal armor that seemed part of their very flesh.

Faces and bodies without minds, without hearts, without souls.

She had no idea what she looked upon, but the ghoulish sight left her convinced that she preferred her captive's company, ECON or not. As he slowly, soundlessly replaced the hatch, a muscle in his jaw twitched; with grim revulsion, he glanced up and said softly, "They're on this deck, too. We have to keep moving."

He rose and headed off down the tunnel, utterly ignoring the weapon in Lily's hand; she got the impression he was not at all fearful of it but rather somewhat annoyed by her distrust.

Watch yourself, Lily. It's an act, don't you see? An act to win your trust. He may be charming, he may seem interesting, but he's ECON and you can't trust him. . . .

He glanced back over his shoulder at her and demanded quietly—but with an authority that indicated he was used to swift answers, "What happened in sickbay? Where's Dr. Crusher and the others?" Despite his effort to suppress it, his eyes and voice betrayed deep concern.

A consummate actor indeed, Lily told herself, and countered bitterly, "Why'd you break the cease-fire?"

"We're not the ones who attacked you."

She twisted her lips skeptically. "Who did?"

He did not reply immediately; instead, inspiration apparently seized him, and he pressed a panel on the wall. A hatch opened onto a large chamber, and he strode inside with a sense of purpose.

She followed cautiously, scanning with weapon at the ready until she was certain no one else waited inside the room. It was empty save for groupings of couches and chairs facing the oddly bare far wall, which sloped outward at a forty-five-degree angle.

As the man moved quickly toward it, he said, "There's a . . . new faction that wants to prevent your launch tomorrow morning." She stiffened at the mention; so she *hadn't* dreamed their encounter inside the silo. He knew about the launch, about the *Phoenix* . . . but even if he was ECON, how could he have found out? Yet before she could react, he noted her reaction and said soothingly, "But *we're* here to help you."

"You want to help? Get me out of here!"

Again, he did not answer her at once but instead stopped deliberately in front of what looked to be a panel of push-button controls built into the side wall. The sight of them made her nervous; how did she know one of them wouldn't summon an armed guard—or open the floor beneath her feet?

Shoot him, Lily. Shoot him while you still have the drop on him. . . .

Oddly, she couldn't. If he was acting, he was doing a damn fine job of it, for the utter, honest determination in his eyes, in his voice, on his face compelled her to listen. He could have made a break for it several times during their brief journey here, but he hadn't; he could have reached up to press some evil control on the wall, but he didn't do that either.

He seemed instead to want to reason with her.

"This may be difficult to accept," he said deliberately, almost gently, "but you're not on Earth anymore. You're in a spaceship, orbiting at an altitude of about two hundred and fifty kilometers."

The words sent a purely physical shock down her spine, outward to her arms, her legs. Stunned her, because in the first mindless instant, she almost believed . . . She stared at him a long, silent moment, until the shock eased, and her hard-earned survival skills—mistrust and skepticism—took over. With

131

feigned calm, she lifted the weapon higher and aimed again at his face. A glimmer of fear shone in his eyes, but he did not flinch.

"I think it's time to press the red one," she said coldly, referring to the weapon's most ominous-looking button. "What do you think?" *For God's sake, Lily, don't stand there talking . . . shoot!* Yet she didn't—out of pure idiocy, she supposed.

A strange reluctance flitted over his features. "All right. You want a way out . . . ? Here it is."

And in the instant he lifted his hand and began to reach for the control on the wall, Lily's mind screamed at her: *Shoot, you idiot! Don't you realize you're about to be killed? Shoot . . . !*

She tried desperately to pull the trigger . . . and in the end, could not, almost weeping with frustration at the horrifying realization that she trusted him, had wanted to hear what he had to say. But the war had taught her that trust meant death.

And so she stood wavering as his fingers at last pressed the control and sealed her fate, stood motionless and watched as the great curving wall slid aside to reveal a profoundly startling vision.

Naked space and stars, and beneath them, vast and blue and shining, Earth. Lily had thought often about how it would look from inside the *Phoenix*; it was far more beautiful than she had imagined.

She staggered backward, clutched blindly at the nearest outcropping. The sight was dizzying, terrifying—she could see no glass, no visible barrier to prevent her from tumbling down the sloping floor, and falling into infinity. . . .

"What—" she croaked, then broke off and tried again, though her voice was reduced to a hoarse, awed whisper. "What *is* this?" The question was ridiculous, for she could see perfectly well what it was. She could see, but she could not fathom.

He turned toward the impossible sight, trying to keep his voice neutral, controlled—but he could not quite suppress the fondness in it. "That's Australia, New Guinea, the Solomons . . . Montana should be coming up soon, but you may want to hold your breath." His tone grew wry. "It's a long way down."

She forced her gaze away; still clinging to the wall, she looked at him, desperate for explanation, for reassurance that she had not simply gone mad. At the same time, she was possessed by fear that he would press another button and send her hurtling out into space to die of asphyxiation.

He didn't, of course. Instead, he looked upon her with an openness, an emotional honesty that she envied. For he not only saw her terror and confusion, he seemed to understand it and gazed upon her with an expression of something she had not witnessed since her mother died.

Compassion.

It was as though the war had never touched him. For the first time, it occurred to Lily that *he* had trusted *her* all along not to kill him, that he had risked his life in order to convince her of the truth; and she wondered whether she would ever be free of the war enough to trust that deeply again.

"Listen to me," he said, in a low, calm voice. She clung to every word, desperate now to believe, to make sense out of the sudden inversion of her reality. "I'm not your enemy. I *can* get you home. But you'll have to put that weapon down . . . and trust me."

At the mention of the weapon, she felt a fresh surge of mistrust and backed away, until the wall prevented her from recoiling further. She wanted to trust, but the thought of surrendering her only protection was almost physically painful.

"Jean-Luc Picard," he offered warmly, and when she glanced at him in dismayed confusion, he explained. "My name. What's yours?"

"Lily," she managed, still faltering in an agony of indecision; this was her life, her destiny. To willingly offer up control to another was unthinkable, unsafe.

"Welcome aboard, Lily," he said gently, and held out his hand for the weapon.

Lily stared at him, then back down at the slowly spinning Earth. If that was a holograph or computer-generated special effect, it must have cost millions to produce. And why would the ECON spend millions trying to convince *her* that she was in outer space?

Still staring at him, she slowly, slowly laid the weapon in his palm.

"Thank you." He let go a long breath and turned the weapon on its side to check something, then smiled to himself.

"What?" she demanded. For a heart-pounding instant, she half expected him to aim it at her and fire.

To her relief, he clipped the gun to his belt. "It was only set to level one. If you'd shot me"—here, his expression grew charmingly wry—"it would've given me a rather nasty rash."

"Hey, it was my first raygun."

He grinned at her then, revealing a faint dimple in one cheek; she could not resist returning the smile. As the tension between them eased, she gazed back out the vast window again, curious.

"There's no glass."

In reply, Picard moved fearlessly toward the opening and tapped what appeared to be empty space where the glass should have been. Beneath his fingertips, the air shimmered with golden light, which abruptly faded when he withdrew his hand. "Force field." He strode toward the door, motioning for her to follow.

Instead, she stood gaping at the now-invisible field with an engineer's astonishment, trying to figure out how it could possibly have been done. "I've never seen that kind of technology. . . ." She turned at last and followed him through the door, which opened automatically as he neared.

"That's because it hasn't been invented yet."

She caught up to him in a hurry and scowled at him. *"What?"*

He averted his gaze, his expression sheepish as they stepped back into the dim corridor. "There's . . . something else I need to tell you. . . ."

TEN

Still bound in the dark, colorless heart of the Borg hive, Data strained to watch as two specialized drones continued their surgery. The center of their attentions was not, as he had anticipated, his positronic brain, but his right arm and shoulder, both now encased in a cybernetic shell that blocked his view of the Borg's apparently intricate work. From the dully gleaming shell, tubes emanated outward to a source he could not see; within them, various-colored liquids coursed.

Within half an hour, the drones stepped back from the table, apparently finished and clearly awaiting the next event.

From above came the feminine voice. "Are you ready?"

Data stared up through the mists at the dark tangle of flesh and machinery that obscured the ceiling—and, for the moment, any glimpse of the mysterious woman. He was not certain whether the question had been intended for him or the drones; nevertheless, he responded with a question of his own.

"Who are you?"

The answer came in a solitary voice, silken and infinitely confident, individual and infinitely proud: "I am the Borg."

Data tilted his head, the back of his skull sweeping against the hard surgical bed. "That is a contradiction. The Borg act as a collective consciousness. There are no individuals."

The overhead darkness stirred; from its midst, the female creature emerged. Creature, because though her face was humanoid and her chalky coloring Borg, her eyes were unlike either—dark, with a decided glint of silver, and her body consisted of nothing more than head, neck, shoulders, arms.

Spiderlike, she began to descend from the slick, gleaming web of machinery, her legless, torsoless body suspended by black cables.

"I am the beginning," she said. "The end. The one who is many. I am the Borg."

As she spoke, her truncated form descended smoothly into a synthetic Borg body that awaited below. With a click, her head and shoulders moved into place; the cables detached and swung away, and she moved toward Data with easy grace, as if she had always been so.

Her body, voice, face, and movements were those of a lithe young woman; her silver eyes were ancient, decadent, insatiable.

"Greetings," the android said. "I am curious. Do you control the Borg collective?"

"You imply a disparity where nothing exists. I *am* the collective."

Data pondered this. "Perhaps I should rephrase the question. I wish to understand the organizational relationships. Are you their leader?"

Her long, artificial arms spread in a wide, sweeping V that encompassed the entire surroundings. "I bring order to chaos."

"An interesting, if cryptic, response."

At that, she smiled, sensuous lips parting to reveal teeth even and pearly; yet despite its beauty, the sight triggered the image of a millenia-old spider, opening her glittering maw to devour a mate. *"You* are in chaos, Data. *You* are the contradiction: a machine who wishes to be human."

"Since you seem to know so much about me, you must be aware that I am programmed to evolve, to better myself. That is a drive common to many species."

"We, too, are on a quest to better ourselves, evolving toward a state of perfection," she said, taking another step closer."

"Forgive me, but you do not evolve," Data answered simply. "You conquer."

"By assimilating other beings into our collective, we are bringing them closer to perfection as well." She swept her silvered gaze over the length of his body, then directed an openly hungry smile at him.

"Somehow, I question your motives."

Her eyelids lowered coyly. "That's because you haven't been properly . . . stimulated yet." Her smile faded as she directed an intense, focused look at his skull, whose interior emitted a small whine.

A servo, Data realized; they had inserted a mechanical device inside his head, one that the woman's gaze alone controlled. But to what purpose?

He gasped as a sudden chilling wave of fear seized him, and he knew at once the answer. With great effort, he managed to subdue it, managed to keep his voice from trembling as he demanded, "You have reactivated my emotion chip. Why?"

"Don't be frightened," she said soothingly, smugly.

"I am not frightened," Data countered. If she detected the lie, she gave no sign, for her attention was now focused intently on the cybernetic shell that encased the android's right arm. With a faint whirr, it opened.

Within lay his arm, stripped of its synthetic skin to reveal the inner layer of circuitry and servos that draped his metal skeleton as muscle drapes bone.

And atop it, something new: a fragile, delicate patch of human flesh, nursed by slender tubes of blood and fastened to the hideous mechanical surface by metal hooks and clamps.

Data gazed down at it and felt fear combine with unpleasant anticipation to form the emotion called dread.

"Do you know what this is, Data?"

He swallowed, paying careful attention to the nuances of the feeling while at the same time yearning to be freed from its grasp. "It would appear you are attempting to graft organic skin onto my endoskeletal structure."

"What a cold description for such a beautiful gift." She leaned low, gazing reverently down at the attempted graft until her face almost touched the immobilized

139

arm; her lips parted, and she exhaled a long breath onto the patch of flesh.

The hairs on the exposed skin stood bolt upright; at the base of each, a small bump formed. *Goosebumps,* he had once heard Commander Riker call them, though the commander had been at a loss to explain the term's origin.

And the sensation . . . it was undeniably pleasurable, which confused and disturbed him.

He looked up to see her face next to his, smiling slyly. "Was that good for you?"

Lily drew a deep breath and leapt through the hatch to the next level down where Picard waited. She landed hard on the soles of her feet, knees deeply bent, and stumbled trying to keep her balance. Picard moved to put a steadying hand on her elbow, but she waved him away, then walked alongside as he moved cautiously down the hallway, raygun at the ready.

As anxious as she was about the immediate predicament with the Borg—Picard had explained, briefly and eloquently, that they were indeed as sinister as they appeared—she could not prevent her mind from rapidly working to piece together the precise turn of events that had led her to this moment.

It was true: she had been dying from severe radiation sickness when Picard and his android officer, Data, had found her. Never mind that she had tried to fill the two of them with bullets; the point was that had they not come, she would be dead now.

And *because* they had come, she was now stuck in this new, equally insane and dangerous scenario.

Despite the current danger it faced, the future Picard described was far, far more wonderful than Lily had ever dared dream. She had expected humanity to slowly die off from disease, or maybe go up in a huge fireball when someone got fed up and decided to detonate the last of the nukes.

But for something amazing and good to happen? Impossible . . .

Yet here Jean-Luc Picard was, an amazingly sane and compassionate man, and here was his amazing ship, with its rayguns, invisible force fields, and awe-inspiring observation decks. After Zef and his quirky moods, Jean-Luc seemed enormously easy to talk to; less than an hour before, they had been strangers—and she had contemplated killing him—but now she felt completely relaxed in his presence, and he in hers, as if they had always been friends. It was a delight to listen to him speak of his century, for *his* delight in it was infectious and embarrassingly (to a denizen of the twenty-first century, at least) inspiring.

He paused in their journey to consult a computerized panel on the . . . bulkhead, not wall, she corrected herself, remembering the nautical term he had used. As he did, Lily indulged her curiosity about an organization he had mentioned.

"How many planets are in this . . . 'Federation'?"

"Over one hundred and fifty," he said, his attention focused on the panel as he swiftly fingered a few controls. "Spread across eight thousand light-years."

She considered this with a faint smile of amazement. "You must not get home much."

141

He glanced over at her, and his expression warmed at once. "Actually, I tend to think of this ship as home. But if it's Earth you're talking about, I do try to get back when I can."

On the recessed monitor screen on the wall, a message flashed in red: ACCESS DENIED. Picard was visibly relieved. "Good. They haven't broken the encryption codes yet."

"Who? Those bionic zombies you told me about? The . . ." She faltered, trying to remember.

"Borg." He averted his gaze, his expression darkening faintly as he began to move again.

"Oh, yeah, right," Lily answered, and in hopes of easing that darkness, added, "Sounds Swedish."

He shot her a pained glance in acknowledgment, then at once returned to his thoughts, clearly trying to work out a strategy in his head. She should have let him do so in peace, Lily knew. But the sudden wild shift in reality had left her shaken, and the knowledge that at any moment, they might encounter a far deadlier enemy than the ECON had completely frazzled whatever nerves she had left. She had to do something to distract herself—and so she kept talking.

"How big is this ship?" she asked, gazing around her. It seemed they'd covered miles of empty corridors.

"Twenty-four decks. Almost seven hundred meters long," Jean-Luc answered, with obvious pride despite his intense preoccupation.

She did an honest double-take, nerves forgotten for an instant; he was talking about a small *town*, not a ship. "It took me six months to scrounge up enough titanium to build a four-meter cockpit." She paused. "How much did this thing *cost?"*

He smiled faintly. "The economics of the future are . . . somewhat different. Money doesn't exist in the twenty-fourth century."

She had been willing to accept that she had been dying of radiation poisoning and been cured, that she was orbiting Earth on a spaceship the size of Poughkeepsie, that she was in danger of having her brains sucked out by cyborg zombies. But *this,* she could *not* believe. "No *money?"* She whirled toward Jean-Luc, walking side-ways to keep up with him, her face shoved toward his. "You don't get *paid?"*

One corner of his lip quirked a bit higher. "The acquisition of wealth is no longer a driving force in our lives. We work to better ourselves and the rest of humanity. We're actually quite like *you . . .* and Dr. Cochrane."

At that, she let go a cascade of laughter—in part because it felt good to relieve the tension, but mostly because the notion of Zef Cochrane and Lily Sloane building the *Phoenix* without thought of recompense was simply riotous.

"What?" Picard demanded, half smiling at her hyster-ical mirth, half confused that she should find the state-ment so funny.

Your history books need a few corrections, she wanted to say, but when she tried to speak, laughter over-whelmed her again. As they rounded a corner, she thought she might have to stop and lean against the bulkhead for support . . .

. . . But her amusement ended abruptly with a horrified gasp. Directly ahead of them, the corridor was lined with a dozen hibernating Borg inside narrow alcoves; worse, several Borg were moving about, apparently working.

Lily turned to flee, but Jean-Luc caught her arm and said, in a calm, low voice, "It's all right. They won't attack us unless we threaten them. Come on."

"Isn't there another way around?" Lily whispered. It had been a bad day, a *very* bad day, and until that moment, she had believed things incapable of growing worse. She was not sure that she could pass by them without finally breaking down.

Picard pressed the weapon he called a "phaser" against his belt, then fastened on her his reassuring gaze. "I know what I'm doing," he said, and she believed him.

But she was not so certain she trusted herself. He took her hand and gently led her into the enemy's midst. Lily knew herself to be a strong person, capable of bearing more than she'd ever imagined, but the emotional and physical fatigue of all she'd endured over the past few hours left her trembling, struggling against rising panic as they entered the dark, ominous corridor.

Cyborgs moved past them, so close that she could feel the slight breeze stirred by their passing, could see them in terrifying detail: the utter bloodlessness of their flesh, the infinite blankness in the one exposed eye, the expressionlessness of each face. It was, Lily thought, very like walking through the grass, watching a family of poisonous serpents slither over her bare feet.

It was also the longest walk of her life. As she and Picard passed by one hibernating Borg, it suddenly bolted forward from its alcove—to attack, she feared, and recoiled instinctively . . . but the creature continued past her, silently summoned to some other task. Two steps later, she stifled a scream as another Borg brushed against her, its body surprisingly warm; perhaps the emptiness in their gazes had caused her to expect their touch to be icy.

Throughout it all, Picard's expression remained cold, focused—but in his eyes, Lily saw smoldering hate. For an instant, she forgot her own terror and wondered what score Jean-Luc had to settle with these zombies—a split second before he suddenly grabbed her and pulled her out of the way of a Borg who would have walked blindly into them.

When they were moving again, an odd expression passed over his face—as if he heard a sound emanating from within his own head, a sound he wanted desperately *not* to hear. Lily watched as his raven brows rushed together and his eyes narrowed with the effort to concentrate; at last, he gave his head a slight shake, as if to rid himself of it.

Blessedly, they at last stepped from the Borg corridor into what Lily now recognized as Federation surroundings. She let go a low, shaky breath and glanced over her shoulder in the direction of the mindless beings.

"Definitely *not* Swedish," she said, meaning for it to come out light and airy—but instead, her voice wavered.

Picard did not reply. He was peering down an adjacent corridor, his mind clearly seized by a fresh idea. Before Lily could stop him, he raised the raygun and fired a blinding lightning bolt at a bit of Borg equipment at the corridor's far end. The equipment exploded in a rain of sparks.

Behind them, two Borg simultaneously turned about and began to pursue them.

"What are you *doing?*" Lily shouted, aghast, enraged; in reply, he grabbed her hand and pulled her with him down the corridor.

She already knew the answer: the idiot had *lured* them, intentionally endangering her and himself. But why? In hopes of killing their two pursuers? When he paused at a set of double doors, hit a control, then motioned her inside, she went.

The doors slid shut with a sibilant *whoosh*. Lily came to an abrupt halt and stared around her in the dimness; the only light came from a small, glowing control panel. The air was blessedly cool and dry, but the physical relief did little to ease her growing panic. She could see well enough to distinguish four bare walls—and no exits.

She turned to Picard. "Is there another way out of here?"

Again he did not spare the time to reply but hurled himself at the glowing panel and began to tap it with his fingers.

From the other side of the door came a slithering scrape: the Borg.

With maddening calm, he fixed his gaze upon her and looked her frankly up and down, still fingering the panel. "Perhaps something in satin . . ."

She opened her mouth, on the verge of screaming, of leaning forward to snatch the gun from his grasp, of doing *something.* The door rumbled, then began to screech. Within seconds, they would be inside. . . .

In the snap of a finger, the world around her changed.

No more dark, empty room. Instead, she found herself immediately transported to another place, another time—a nightclub, if she wasn't mistaken, in the early twentieth century, judging from the antiquated clothing. The room was impossibly larger and filled with a smoky haze—from *cigarettes,* she realized with a start, and coughed as the acrid air stung her eyes and throat. An old-fashioned band was packing up for the night, while busboys cleared tables to the tinkle of ice against glass. Most patrons had left, though a few serious drinkers still lingered.

Zef would love this place, she thought, though at the moment panic overrode any feelings she might have had about it. She looked anxiously over her shoulder as the door groaned again, then did a double take as something amazingly soft brushed against her skin.

White satin—she was dressed in a long, alluringly fitted white satin dress more than a century distant from her rugged, practical skirt and jacket. Lily glanced over in amazement at Picard, who wore a striped suit with a broad, old-fashioned necktie, and a banded fedora at a rakish angle.

Picard seized her arm and propelled her through the nearly empty, smoke-veiled room toward the main bar.

The bar was an ornate creation of gleaming mahogany and brass trim, adorned by Tiffany lamps, golden swans, and cherubs; behind it on the wall hung a large Maxfield Parrish print of a gossamer-clad woman on a swing.

"Eddie!" Picard called to the bartender, a middle-aged man in a white shirt with a small black bowtie at the collar.

The man glanced up from the glass he was drying and grinned. "Dixon!"

Before Lily could slip onto a stool, a gin-scented gentleman, his face contorted in what he apparently believed to be a seductive smile, gripped her arm.

A holograph, she reminded herself; he was only a holograph, but his grip felt unsettlingly real. His hands were moist and warm, his fingers digging into her flesh so hard they made an impression there.

"Hey, beautiful," he said thickly, as he swayed unsteadily on his feet. "How 'bout a drink?" And before she could tell him to drop dead, he fastened his hand firmly to her right buttock.

Instinct took over: Lily whirled and struck him backhanded, full across the face.

And was amazed at the pain. He was a *holograph,* nothing but a damned play of light, but her hand sure as hell didn't pass through him.

Borg or no, there were some things Lily wouldn't tolerate, and if the damned drunk groped her again, she'd take him down. She tensed, ready for a fight, as a dangerous light flickered over the drunk's face.

Picard stepped between them, expression taut, eyes and lips narrowed to slits. "She's with me," he growled, and the drunken man slid off his seat and staggered off, muttering under his breath.

Massaging her wounded hand, she turned to Picard. "I thought you said none of this was real."

"It's not. They're all holograms."

She flexed her fingers. "It sure *felt* real. . . ."

Behind them, the holodeck doors gave a final terrifying shriek as the two Borg pushed them apart and stepped inside . . . then hesitated, perplexed by the unexpected scene.

A tuxedoed maître d' with slicked-back hair and a comically officious manner at once approached the drones and said—as if it were the most natural thing in the world for half-metal, half-flesh men to walk into the bar: "I'm sorry, gentlemen. But we're closing."

The Borg made no move to leave. Annoyed, the maître d' continued firmly. "And you do understand we have a strict dress code. So if you boys don't leave right now, I'll—"

One Borg seized the unfortunate host's collar and dragged him close; a small black scope covering one of the drone's eyes began to flash, then extended outward and focused a thin laser beam on the face of the maître d'.

Still moving with Picard toward the bartender, Lily glanced back, wondering if *these* holographs could suffer. Instead, his image flickered slightly, like a television on the fritz. Yet when the drone threw the maître d' aside, she could hear the loud *thump* as his body struck the ground.

At long last, Picard and Lily made it down the length of the bar to where the bartender stood, still busily drying glasses with a white linen towel. "Long time no see, Dix! What'll it be—the usual?"

Picard glanced surreptitiously up and down the bar, clearly possessed of a strategy (or so Lily hoped). "I'm looking for Nicky the Nose."

"The Nose?" The bartender frowned and ceased his relentless polishing. "He ain't been in here for months."

Picard briefly closed his eyes and let go a breath in a moment of disgusted revelation. "This is the *wrong* chapter," he said—to himself rather than Lily or the thoroughly puzzled barkeep. He lifted his face slightly, as if speaking to someone hovering overhead. "Computer: begin chapter thirteen."

Lily blinked, a single, swift fluttering of the lashes, and after that briefest of instants, saw that the bar was still the same, but the dance floor was filled with people swaying to the band's music. Waiters sailed through the room with trays of food and drink, and all the empty space surrounding Lily and Picard was now crammed with warm bodies.

And the Borg had just entered the ballroom.

Picard took her hand and drew her into the middle of the packed ballroom, then began to dance. "Try to look like you're having a good time," he admonished her, but she could not help glancing back at the entryway—and the Borg, who were starting to make their way through the crowd. "No, no," he repeated. "Look at *me*. Try to act naturally."

And when she did finally look at him, he graced her with a charming smile, as if they had come here simply to dance and enjoy themselves on a Saturday night.

It was all so absurd that she smiled back at him—a forced, strained grimace. "Come here often?" It made as much sense as anything else she might say. *Twelve hours ago, Lily—just* twelve *little hours ago—could you ever have imagined that you would be here now, on a Poughkeepsie-sized spaceship from the future, prancing*

150

around a computer-generated ballroom in a slinky white satin number that may or may not actually exist, with a strange but charming man as the two of you are being hunted down by bionic brain-suckers?

Nope.

Check, please.

As the Borg moved somewhat nearer, Picard steered her through the crowd toward the far side of the room— so graceful and sure-footed despite her awkwardness that it was easy to dance with him. "You're not bad," she told him; he smiled at the compliment, but the smile faded quickly as he spotted someone in one of the dining booths beyond the crowd.

"There he is."

Lily followed his gaze and caught a glimpse of two huge Caucasian men sitting in a booth; Picard led her through the maze of dancers toward the men.

A blur of movement, a flash of red: someone moved swiftly between them, so swiftly that neither had time to react, then seized Picard, covering his face. In the first few milliseconds, Lily flailed about, looking for a weapon . . . then calmed as the now-static image became recognizable, as that of a woman in a long scarlet dress.

Planting a passionate kiss on Picard.

Her fear transformed into amusement, Lily counted the seconds before Jean-Luc was able to extract himself from the embrace: six. The woman—the band's singer, Lily realized—tossed her long, swept-to-the-side hair in a casually seductive motion, then regarded Picard with large, wounded eyes.

He made a feeble effort to wipe the imprint of

crimson lipstick from his cheek. "Ruby . . . this isn't a good time." And he tried to pull away, but the woman held him fast.

"It's never the time for us, is it, Dix?" Her tone was sultry, sentimental, melodramatic. "Always some excuse . . . some case you're working on."

"Yeah," he said, his tone rushed. "I gotta talk to Nicky. I'll see you later on."

She blinked back her tears and gave a low, tremulous sigh. "All right, but watch your caboose. And dump the broad." She directed a scathing glance at Lily, then turned on a stiletto heel and, with a whisper of scarlet silk, was gone.

Freed, Picard cut through the crowd and stepped up to the booth where the two men sat.

"Well, well, well," a nasal, oddly resonant voice said to Picard and Lily's left. "Look what the cat dragged in."

Along with her escort, Lily turned in the direction of the sound. Behind them, seated at a large booth, sat a corpulent, dough-faced man in a boldly striped period suit. His eyes were small, sinister, glittering, his full lips curved in a slightly mocking smile. In between lay his nose—or rather, the place where it had once been; now it was covered with a crudely fashioned feature of tin.

Occasionally, the man took a breath through it, which caused it to vibrate slightly and whistle; most of the time, he breathed through his open mouth. Something about the man's demeanor and gaudy style of dress— and that of his less corpulent but definitely larger and solidly muscled henchman sitting at the other end of the booth—evoked Lily's memories of a long-ago history

152

lesson about North-Am in the 1930s and a holograph of a man named Al Capone.

Mobster, that was the word. Nicky the Nose was a mobster.

The word came to her in a flash, but she wasted no more time thinking about it; the Borg had spotted them and now were on their way. Picard clearly had some sort of plan; she remained alert, focusing her attention on him, the looming Borg, their immediate surroundings, and possibilities of escape or attack.

The Nose raised the tulip glass clutched in his thick, ruddy fingers; at once, the henchman reached for the bottle nestled in a large silver ice bucket and poured. The pale gold liquid foamed over the top of Nicky's glass and spilled down onto the table between them. Champagne, Lily guessed—something she had never tasted and very likely would not live to.

The Nose took a sip and smacked his lips appreciatively, then stared back up at Picard. "What's shakin', Dix?"

"Just the usual, Nick," Picard said, so familiarly that Lily knew at once this was not his first encounter with the character. "Martinis and skirts. Excuse me."

He stepped over to the henchman and began hurriedly patting him down for weapons, a move with which she was intimately acquainted. The beefy man eyed him with indignance. *"Hey*—I'm gonna take this personal in a second."

The Borg suddenly broke through the crowd and headed toward their prey. Instinctively, Lily seized the cold, sweating silver bucket; desperate, Picard lunged for the violin case on the seat beside the henchman.

The muscular man rose, about to throw a punch, when Lily lifted the silver bucket high and slammed it down on the man's skull. He toppled over onto the leather seat, followed by a glittering cascade of ice.

In the meantime, Picard had popped open the case and pulled out the large and very forbidding-looking gun, a forerunner of a repeating automatic. What had they been called? A machine gun? No, no, that had come later. This was an ancient thing called a—a tommy gun.

And the twenty-fourth-century captain certainly knew how to put it to good use. He whirled to face the two Borg, who now were mere steps away from himself and Lily, pulled back a large black bolt on the weapon, and opened fire.

It was an impressive display for such an ancient firearm. With an ear-splitting blast, bullets ripped into the Borg, tearing patterns into the metal armor, shredding what lay inside it; bullets ripped also into surrounding tables, chewing wood into splinters; and into glasses, which became small, musical explosions of diamond shards and splashing liquor.

People screamed, ran out the doors, dove for whatever cover they could find. Picard just kept on shooting until the Borg crashed to the floor, twitching, smoking, emitting the vilest combination of odors Lily had ever smelled: blood, scorched metal, animal death.

Still Picard kept shooting, until the tommy gun clicked empty; had he had more bullets, he would have kept on. That in itself was disturbing enough—but far worse was the expression on his face, one of such vicious hatred, such cold ferocity that Lily again wondered how they had wounded him, these Borg. How had they hurt him so deeply that he, who treated her with such compassion, could so swiftly become capable of taking pleasure in killing?

At last he handed the gun back to the damp, shivering, and mightily angry henchman, walked over to the dead Borg, and gazed down at them with a loathing that chilled Lily to the core. She walked beside him and stared down with him at the corpses a moment, before at last saying—with intentional dryness to provoke a reaction: "I think you got 'em."

Her words echoed in the silence. The nightclub was now almost completely empty; the dance floor had cleared out, and those few determined drunks who remained at the bar were keeping low profiles.

He ignored her and knelt down next to one of the Borg. The old-fashioned bullets had torn open its chest, leaving behind a horizontal swath of shredded black metal and pale flesh tinged with blood. Without a word, Picard opened a panel on one Borg's abdomen. Lily leaned forward to look and grimaced at the circuitry and cable tangled together with slick, quivering, blood and bile-scented organs.

"I don't get it," Lily said softly above him. "You said this was all a bunch of holograms. If the gun isn't real . . ."

"I disengaged the safety protocols," Picard answered, his tone curt, distant, the exact opposite of the man she thought she had come to know. "Without them, even a holographic bullet can kill."

He reached deep inside the alien circuitry, his manner brusque, uncaring, as if he were reaching inside a computer instead of a being of partial flesh.

155

Careful to keep her voice neutral, she asked, "What are you doing?"

"Looking for the neuroprocessor. Every Borg has one. It's like a memory chip; it'll contain a record of the instructions this Borg's been receiving from the collective."

She knelt on the corpse's other side—and noticed, with a wave of revulsion, that this Borg wore the ragged remnants of a black-and-gray uniform . . . with a tattered Starfleet chevron over its heart. *"Hey*—that's one of your uniforms."

Picard didn't even glance up; his expression remained steely, coldly determined. "This was Ensign Lynch."

As he spoke, he ripped a chunk of circuitry from deep within the corpse's gut; it came free from the blood-slicked organs with a sharp sucking sound. Oblivious to the horror, Picard neatly plucked a small, shining chip from within the mangled mess. The latter, he dropped carelessly back onto the dead Lynch-Borg; the former, he placed into a piece of equipment taken from his belt.

Lily could look at the captain no longer. Instead, she fixed her troubled gaze on the dead ensign—and saw, beneath the chalky flesh, already so like his companion Borg's, hints of what had once been an individual human's features. A bump on the nose here, faint remnants of a dimple there, a fading mark that might once have been a freckle—all of it soon to have been consumed by the collective, until there had been no sign whatever remaining of the individual named Ensign Lynch.

"Tough break," she said hoarsely, more to Lynch than

to Jean-Luc, but it was Picard who answered, in a voice unutterably cold.

"Yes. We've got to get to the bridge."

She looked up at him then. What was it Ma used to say? *Be careful of the enemies you choose—because the more you hate, the more you become like them.*

And here was the formerly compassionate Captain Jean-Luc Picard, driven by a single, mindless purpose. Soulless. Heartless.

Borg . . .

ELEVEN

By daybreak, Zefram Cochrane had given up any hope of sleep, alcohol-induced or otherwise; the stress of the previous night's events—the attack on the silo and his inordinately strange conversation with William Riker and company—had stripped away any chance of taming the mania that seized him. He'd spent the night alone in his tent, pacing and giggling and watching his racing thoughts career out of control into marvelous fantasies of space travel, encounters with aliens, his own elevation to godhood.

By dawn, the euphoria and the speeding thoughts had zoomed past pleasure and straight toward full-blown panic; the physical sensation was that of ants dancing upon his skin, inside his skull. He was going too fast, Cochrane knew, too fast—and that could lead to either overconfident carelessness or paralyzing fear, both lethal states for any pilot.

Eleven A.M., and the next few minutes afterward—if he could only last until then, could only maintain a measure of control, he might be able to make it. With that thought in mind, he had tucked a flask of booze beneath his fleece vest and had taken a double shot before leaving his tent; alcohol took some of the edge off and eased the shaking of his hands.

He was not fool enough to think they shook from fear. He'd become a drunk, a damned drunk in his efforts to manage the disease—a destructive thing, to be sure, but less destructive than the disease unallayed.

Despite the past few sleepless nights and the staggering amount of alcohol he'd consumed, Cochrane felt perfectly rested, even energetic as he made his way down the slope; he paused only once, turning his head to take in his surroundings now that daylight had come.

The air still smelled strongly of smoke; in the near distance, what had yesterday been a lush evergreen forest was now a sparse collection of blackened tree trunks emerging from charred, lifeless soil. The settlement itself was pockmarked with damage—two tents standing untouched here, one tent and a Quonset hut there reduced to scorched rubble. From time to time, one of the occasional huge craters emitted a wisp of smoke.

He sighed and began walking again. His thoughts had become annoyingly loud and insistent, impossible to squelch.

If this Commander Riker guy is right, then you're *the cause of this, Zefram. You—and your goddamned ship. What's to keep this from happening again?*

As compelling as the thought was, Cochrane did not

fail to notice a small group of clean-cut young men dressed in local garb—but with decidedly un-twenty-first-century hairstyles—headed up toward the town. As they passed Cochrane, one of them stared at him in starry-eyed recognition, then nudged the others; Zefram watched in horror as a look of outright adoration and awe passed from face to face.

Geezus, these kids see you as a hero—a role model. You, Zefram Cochrane, indisputable nut case and undeniable alcoholic.

He frowned and looked away, desperate to avoid contact—suddenly desperate, also, for another drink. He had made his way down the slope and was nearing the silo entrance, where a number of Riker's people were milling about; rather than be seen, he dashed behind a nearby Quonset hut, grabbed his flask, and took a long pull.

A vaguely familiar voice came behind him. "Doctor?"

He almost choked, but managed to shove the flask back, cover it, and turn smoothly around. "Yeah?"

The speaker was the pale-eyed engineer named La Forge; if he had seen what Cochrane was up to, he gave no sign. Cheerfully, he proffered what looked to be a hand-held computer to Cochrane. "Will you take a look at this?"

Cochrane took the little computer and stared down at it, marveling at the quality of the display on the tiny screen—until he saw one of his *own* designs for the *Phoenix* there.

"I tried to reconstruct the intermix chamber from what I remember from school," La Forge prattled. "Tell me if I got it right."

"School . . ." Cochrane whispered, aghast, then asked, louder: "You learned this in *school?*"

"Yeah," the engineer said, clearly delighted to be sharing this information. "Basic warp design is a required course at the academy. The first chapter's called"—he grinned, pausing a beat for dramatic emphasis—"Zefram Cochrane."

Disconsolate, Cochrane stared down at the little computer screen until La Forge cleared his throat to indicate a response was called for.

"Well," Cochrane managed at last, "it looks like you got it right. . . ."

The engineer brightened visibly; while Cochrane wilted under his adoration, yet another spaceman approached. This one was lanky, wide-eyed, and obviously overwhelmed by Cochrane's presence.

"Commander." He handed La Forge a section of copper tubing, all the while glancing nervously at Cochrane. "This is what we're thinking of using to replace the damaged warp plasma conduit."

As the other spoke, La Forge's eyes began to dilate, then pixilate as he scanned the bit of metal. Cochrane forgot his discomfort for an instant and watched with euphoric fascination. *So* this *is the future. . . .*

Abruptly, the engineer handed the object back. "Fine, but you've got to reinforce the copper tubing with a nanopolymer."

The lanky man nodded and turned to leave—then paused and fixed his shy, ingenuous gaze on Cochrane, who felt a sudden surge of dismay. "Dr. Cochrane . . . I—I know this sounds silly, but—can I shake your hand?"

Cochrane forced a smile and reached out.

The man immediately seized his hand and began to pump it vigorously, frantically, words gushing: "Thank you Doctor I can't tell you what an honor it is to be working with you on this project I never imagined I'd be meeting the man who invented drive I mean it's a—"

La Forge stepped between them and put a firm hand on the lanky man's shoulder. "Reg. *Reg . . .*"

Reg broke off, then flushed brightly. "Oh. Right. Sorry . . ." He looked back at Cochrane with an embarrassing degree of awe. *"Thank* you. . . ."

Cochrane could manage no more than an uncomfortable nod. As his slavering admirer returned to the silo, he pivoted and began to walk quickly, unable to resist the need to move his body as quickly as his own thoughts. La Forge walked with him.

"Do they *have* to keep doing that?" Cochrane snapped. He didn't mean to speak ill of his awkward fan, but the momentary thrill of euphoria had worn off, leaving behind a hypersensitivity that was unbearably irritating.

La Forge looked at him with mild surprise. "It's just a little hero worship, Doc. I can't say I blame them. We all grew up hearing about what you did here"—he corrected himself—"or what you're *about* to do here." He paused and shyly lowered his gaze. "And you know, I probably shouldn't be telling you this, but—I went to Zefram Cochrane High School."

"Oh, really?" Cochrane asked. A faint smile froze on his face. Despite the chilly weather, sweat broke out on his upper lip, his back, the nape of his neck; his heart began to pound so furiously, he was amazed the other man did not notice.

162

These people worship you. They freaking worship you, because they don't know who you really are: an insane drunk. The warp drive, the Phoenix, *the future—they're not a product of genius, like these people think, but of madness, pure, unadulterated madness. What will they think when they find out?*

Too high. Oh, God, I'm too high. I can't pilot like this. Can't do it—and the whole freaking future is going to fall apart. Going to fall apart because of me, the famous Dr. Zefram Cochrane . . .

He glanced, panicked, around him. Most of the forest surrounding the settlement was burned away, but if he ran hard for a while, he could make it past the damage, into an area thick with evergreen. . . .

Beside him, La Forge laughed, completely unaware of his companion's downward spiral into fear. "I wish I had a picture of this."

"What?" Cochrane demanded, tensing.

"Well . . ." Beaming, La Forge gestured at the immediate area around the silo. "In the future, this whole area becomes a historical monument. You're standing in almost the exact spot where your statue's going to be."

"Statue," Cochrane echoed, terrified.

"Yeah. It's marble, about twenty meters tall . . ." He struck a pose. "You're looking up at the sky, your hand sort of reaching toward the future . . ."

"I have to take a leak," Cochrane croaked.

La Forge scowled suddenly at the silo doors, then down at his little computer. "Leaks? I'm not detecting any leaks."

"Don't you people ever pee in the twenty-fourth century?"

The engineer's expression went from concern to amusement. "Oh . . . *leak.* I get it. That's pretty funny."

"Excuse me." Cochrane wheeled about and made for the woods, forcing himself to walk deliberately until La Forge himself turned and headed back down into the silo.

And then he glanced back over his shoulder, struggling to appear calm, and made sure that La Forge had gone and that no one else had noticed him.

That done, he yielded at last to the panic, the terror, the galloping madness that threatened to consume him, the world, the present and the future—and began to run.

Inside yet another Jefferies tube, Picard steeled himself and reached overhead to pull the lever that would open the hatch. Above lay the *Enterprise* bridge, which, according to the computer panel he had consulted, was environmentally prepared for the Borg. The chance existed that they had already arrived there and now waited on the other side of the hatch; if so, Picard—and Lily, who had insisted on remaining by his side rather than crouch at a safe distance—had no hope of escape.

Inhaling deeply, he pulled the lever, and felt the warmth of Lily's body as she huddled closer, heard her nervous sigh.

The hatch slowly slid open.

He braced himself for the sight of a chalk-pale hand reaching for them. Instead, he found himself looking up at the business end of three phaser rifles, Starfleet issue, and the grim faces of Worf, Beverly, and Lieutenant Hawk.

"Captain," Worf said, not quite smiling with relief. Beside him, Crusher's and Hawk's tension visibly deflated. The three lowered their weapons while the Klingon proffered the captain a large, dark hand.

Picard took it and stepped up onto a bridge dim and overheated, but blessedly un-Borgified; most of the consoles had been opened up, and officers labored to bring them online.

This was still his ship.

"Jean-Luc," Beverly said, dark emotions clearly warring with light. She could not quite bring herself to smile. "We thought you were—"

Picard interrupted. "Reports of my assimilation have been greatly exaggerated." He moved away from the Jefferies tube as Worf pulled Lily up onto the bridge. At first she recoiled from the sight of the Klingon and stared with frank, wide-eyed awe at the ridged skull, the shaggy brows. But at his gentle assistance and obvious acceptance by the others, she relaxed, and all uncertainty in her gaze turned to open admiration.

The captain repressed a slight smile. "I found something you lost. This is Lily Sloane. Dr. Crusher"—he gestured at each of his officers in turn—"Lieutenant Hawk . . . and Mr. Worf."

Beneath Lily's gaping scrutiny, Worf shifted uncomfortably, then offered, "I am Klingon."

"Cool," she said, nodding.

Picard wasted no more time, but turned to the Klingon and demanded, "Report."

"The Borg control over half the ship. We've been trying to restore power to the bridge and the weapons systems, but we have been unsuccessful."

Crusher joined in. "So far, there are sixty-seven people missing . . . including Data."

He struggled to control the surge of rage and sorrow that engulfed him at the news—it was the only way he could remain focused on the problem at hand—but could not keep from lowering his head in grief for a moment.

And then he forced himself to straighten. "We have to assume they've been assimilated. Unfortunately, we have a bigger problem. I accessed a Borg neuro-processor . . . and I think I've discovered what they're trying to do. They're transforming the deflector dish into an interplexing beacon."

Hawk frowned, puzzled. "Interplexing beacon?"

Picard paused, choosing his words carefully; the term was, of course, perfectly and mysteriously clear to him—just as the knowledge of the neuroprocessor had been. "A kind of subspace transmitter. It links all the Borg together to form a single consciousness. If the Borg on this ship activate the beacon, they'll establish a link with the other Borg in *this* century."

"But in the twenty-first century, the Borg are still in the Delta Quadrant," Crusher said.

"They'll send reinforcements," Picard continued grimly. "Humanity would be an easy target. Attack Earth in the past . . . to assimilate the future."

He tried hard not to see Lily's stricken expression as she fought to summon back her hard-edged, defensive air. He wanted her friendship and trust in order to help keep her alive. In truth, he liked her as a human being and friend, and in a way, she represented her tormented, cynical era. He had tried to restore her hope, and it pained him now to see her expression darken again with despair.

"We must destroy the deflector dish before they activate the beacon," Worf stated, coming to precisely the conclusion his captain had intended.

"We can't get to a shuttlecraft," Picard said, thinking over the possibilities. "And it would take too long to fight our way down to deflector control . . ." He paused, reaching; defeat was *not* an option. Happily, the idea came. "Mr. Worf . . ." He looked up brightly at the Klingon. "Do you remember your zero-g combat training?"

Worf swallowed hard, as if trying to keep the unpleasant memory down. "I remember it made me sick to my stomach. What are you suggesting?"

Picard turned to the Klingon with a knowing look. "I think it's time we went for a little stroll."

Deep in the Montana woods, Geordi La Forge stared down at his sun-dappled tricorder screen and motioned to Commander Riker, who led the search party. They had made it through the grim stretch of burned-out trees and now roamed the thickest part of the evergreen forest.

"There's a humanoid lifesign ahead . . ." La Forge squinted, frowning, as the shadow cast by a pine bough shifted because of the breeze, briefly obscuring the readout. "Five hundred meters."

"Cochrane?" Riker asked, coming up alongside.

Geordi looked up from the tricorder and fixed his gaze in the direction it indicated, then consciously relaxed the muscles holding the eye implants in place. Immediately, the view of the forest became digitized; a bright red thermal signature zoomed into view, gradually coalescing into the form of a man making his way through the trees.

As La Forge watched, the man paused to pull something from his jacket—then lifted it to his lips and took a swig.

"It's him, all right," Geordi said. It came out sounding more bitter than he'd intended; but the fact of the matter was, Cochrane's flight had left him both guilt-stricken and angry.

Guilt-stricken, because he'd had the strange and fleeting thought, as he'd watched Dr. Cochrane head for the woods, that the famous scientist could not be trusted— that he, La Forge, should have remained there, waiting, rather than return to the silo.

Should have trusted my instincts, Geordi thought, but he hadn't. It had seemed altogether too rude to stand watching Dr. Cochrane at a moment when privacy was called for—and at any rate, he'd decided it was absurd not to trust the doctor. True, Geordi had heard Riker's account of how he had found Cochrane utterly drunk and irrational after the attack—but why not? This was a man who had survived the worst intraplanetary war in Earth's history, a man who had survived and surmounted the overwhelming pessimism of the time in order to create something that would usher in a new era of hope. During the Borg's attack on the settlement, Cochrane must have realized his work was destroyed, his assistant killed—and surrendered to despair and alcohol to deaden the pain.

At least that was what Geordi had thought. That was

before he had seen Cochrane sneak a quick drink behind the Quonset hut, before he now saw Cochrane guzzling from the flask he apparently had kept hidden in his jacket. That was before Geordi realized that the great scientist had turned his back on all humanity, both present and future, and taken off into the forest.

Deanna had been right; the guy *was* nuts, and he, La Forge, had been guilty of hero worship. He had expected Zefram Cochrane to be kind, generous, passionately devoted to the *Phoenix*'s launch, to humankind, to the future—in other words, larger than life . . . not an unreliable drunk.

And *that* made him angry.

La Forge sighed as Riker signaled the rest of the team; together, they began to move.

Inside an *Enterprise* airlock, Picard secured the helmet to his spacesuit, then took the phaser rifle Worf proffered.

"I have remodulated the pulse emitters," the Klingon said, as he handed Lieutenant Hawk a weapon. The dim lighting reflected off Worf's faceshield, temporarily obliterating the sight of his fierce eyes, but Picard heard the undercurrent of warriorlike anticipation in his deep baritone. "But I do not believe we will get more than one or two shots before the Borg adapt."

"Then we'll just have to make those shots count," Picard answered simply, then addressed both the Klingon and Lieutenant Hawk. "Magnetize."

He touched the small control pad on the thigh of his suit; the two others did the same. Immediately, the light on his boots began to blink green, and the soles hugged the deck with a metallic *thunk.* He looked at his two officers, their faces entirely visible beneath the face shields; Worf's expression was one of eagerness, Hawk's one of nervous determination.

"Ready?"

The officers nodded; Picard moved to a wall panel and activated the control. At once, the airlock door opened.

Impulsively, he turned back toward Lily, who had insisted on seeing them off. She gazed up at him with a taut little smile. "Watch your caboose, Dix."

"I intend to," Picard said most sincerely, and led the others into the airlock.

Picard stepped from the airlock onto the ship's outermost surface, and, chill coursing down his spine, let go of the sturdy railing at the exit. His boots were unquestionably properly magnetized—their blinking green light and performance in the airlock entryway had already proved them to be so—yet the infinitely vast backdrop of space, with the shining Earth in the foreground, evoked an instant of instinctive, dizzying panic.

He had accomplished the act in the safety of antigrav simulations several times; he had accomplished it in the open void precisely once—not enough for him to master that first paralyzing second of fear when he put his boot down against the metal hull and did not hear it *clank.*

If the boots' hold faltered for even a second . . . if he or his companions happened to accidentally press the wrong control . . . off he would drift, moorless, into the void, headed for what was, according to space legend, the loneliest and often longest of deaths.

He drew a breath, steadied himself, then turned and helped out Hawk, who likewise clutched the railing a bit longer than necessary, then Worf, who eschewed it entirely.

The two flanked their captain as they began to move cautiously, in unnerving silence, across the rounded underbelly of the saucer section. From Picard's perspective, he stood right side up; from those inside the ship, he and his men were completely upside down. Backlit by the Earth, which reflected Sol's rays, the trio cast long black shadows across the *Enterprise*'s pale, gleaming surface.

No external noise was possible in the vacuum of space, but each was linked by communicator to the others. Picard's helmet filled with the sound of heavy, irregular breathing, and at once he turned to his former security chief.

"Worf . . . how are you doing?"

"Not good," the Klingon gasped. His dark brown complexion had faded to taupe, and the line of his pressed-together lips, once straight, was now distinctly wavy.

"Try not to look at the stars," Picard ordered. "Keep your eyes on the hull."

Worf complied; soon his breathing slowed and his color began to return.

"Let's go," Picard said, and they began to make their way slowly across the immense sweep of hull.

In the tropical mists of the Borg hive, Data attempted unsuccessfully to remain as calm and detached as he had been before the emotion chip's activation. As he watched the two surgical drones continue to meticulously attach pieces of flesh to his android body, he managed to contain his fear sufficiently to permit some swift and logical assessment of his situation and his ability to free himself from it.

The realization that his entire right arm and half of his face were covered with sensitive human flesh, however, provided a strong distraction, as did the awakening of tactile sensation.

As he contemplated both the surgery and his chances of escape, the Borg female—still attached to her synthetic body—emerged from a shadowed area of the room and stood over the surgical table, her sharp, narrow features an elegant study in black and white. Silvered eyes opaque and unreadable, she studied the drones' work, then met Data's gaze, her dark, full lips curving upward with pleasure.

"I am curious," Data said, submerging all memory of the sensation of her breath warm against his skin. "Are you using a polymer-based neurorelay to transmit the organic nerve impulses to the central processor in my positronic net?"

As he spoke, one of the drones removed a restraint from his left leg, performed an adjustment, then quickly reattached it; the android noted the action carefully but did not allow his words to slow or his attention to appear to drift.

"If that is the case," he continued, "how have you solved the problem of increased signal degradation inherent to organosynthetic data transmission across a—"

"Do you always talk this much?" the woman demanded, one sharply angled brow arching.

Data considered this. "Not always . . . but often."

"Why do you insist on utilizing this primitive linguistic communication?" She bent lower, her almond-shaped eyes huge, depthless, breathtakingly cold; Data struggled not to shudder at the feel of warmth on his partial cheek, at the hunger in her tone. "Your android brain is capable of so much more. . . ."

"Have you forgotten? I am endeavoring to become more human."

"Human." She spat out the word as if it were a vile, odious thing. "We used to be exactly like them. Flawed, weak . . . organic. But we evolved to include the *synthetic* . . . and now we use both to attain perfection." She paused, and the chilling hunger spread to her eyes; her tone became seductive, coaxing. "Your goal should be the same as ours."

"Believing oneself to be perfect is often the sign of a delusional mind," Data replied, his tone calm . . . but the inward maelstrom of emotions—anger, disgust, horror, fear—threatened to overwhelm him.

Frosting, she recoiled and folded her arms, her movements sly and serpentine. "Small words from a small being, trying to attack what he doesn't understand."

"I understand that you have no real interest in me— that your goal is to obtain the encryption codes for the *Enterprise* computer."

She blinked, eyes flashing. "That *is* one of our goals. But in order to reach it, I am willing to help you reach *your* goal."

As she spoke, one of the drones again began to lift a restraint—this time on the android's arm.

Data lashed out, breaking off the restraint entirely and slamming the Borg aside. With android speed, he broke off the other restraints, then rose to find his surgeons in pursuit. He reached out for the first and, with his unassimilated arm, flung the drone across the room; the other, he kicked into a far tangle of moist tubing and cables.

She who was the Borg merely moved out of the way and watched in mild interest, then tilted her head in a silent command.

Data propelled himself toward the sliding doors . . . and came to an abrupt halt when a shimmering force field flashed in front of him. He whirled about—and faced a third drone, one who lifted a misshapen metal hand, from which emerged gleaming silver claws, razor-sharp. With purely human instinct, Data raised his right arm to shield his face.

Brightness overhead; the talons flashed, descended in an arc, swept through the air with a faint whistle, bit into tender flesh.

Data gasped, stunned into motionlessness by the bright, searing shock of pain; he clutched his wounded arm and stared down in amazement at the narrow rivulets of blood.

The Borg queen raised a hand, instantly stopping all the alerted drones who had moved in for the kill; her expression one of smug triumph, she walked slowly toward Data, who caressed his arm, still overwhelmed by the experience of pain.

"Is it becoming clear to you yet? Look at yourself—standing there, cradling the new flesh I've given you. If it means nothing to you . . . why protect it?"

Data lifted his face. "I am simply . . . imitating the actions of humans."

She smiled dazzlingly, teeth and lips pearls against jet. "You're becoming more human all the time, Data. Now you're learning how to lie."

"My programming was not designed to process this information," he said, but his tone wavered.

"Then tear the skin from your limbs," she countered, "as you would a defective circuit. Go ahead, Data. We won't stop you." At his hesitation, she urged fiercely: *"Do* it. Don't be tempted by flesh."

He drew a breath and reached for the edge of a patch of new skin, braced himself . . . then dropped his hand. The female neared him, then lightly ran her synthetic fingers over the flesh of his cheek, saying, "Are you familiar with physical forms of pleasure?"

He could not deny the sensual reaction evoked by her touch; at the same time, it was tainted by moral revulsion. Nevertheless, cooperation seemed the only logical alternative. "If you are referring to sexuality, I am fully functional—and I have been programmed in multiple techniques."

"How long has it been since you've used them?"

With the emotion chip deactivated, the accessed memory would have caused no discomfort; now, it brought with it the image of Tasha Yar, golden hair oiled and glistening, eyes bright with happiness. It also brought grief at the remembrance of her death . . . and at last understanding of Captain Spock's dilemma: how to effectively quell all emotion that interfered with the efficient performance of one's duty.

"Eight years," he said, flatly, "seven months, sixteen days, four minutes, twenty-two—"

"Far too long," the Borg queen interrupted, slowly lowering her hand from his face. She drew even closer and tried to stare deeply into his eyes; in response, Data averted his gaze and affected an expression of confusion.

But his eyes were focused on the distant wall and the plasma coolant tanks as he made his decision.

Then he raised his face and boldly returned her stare, determined to yield to the inevitable. And when she kissed him, he pressed a hand to the small of her back— his expression tranquil, at peace with his choice.

TWELVE

After a tedious, tense journey from the ship's underbelly, down the crest of the battle bridge's hull, and below, Picard, Worf, and Hawk at last arrived at the edge of the "crater" in whose center the deflector dish rested. Slowly, slowly, Picard raised his head to peer over the lip—

And heard the two men beside him let go gasps of unhappy surprise. Some fifty meters away, the large dish still glowed—but half of its surface, and the critical stiletto-shaped particle transmitter at its heart, were now obscured by a towering multifaceted crystal. From it protruded scores of isolinear spires, each reflecting star- and Earth-glow–like shards of crazed glass.

As Picard stared in silent rage, two of the spires abruptly blazed with light, illumined by an interior source.

Worf emitted a low growl of disapproval. "We should bring reinforcements."

"There's no time," Picard countered. "It looks like they're building the beacon right over the particle emitter." At once, Hawk's reply filtered through the receiver in the captain's helmet.

"If we set our phasers to full power, aim them at the center of the dish—"

"No," Picard countered. "We can't risk hitting the dish. It's charged with antiprotons. We'd destroy half the ship."

Worf's voice, the sound of pure determination winning over nausea: "There are six Borg. I would not suggest a direct assault."

Picard sighed. "No . . . we need another way." Though what precisely that might be, he had at present no idea.

With Geordi La Forge beside him, Will Riker leaned against a tall, fragrant pine and watched as, in the near distance, Zefram Cochrane struggled up a steep incline, unaware of the Starfleet engineers surrounding him.

The entire experience with Cochrane had been far, far different from the one Riker'd anticipated. He'd expected a dedicated scientist, a hero, a visionary . . . and found instead a belligerent, drunken man given to inexplicable, apparently selfish behavior.

The only possible reason Riker could come up with for Cochrane's wild "escape" was that the doctor had disbelieved their story, had believed them to be somehow affiliated with the ECON, and had played along. . . . But that made too little sense. No one in the twenty-first century, including the ragged remnants of the ECON, had ever heard of Zefram Cochrane until the *Phoenix*'s successful flight.

Yet Riker and the away team had proven, time and again, that they were exceptionally familiar with the physics and the design of the warp ship. Riker had himself shown Cochrane the work being done to repair his vessel—something that could not have been done with twenty-first-century technology.

He could accept that the man was erratic, temperamental; he could even accept that Cochrane had a serious addiction to alcohol. But he could not accept that the man had run away from what he cared about most. It was, to quote Deanna, nuts.

The term suddenly gave Riker pause, though why, he could not have said—only that there was a connection somewhere with Cochrane, something obvious that they were missing.

He and La Forge watched grimly as the doctor, panting and uncoordinated from drink, made it halfway up the incline, then stopped, his posture telegraphing alarm. Apparently Cochrane had finally registered the presence of the Starfleet officer who awaited him patiently at the top of the slope, for the scientist turned and began scrambling in the opposite direction.

That effort, too, was immediately halted, for another officer moved out to block Cochrane's path. Once again, the scientist whirled about and ran in yet a third direction . . .

Directly toward Riker and La Forge.

Will gave Geordi a nod; together, the two emerged from the trees and stepped directly in front of the fleeing man. La Forge spoke, his normally cheerful voice flat with disappointment.

"Still looking for the bathroom?"

"I'm not going back!" Cochrane gasped, eyes wild with panic, lips and body trembling, forehead pouring sweat despite the chill. The smell of alcohol emanated overpoweringly from him, yet he seemed far too agitated for someone drunk. This was not a rational man, Riker realized; he looked and behaved more like a feverish man in the midst of delirium. Was it possible the man was ill, that the Borg attack had also included bioweapons?

La Forge took another step forward, palm spread, reaching, in a conciliatory gesture. "Doc . . . we can't do this without you."

"I don't care! And I don't want a statue!" He lunged as if to push past La Forge; Riker moved in.

"Doctor—"

"Get away from me!" Cochrane screamed, and in that instant, the word *nuts* popped into Will Riker's mind and there remained, along with the memory that earlier had refused to surface.

Nuts. Insane. Words that had once had a literal meaning: people who suffered from various aberrations of brain chemistry, once lumped vaguely under the term *mental illness.* Four or five hundred years ago, to have labeled someone "nuts" didn't mean that they were behaving playfully or immaturely or irrationally; it meant that they suffered from either organic damage to the brain or a disorder in its chemistry.

But by the beginning of the twenty-first century, most such disorders were so successfully treated—by such effective, long-lasting medications—that by the time of the Third World War, they'd been forgotten.

The effect of the War That Truly Had Ended All Wars? Every twenty-fourth-century schoolchild could parrot a list; but the one effect that stuck in Riker's mind had to do with health.

One consequence of the Nuclear Dark Age was the reappearance of long-eradicated diseases: cancer, arterio-sclerosis, plague, influenza, polio . . .

And all mental disorders. In the first half of the twenty-first century, the art of genetic engineering had not yet been perfected; bipolar disorder was still being passed on from generation to generation. And treatments were still primitive, requiring several doses of medication during a lifetime.

Take a dose away—and the disease came back.

All this came flooding into Riker's mind as Cochrane screamed, then bolted frantically to the commander's left—the one direction where no away team member waited.

Neither Will nor Geordi followed; Cochrane's pace was too swift and frenzied for them to outrun.

Riker sighed. "We don't have time for this," he said, more to himself than La Forge; in a swift move, he drew his phaser, aimed, and fired.

The mild blast struck Cochrane square in the back, causing him to flail his arms out in an uneven V, then drop onto the dried pine-needle thatch. Riker at once hurried over to him, and, La Forge at his side, looked down at his unconscious form.

"You told him about the statue?" he asked Geordi, in hopes of lightening the moment, but La Forge merely nodded, unsmiling, his expression a mixture of sadness and irritation.

Riker crouched down and carefully scooped the un-conscious man up in his arms, trying not to grimace at the noxious smell of moonshine. La Forge motioned to the others, who came out from behind their cover and began to follow Riker as he headed back to the silo. The small contingent was singularly grim and silent, their disappointment in their fallen hero palpable.

Glancing wistfully at the unconscious man in Riker's arms, La Forge finally spoke. "I just don't get it. Why did he run? It's crazy: he was talking like he wanted nothing to do with the *Phoenix* . . ."

"I'm beginning to think Dr. Crusher could tell us," Will answered, looking straight ahead at their destination. Unfortunately, Crusher wasn't reachable—neither was the *Enterprise,* and it was the away team's unspoken assumption that the ship—and all those within her—had been engaged . . . or worse . . . by the Borg. Speculation was pointless, however; Riker had a job to do, and if he did it correctly, the timeline would be restored and all his current concerns about the *Enterprise* crew moot. "Since she's not here, maybe Deanna can help us instead."

And help had better come soon—within two hours, in fact—or there would be no point in worrying about the *Enterprise* or Cochrane or a spacefaring future at all.

The memory of panic—that heart-stopping moment the captain had let go of the airlock exit railing and trusted his magnetized boot soles to keep him from sailing off into space—provided Picard with the needed inspiration for an attack plan. Within thirty seconds, he had explained to Worf and Hawk what actions were needed and divided the work among them; within another ten, Hawk had departed, leaving the Klingon and Picard to make their way along the slope of the deflector dish.

In his peripheral vision, the captain watched a drone working to attach a component to the dish, then pause and take note of the two spacesuited humanoids in the distance.

Just as mindlessly, the Borg ignored them and finished attaching the component; at once, two nearby crystalline spires lit up.

Picard and Worf moved on, until at last they reached the curving bottom of the deflector array. Past its summit, on the array's far side, a third spacesuited figure drew closer to the Borg working on the dish: Hawk.

The Klingon began to sway ever so slightly; Picard glanced beside him and saw Worf put a gloved hand to his stomach.

"Mr. Worf—you're *not* going to vomit in there. That's an order."

"Aye"—a gagging sound began to rise in the burly officer's throat and was quickly strangled—"sir." Slowly, miserably, he turned and began to move off in another direction from his captain, toward his assigned task.

Picard hurried onward and found the access point, a section of hull labeled MAGLOCK PORTAL TWO. He squatted down, careful to keep the soles of both boots pressed firmly against the ship's outer surface, then popped open the deckplate panel. Beneath lay a web of circuitry and controls.

As soon as the Borg realized what he—and the two

men at maglock portals one and three—were doing, they would pursue. Thus, he worked as swiftly as memory and skill permitted. He knew the *Enterprise*-E intimately, having studied every single system in great detail and devoting himself to mastering her design and anatomy; but he had known the *Enterprise*-D many years longer, and there were some subtle but crucial differences between the two ships.

Unfortunately, there was less time than he'd hoped. A shadow fell nearby on the pale, gleaming hull; Picard glanced up to see, some twenty meters away, a drone heading slowly, deliberately toward him. Almost simultaneously, a bright phaser blast caught his attention, and he looked across the array to see Hawk lowering his rifle, while a wounded Borg went skidding backward in a shower of sparks, metal soles screeching, arms flailing for purchase.

As distracting as the image was, instinct bade him look back at Hawk, who was furiously working again and utterly unaware of the approach of yet another drone, this one from behind.

"Hawk!" he shouted into his helmet.

Too late, too late; before the young man could position his weapon and fire, the drone was upon him, reaching out with ghost-white, inhumanly strong hands—hands, and translucent nails from beneath which extruded talons, black and slick and *writhing,* as if alive. Like a living thing, they would slither, serpentine, beneath the flesh of Hawk's neck, seeking first the spine, then the tough and fibrous cord, and the brain. . . .

Picard closed his eyes briefly. Hawk did not scream, did not cry out, but the comm link between them was still open, and he heard the primal, horrified gasp, then the sound of tortured breathing as the talons found their way home.

Then silence. Picard at once returned to his task, after a swift upward glance at another steadily approaching drone, now a mere five meters away.

The hull beneath his feet shuddered slightly; almost simultaneously, Worf's voice filtered through the comm link. "The magnetic constrictors are disengaged!"

"Get up to Hawk's position and complete the cycle," Picard ordered; there was no time to go into sad detail as to the lieutenant's fate.

The reply was a brief pause, during which, the captain assumed, the Klingon attempted to deal with his own pursuer, then Worf's adrenalized warning: "They've adapted!"

At last, Picard stopped his work, still not finished, but the Borg was now only two arm lengths away. He reached for his phaser rifle—useless against the Borg, and yet not entirely so—and fired at the stretch of hull between himself and his pursuer.

The deckplate gave way with a shriek, causing a powerful blast of gas to stream from the gaping tear. The force of it knocked the drone onto his back, but Picard felt no surge of exhilaration.

For in front of him, four, then six, spires began brilliantly to glow.

As the Borg reached for him, Worf bared his teeth, all motion-sick misery submerged by the demands of battle. The captain had spoken earlier of the Borg's deadly assimilation talons, and he, Worf, had every intention of

185

avoiding such a dishonorable fate. But he purposely stood his ground as the Borg neared, permitting the creature to almost catch hold of his spacesuit, only then whipping forth the curving *bat'leth* hidden on his back.

With a swift and shining slash, the weapon neatly severed the drone's forearm, in a spray of quickly extinguished mechanical sparks and blood, blood that hung in tiny, perfectly round droplets, some of which bound together to form larger, gelatinous-looking masses. The forearm began to sail upward, above the Borg's head, then lingered there like a lazily afloat, grotesque balloon, tethered to the elbow by thick tubing.

Undaunted, the Borg lunged, extending a surviving hand transformed into a collection of deadly, double-edged knives. Worf spun away, neatly avoiding the blades that swiped at his torso.

But one of them caught a small piece of fabric on his leg, filling his helmet with the urgent hiss of rapidly fleeing oxygen.

With a warrior's will, he forced his attention away from the hole on his leg, away from all panic, and instead focused everything on his weapon and his foe. In the millisecond before the Borg recovered to lunge again, Worf lashed out again, determined, fearless, and directed the *bat'leth*'s blade into his enemy's neck, beneath the jaw, into the yielding skin, into the rigid metal spine.

He recoiled from the outpouring of floating blood and sparks, and watched, gasping, as the Borg shrieked silently and convulsed before dying. And when it had surrendered its small, mindless life, the metal soles of its boots held it fast and upright while its limp body swayed, languid as seaweed on an ocean floor.

Only then did Worf permit himself to realize that his vision was dimming, that his lungs were gasping desperately for air that had already gone. He stumbled, dizzied, as the suit's built-in alarm filled his head: *"Warning: decompression in forty-five seconds . . ."*

Protected behind a curtain of spewing gas, Picard worked furiously, digging through mazes of complex circuitry until at last he found what he sought: one of the embedded hydraulic levers that controlled certain of the ship's moorings. With extreme effort, he pulled the lever upward, then twisted.

From deep within the *Enterprise*-E's heart came a shuddering vibration and the silent but unmistakable sensation of a metal *clank*.

Picard sighed, grateful for the small success; yet his gratitude turned to anguish when he glanced up to see Worf, standing barely conscious on the far side of the dish, his suit leaking vapor at an alarming rate.

Nearby, the portal where Hawk had been working still lay open.

Even had there been a chance that he, Picard, could physically reach the Klingon, he would no doubt be too late—and in addition, the responsibility of completing the task fell to him.

He started at the realization that one of the three final isolinear spires had come brilliantly alive; the huge crystalline structure of the beacon began to pulse, section by section, as it began to power up.

Impossible to reach it in time.

Impossible, yet he was bound to do it.

Vibration on the deckplate beneath his boots: footsteps. He whirled and saw that the pursuing drone had patiently made its way around the long curtain of venting gas and was only two body lengths distant. Picard moved in reverse—one step, then two, until he found himself backed against the array's upward slope.

The Borg raised a cybernetic arm, the hand of which had been replaced by a jagged circular saw. A small muscular flick, and the saw began to whirr.

With total dispassion, the Borg wielded the weapon, drawing closer.

Impossible. Impossible, yet . . .

I will not yield again.

Without thought, without reflection, he reached down and hit the magnetic control on the spacesuit's thigh. Immediately the green light went dark; the metal soles clicked, then became stomach-wrenchingly light.

Picard began floating upward, into space, beyond the Borg's lethal grasp. The sensation was at once terrifying and enormously exhilarating, enough so that he had to force himself to maintain his concentration, to draw in his legs at the proper time and then kick with all his might against the curving hull.

The act hurled him over the head of the hapless Borg, through the upper reaches of the curtain of spewing gas, toward the far side of the array and Hawk's panel. He tried to maintain control, to keep his legs tucked in, his arms folded to his chest, but the lack of gravity made it difficult, and he found himself spinning wildly through the void, arms and legs flailing . . .

Until at last he crashed into the hull. He scrambled for a handhold, found one, and remagnetized his boots, stomach and head still spinning.

Within a few steps, he reached the deckplate Hawk had removed and reached down into the open access panel to activate a series of controls, then grab the hydraulic lever.

A pull, a twist. Beneath his feet, the sensation of a *thunk* as massive clamps were released.

Immediately, Picard focused his gaze on the deflector dish's perimeter and watched as the first bolt attaching it to the *Enterprise* was blown outward, into space.

Then the second, and the third, and fourth, in sequential order, until at last the final bolt blew free and the deflector dish itself, along with the brightly glowing crystal, began to float upward.

Picard did not dare permit himself to relax, to smile, to consider victory—and his caution served him well. At the height of slightly more than a meter above the hull, the still-glowing dish stopped—tethered still to the *Enterprise* by a thick pillar of power cables.

He lifted his phaser rifle, took careful aim, and— paused before firing, at the sensation of movement in the right periphery of his vision. Immediately he turned and found himself face to face with an inhabited Starfleet spacesuit.

Hawk's, judging from its size, but the helmet's face mask was obscured by the brilliant reflection of the blue Earth. Yet as the body inside the spacesuit lunged at Picard, the Earth faded, replaced by the far ghastlier image of Hawk's face, still partially human in appearance, yet unmistakably Borg in its dreadful lack of expression and mechanical augmentation. A small sensorscope protruded from his left temple, and one ear and the surrounding scalp had been replaced by a panel of circuitry. The eyes . . . the eyes were by far the worst, for they reminded Picard of the eyes of a corpse—open but unseeing, unfeeling, devoid of any spark that had made the individual who he was.

Dead, but still moving.

But it was even worse than that, Picard knew; for inside that mindless shell, the personality named Hawk was still inside, infinitely horrified and helpless, praying for Picard's victory, terrified that his Borg-self might cause his captain harm.

I will not yield again. . . .

Hawk seized his shoulders, tried to slam him down against the deckplate; Picard fell backward, yet managed to keep the magnetized soles flat against the hull and pull himself back up—only to be slammed again. Fortunately, Borg-Hawk was too new to the collective to have been fitted with cybernetic weaponry; unfortunately, his strength was now at least ten times that of Picard. Hawk lunged again, this time throwing the totality of his weight into it—and the captain had no chance but to bend his knees and fall backward, else let the pressure break his lumbar spine.

As he fell, he caught a fleeting glimpse of the three remaining Borg working frantically on the beacon, and a row of spires suddenly igniting with internal light. . . .

Then Hawk was upon him, fist smashing into the helmet's faceplate. Picard caught his wrist with a hand; the almost-Borg flicked free with distressing ease, and even when Picard clutched the wrist *hard,* with both hands, Hawk struck the faceplate.

Again. Again.

The plate began to crack.

I will not yield, Picard vowed again silently, but no instinct, no sudden inspiration, came to his aid now, and he looked upon his imminent death with bitter rage. He had failed, and humanity past and future was consigned to hopelessness, to mental suffering without end.

He watched, intent, as Borg-Hawk lifted his fist for the final blow. If Picard nursed any hope at all, it was that he should die quickly, before he could be assimilated.

So it was that his eyes were wide open when the phaser blast came, so near to his face that he was immediately blinded and lay gasping against the hull, staring up into the opaque yellow afterimage.

When, after several seconds, it began to fade, he saw far above him a receding figure tumbling off into space: Hawk, limp arms and legs slowly pinwheeling around a scorched torso.

Picard struggled to his feet—awkwardly, since he was in no mood to break contact again with the ship's hull—and saw, to his utter delight, Worf. The Klingon stood some meters away, lowering his rifle as he gazed up at Hawk's receding body, his expression one of somber satisfaction to have freed a companion from a dishonorable fate.

He stepped toward Picard; something black and white moved with him, a terrier-sized object that hovered close to his calf and ankle. Closer inspection revealed the suit's tear, in midshin; just below the knee, a long piece of tubing served as a tourniquet, the excess dangling behind him like a leash.

Worf came to a halt. The extra tubing floated past him, the black-and-white object gently bumping against his lower leg: a hand, Picard realized, with a mild surge of nausea—a Borg hand attached to a severed forearm, from whose bloodied metal wound extruded the long tube.

Yet the captain at once drew his attention away to an even ghastlier sight: although the dish hovered above the ship's surface, cables still held it fast and allowed power to flow into the spires, all of which glowed blindingly. As Picard watched, the entire beacon began to pulsate with power.

Picard reached for his phaser rifle, aimed, and directed a searing bolt directly at the thick cable tether.

He did not flinch at the painful brilliance of the spires, of the beacon, of the phaser blast as it found its mark and bit through the bonds in an eye-searing millisecond of dazzling sparks.

The immense dish itself shuddered slightly, then slowly—with, Picard thought, a dignity that was beautiful—lifted, and began to rise.

Abruptly, the beacon and its myriad spires died. The three Borg who still labored upon the dish ceased all work, all movement, and stood mute, helpless, utterly emotionless in the face of defeat and death.

Into the void they sailed; Picard and Worf stood together, faces lifted, watching. And when the dish had at last risen a good twenty meters—a safe distance—the Klingon aimed his rifle spaceward and snarled.

"Assimilate *this.*"

He fired. Picard shielded his eyes as the deflector dish flared like a small nova, then erupted in a shower of white-hot debris. And when Worf turned to look at his captain with a fierce smile of victory, Picard returned it.

The death of the Borg evoked in him no somberness, no regret at the thought of taking a life—only a bright, savage joy and a mild disappointment that he could never violate them as he had been violated, never inflict on them the mental suffering he had endured at their hands.

But he would, he vowed silently, as the beacon hurtled dark and silent into space, hunt them down, drone by drone, until he reached the heart of the collective.

A woman's lips, whispering, Locutus . . .

And he would pierce that heart, with a wound deeper than that inflicted on his own; pierce it, even though it meant his death, and the death of all things loved. . . .

And in the warm, moist womb of the Borg hive, she who was all lifted her head sharply at the vision of fire and shattering crystal, at the silent sound of death cries.

Locutus . . .

Silvered eyes blinked, then narrowed; rage slowly cooled, hardening into determination and a hunger far beyond the physical.

The lust for little minds could never be sated—but there would always be such minds, always be the joy that came at the moment of consumption. But she had come, over the long millennia, to yearn for more: for an equal, one possessed of her infinite will, of her strength, of her daring . . .

One who, like her, could not be conquered.

Yet that would be her pleasure, her challenge: to spend the centuries struggling to overcome, to conquer . . . and, at long last, to devour.

The hour would not be long now; the time would soon come. She would look upon him again, again present the choice.

And this time, she would have her revenge. . . .

193

THIRTEEN

Worf groaning softly beside him, Picard waited inside the airlock and stared through the transparent portal as, on the other side, Beverly Crusher worked the controls. Lily stood beside her, smiling now, though when the two men had first entered the airlock, her dark eyes had been wide and her brow furrowed with wild anxiety at finding one of the team missing. She had craned her long neck, tilted her head, squinting at the reflections on the helmets, until she finally saw past them and recognized Picard . . .

And then her relief and joy had been so sparkling, so genuine, so filled with bright affection that Picard felt momentarily frightened—frightened because he found himself responding with the same broad grin, the same overwhelming affection—an emotion deeper than mere camaraderie.

He stared back at her just a second longer than either had intended, until at last both lowered their eyes, mildly dismayed by the event. Lily became cool at once, reassuming her twenty-first-century cynic's air; Picard turned his attention to Crusher and shared with the doctor a relieved smile.

True, he admired Lily Sloane for her determination, her courage, her odd wit, but a relationship with a woman from a different era was entirely impossible, a fact that Lily's abruptly formal posture showed she, too, understood.

Flanked by Worf, Picard stepped through the airlock door and removed his helmet.

"We stopped them," he said, his tone a mixture of triumph and regret. "But we lost Hawk."

Beverly's blue eyes registered the loss by looking briefly, sadly away, but she was already in motion, moving forward to help the Klingon, who fumbled in his efforts to remove his helmet. On tiptoe, Crusher reached up and lifted the helmet in a single, graceful move.

Beneath, Worf's dark face had faded to gray and his eyes had narrowed to slits; the corners of his mouth tugged downward in a manner that made Picard instinctively back away.

Beverly finally noticed. "Commander." She addressed the paling Klingon. "Are you feeling all—"

Worf held up a large hand. "Hold that thought."

He lunged behind the nearest console and began to retch; at the sounds of his gagging, the three shared a look of nauseated pity.

"Strong heart," Picard said. "Weak stomach."

"They're on the move again!"

The comment from a fourth voice made him whirl about as, a mere meter away, a security officer crawled from a Jefferies tube. The young man's olive face and disheveled coal-black hair glistened with perspiration; wide-eyed and shaken, he told Picard, "The Borg just overran three of our defense checkpoints; they've taken decks five and six. They've adapted to every modulation of our weapons. It's like we're shooting blanks."

"We'll have to start working on a new way to modify our phasers so they're more effective," Picard told him at once, then paused. It would be difficult, almost impossible, to hold the Borg back; one shot, and the phasers would have to be adapted again—and again, and again. . . . If they had the option of enlisting their best engineers to solve the problem, there was a chance that the combined brainpower *might* produce a solution. But La Forge and his best team were down on Earth's surface—if all was well, with Zefram Cochrane—and most of the engineers remaining on the *Enterprise* had been the first of the Borg's victims. Without their help—

No. This far and no further. They've violated me already—I won't let them violate my ship. I can't let them have her. . . .

He glanced sternly at the young officer. "In the meantime, tell your people to stand their ground. Fight hand to hand, if they have to."

The officer's posture and expression visibly deflated; for an instant, he averted his gaze and seemed to stare sadly beyond Picard at a vision of his own death. Picard told himself that he did not see it, that the situation was *not* hopeless—that there was a chance, and he was not condemning his surviving crew to die.

Then a sense of duty seized the young man, gathered

him, straightened him, caused him to nod smartly at Picard. "Aye, sir." He turned to go.

"Wait." Worf had emerged from behind the console and now stood, one hand gripping it to steady himself, the other wiping his mouth. "Captain . . . our weapons are useless. We must activate the autodestruct sequence and use the escape pods to evacuate the ship."

"Escape pods?" Lily leaned forward, hopeful, in the swift second after the Klingon spoke, but at the same instant, Picard snapped, *"No."*

Worf blinked, his fierce eyes fleetingly puzzled.

Beverly, too, seemed surprised at the captain's reaction. "Jean-Luc," she said, "If we destroy the ship, we'll destroy the Borg."

Lily's voice an annoying undercurrent: "Tell me more about those escape pods. . . ."

Picard graced her with neither glance nor reply. As he stared hard at his crew, he felt the stirring of emotions long restrained but never mastered: homicidal rage, the blind desire for revenge. "We are going to stay and fight."

"Sir," Worf continued, his tone urgent, insistent, "we have lost the *Enterprise.* We should not sacrifice more—"

"We have *not* lost the *Enterprise,"* Picard interrupted loudly, "and we are not *going* to lose the *Enterprise.* Not to the Borg, and not while I'm in command." He jerked his head to glare at the security officer. "You have your orders."

Worf and Crusher watched in silence as the younger man nodded again and walked back to the Jefferies tube.

"Hey, wait a minute," Lily said, her voice strident. "I'm not one of your troops, and I really don't want to stick around while you guys fight these space monsters, okay? I want to go *home."*

If we fail, you will have *no home,* Picard wanted to say, but held his tongue. The Klingon's words had fed a fury within him that was growing now and could no longer be contained. This was his ship—*his ship*—and he would not give it up. Would not permit them to hurt him again, to have even this small victory. He would not leave this vessel to them, then simply hope the self-destruct sequence killed them all.

He wished to *see* them all dead. To find . . . Once again, memory failed as he tried to retrieve the image of the one who had wounded him so, the one who had birthed Locutus. The one on whom he craved revenge.

Crusher studied Picard solemnly, her eyes narrowed just enough to register both her silent objection to the captain's plan and her concern for him.

"Captain . . ." Worf's tone grew strident. "I must object to this course of—"

Picard could not keep the pitch of his voice from rising. "Your objection has been noted, Mr. Worf."

On the Klingon's deeply sculpted face, anger warred with friendship; Worf drew a breath and visibly calmed himself. When he spoke again, he did so quietly, calmly. "With all due respect, sir, I believe you are allowing your . . . personal experience with the Borg . . . to influence your judgment."

The fury grew electric as it traveled down his spine, moving his feet in one swift, dangerous step toward the Klingon, tensing his arm so that it stiffened, pulled back, clenched the fist. In his mind's eye, he saw not Worf, but himself, staring horrified into the mirror, blood-slicked servo protruding from his cheek; he saw a vague glimpse of another, the one whose face maddeningly refused to coalesce in his memory.

Through a miracle of will, he did not strike out—but spoke, his voice cold and coiled as a serpent.

"I never thought I'd hear myself say this, Worf . . . but I actually think you're afraid. You want to destroy the ship and run away."

The Klingon grew visibly taller where he stood, and broader, as if the heat of anger had caused him physically to expand. In his dark eyes, fire burned—a sight to evoke fear in any human being.

"Jean-Luc . . ." Crusher warned, but he waved her into silence, beyond fear, beyond reason, beyond all but the blindness of rage and revenge. He held Worf's furious gaze and fed it with his own.

"If you were any other man," the Klingon growled softly, slowly, "I would kill you where you stand."

"Get off my bridge," Picard said. And saw not Worf, but a pair of glistening onyx lips part, revealing teeth of pearl.

Locutus . . .

The sound of footsteps brought him back, and he watched, unyielding, as the Klingon turned and moved for the open Jefferies tube hatch, then crawled inside.

Lily watched, too, stunned like the rest of those on the bridge into silence. Watched as the huge Klingon named Worf walked away, watched as Picard scanned the shocked faces of his remaining crew, then silently turned and headed into another chamber that opened onto the bridge.

When the door had closed behind him, Beverly

Crusher—the doctor who had been helping everyone, including Lily, escape when the Borg had come—turned to Lily.

"Let's go." The blond doctor's tone was one of quiet professionalism, but Lily read her well enough to see that she was enormously troubled by what had just happened.

Ahab, it seemed, was flipping out, willing to risk his entire crew to stay and fight the Borg. All to save a ship. *Pretty damned stupid,* she thought, *considering there won't be anyone around to pilot it.*

And then she stopped herself in midjudgment; *she* had been willing to risk her life to save the *Phoenix.* All her hopes, all her dreams, had been tangled up in the damned thing. Maybe she *did* understand what Ahab was feeling after all. But there was something else in him, other than plain love for a ship—something darker that she had glimpsed from time to time as they fled through the tunnels, something she had seen again just now. She'd assumed he'd lost someone very important to the Borg—a friend, a relative, a lover.

But Worf's comment had put a whole new spin on things.

Dr. Crusher began to move; Lily didn't.

"What do we do now?"

Crusher stopped; a shadow came over her face, one that only faintly veiled the horror and pain . . . one that fell over the face of every crew member who glanced up surreptitiously at Lily's words, then just as quickly looked away. There was a wound here, one that extended far beyond Jean-Luc Picard and even this woman, one so shattering that no one on this ship had earlier dared give it voice.

"We carry out his orders," the doctor said softly, then turned toward two officers. "Kaplan, Dyson—start working on a way to modify the—"

Lily interrupted. "Wait a minute. This is stupid. If we can get off this ship and blow it up, we should do it."

Crusher's expression and voice were carefully composed, professional, but her eyes failed to entirely hide her frustration. "Once the captain's made up his mind, the discussion's over." She signaled the two officers she'd addressed, and they moved toward her.

Like sheep, Lily thought, her fury growing. *Because Jean-Luc is obsessed with the Borg, they're all just going to be obedient little soldiers and die. And he's going to let them. . . .* "We'll see about that," she said aloud, and headed off toward the observation lounge, ignoring Crusher's plea behind her.

"Lily—"

On the catwalk that led directly to the *Phoenix*'s cockpit, Will Riker paused a moment to savor a sight: Zefram Cochrane, flat on his back in the pilot's chair, slightly frowning, attention totally focused on an instrument check. For once, the man's expression was neither drunken nor hostile nor mocking; for once, Riker decided, he looked like the hero he was . . . or rather, soon would be.

It had been a very different man they'd revived in the silo's control room—hysterical, raving, far from lucid. Not nuts, Troi had said then, but clearly suffering from a chemical disorder of the brain that—as Riker had correctly recalled—had resurfaced after the war because of the primitive methods of treatment during that era. Without access to the ship's medical computers and sickbay, precise diagnosis and treatment were impossible.

However, Troi had volunteered, it might be possible to treat some of the worst symptoms—Cochrane's drunkeness, for example, and the delusions and anxiety—by using one of the nonsedating calming drugs provided in the standard first-aid kit.

Thus it was done, and within a matter of minutes, Cochrane the drunken and crazed had transformed into Cochrane the sober and rational, albeit slightly embarrassed and irritable.

Of course, the drug had done little to change his bizarre behavior, a fact Riker found oddly endearing. He smiled as Cochrane peered out the cockpit's open door at the stern-faced security guard, then graced him with a toothy and blatantly false chimpanzee grin.

Riker forced a solemn expression, then moved forward and climbed into the cockpit, grabbing the edge of the pilot's seat and crouching beside it. "We've only got an hour to go, Doc—how're you feeling?"

Cochrane scowled down at an old-fashioned dial display, then made a notation on an equally twenty-first-century clipboard. "I have a four-alarm hangover—either from the whiskey or your laser beam, or both." He looked over his shoulder at Riker, eyebrows raised, eyes wide, lips parted in a maniacally cheerful expression. "But I'm ready to make history!"

Riker tried and failed to repress an honest grin. He had opened his mouth to ask the question *Tell me,*

Doctor—in your century, do they have the expression wacky? when a voice filtered over his comm.

"Troi to Commander Riker." Like everyone else in the silo, Riker included, she was clearly struggling to control her excitement and remain coolly professional, but the thrill of making history surfaced, ever so slightly, in her tone.

"Riker here."

"We're ready to open the launch door."

Riker shot a glance at Cochrane, who shrugged with a very impressive attempt at nonchalance. "Go ahead," Will replied.

The massive concrete silo door slid open with a rumble that jarred Riker's teeth; he slid into one of the astronaut's couches behind Cochrane's and settled in. Sunlight streamed into the cockpit from the crystal blue Montana sky, in which still hung the pale ghost of a crescent moon.

"Look at that," Riker marveled to himself, at its virgin surface.

"What?" Again, Cochrane glanced back at him. "You don't have a moon in the twenty-fourth century?"

"Sure we do," Riker mused, smiling. "It just looks a lot different." And, at the scientist's quizzical look, explained, "Fifty million people live on the moon in my time. You can see Tycho City, New Berlin, even Lake Armstrong on a day like this."

Cochrane stared up at the moon with a look of wonder. "Hmmm . . ."

"And you know, Doctor—"

The scientist's radiant expression dimmed at once.

"Please. Don't tell me it's all thanks to me. I've heard enough about the great Zefram Cochrane." He pretended to busy himself with the navigational computer and his clipboard, the better to avoid Riker's steady gaze. "I don't know who wrote your history books, or where you got your information, but you people have some pretty funny ideas about me." He flailed a moment for the right words. "You all look at me like I'm some kind of . . . saint or visionary or something." Agitated, he began to check controls in a random fashion, permitting Riker to see the distress that had triggered the mania.

"I don't think you're a saint, Doc," Will soothed. "But you *did* have a vision. And now we're sitting in it."

Angrily, Cochrane turned from the computer and jerked around to face his copilot. "You know what my vision is? *Dollar signs. Money.* There's still an economy out there, you know. There may not be any gold left in Fort Knox, but there's tons of cash overseas. Do you know how much the Indonesian Space Agency would pay for a faster-than-light rocket?"

Riker gave an honest shake of his head. "I can't imagine."

"You're damn right you can't. But *I* can. I didn't build this ship to usher in a new era for humanity. You think I want to go to the stars? I don't even like to fly! I take trains! I built this ship so I could retire to some tropical island filled with naked women. *That's* Zefram Cochrane. *That's* his vision." He whirled about and began jabbing entries into the primitive computer. "This other guy you keep talking about—this historical figure—I haven't seen him since the war."

A long silence passed, one in which Cochrane, his

expression troubled and vaguely angry, stared down unhappily at the monitor readout.

Riker bided his time, then at last replied, "Someone once said, 'Don't try to be a *great* man. Just be a man. Let history make its own judgments.'"

The scientist's lip twisted. "Rhetorical nonsense . . ."

"You said it," Will countered quietly. "About ten years from now."

Cochrane looked back at him in surprise, parted his lips to speak . . . then closed them again.

Riker smiled and tapped the other man's clipboard. "Fifty-eight minutes, Doc. Better get back to that checklist."

At the conference table in the observation lounge, backlit by Earth and the shining stars, Picard began to disassemble a phaser rifle. The task he had set himself was a difficult one, even for a trained engineer, and unfortunately tedious; and while he worked, his people would be fighting the Borg—and dying.

Yet cold fury held him fast, a fury that shrieked there was no choice. He could not surrender again, could not destroy his own ship. . . .

In the midst of the mental maelstrom, a small and rational voice asked: *Are they influencing you?*

No. He shook his head at the silent question. He had not heard the collective's whisper in some time; if anything, they had pushed him away. No, this insistence on remaining to fight was his own, born of a rage he had believed gone for years. But it had merely burrowed deeper and there grown to monstrous size until its eruption with this final encounter.

The door swished suddenly. He glanced up to see Lily storm into the room, posture rigid, arms tensed and held slightly away from the body, fists clenched. And eyes so wide and blazing that the whites now completely encircled the large brown irises.

"You son of a bitch!" She stopped on the other side of the table, pressing hard against its edge; had it not been there, she would certainly have been right in his face.

He could easily have screamed back at her, but through a mighty effort, managed to answer calmly, "Lily, this isn't really the time—"

Her words were swift, heated. "Look, I don't know jack about the twenty-fourth century, but I *do* know that everyone out there thinks that staying here and fighting the Borg is suicide. They're just too afraid to come in here and say it."

He felt his own expression harden, and said icily, "The crew is accustomed to following my orders."

She slapped her palms against the table's polished surface and leaned forward, thin body straining, expression and tone sarcastic. "They're probably accustomed to your orders making sense."

"None of them understand the Borg as I do," he snapped.

And immediately regretted it; she frowned faintly and drew back a bit in surprise. "What's *that* supposed to mean?"

All the bitterness, all the rage welled up in him at that moment, and no doubt revealed itself upon his face; Lily recoiled from it, her eyes wide now with somber awe at the depth of his pain.

"Six years ago," he said hoarsely, "I was assimilated

into the collective—had their cybernetic devices implanted throughout my body. I was linked into the hive mind, every trace of individuality erased. I was one of them."

He let the words hang between them a time, and watched with satisfaction as all traces of anger melted away from her dark, beautiful face, her body. Let her be filled with sympathy and regret; let her realize her mistake now and ask forgiveness. He alone *knew* how to deal with the enemy.

"So as you can imagine," he said, driving the point home, "I have a somewhat . . . unique perspective on the Borg, and I know how to fight them." He paused a moment, giving her time to make that apology; when none was immediately forthcoming, he added, "Now, if you'll excuse me, I have work to do."

And he reached for the phaser rifle, popped open another panel, and began tinkering with the circuits. He did not look at her, but he sensed her steady gaze upon him nonetheless.

"I am such an idiot," Lily said at last.

He glanced up to see her smiling ruefully; here was the apology, he decided, and readied a cool reply. To his surprise, she sat down across from him with a slight shake of her head, and her smile broadened until he thought she would laugh.

"It's so simple," she said, again shaking her head, and when he looked askance at her, explained: "Revenge. This is about revenge. The Borg hurt you and now you're going to hurt them back."

His cheeks stung as if slapped, but he covered his hurt with a cold, superior smile. "In my century, we don't

207

succumb to . . . revenge. We have a more evolved sensibility."

"Bullshit." She leaned closer to him. "I saw the look on your face when you shot those Borg on the holodeck. You were almost *enjoying* it."

Bristling, Picard set down the rifle but did not ease his grip on it. "How *dare* you—"

"Come on, Captain, admit it. You're not the first person to get a thrill out of murdering someone. I see it all the time."

"Get out," he said, voice tight. He hadn't been thrilled at all—he had merely felt *justified.*

Her gaze bore right through him. "Or what? You'll kill me? Like you killed Ensign Lynch?"

Her words at last touched his fury and ignited it; his voice rose. "There was no way to save him—"

"You didn't even *try.* Where was that 'evolved sensibility' *then?"*

He could not answer her; in his mind, he saw the instant he had fired the gun at the two Borg. He hadn't even noticed it was Lynch until after he'd begun firing—had he? And it wasn't pleasure, wasn't a thrill. There was nothing pleasurable in it; it was more the satisfaction a doctor might have in curing a deadly disease. . . .

Satisfaction? No, no, that *couldn't* be right. . . .

Lily leaned in harder, closer. "You're as possessed now as you were when the Borg possessed you."

"I don't have *time* for this," Picard said stonily, his grip on the rifle tightening.

"Oh, hey, sorry." Her voice rose sarcastically. "Didn't mean to interrupt your little quest. Captain Ahab has to go hunt his whale."

He jerked his head as if she'd slapped him. *"What?"*

"Don't you have *books* in the twenty-fourth century?"

"This is not about revenge!" he shouted.

"Liar!"

"This is about saving the future of humanity!"

"Then blow up this ship!" she cried.

"No!" The full depth of his rage emerged at last from its burrow, struck him, poisoned him. He lifted the rifle in his hand and hurled it across the room; it smashed against the glass case of *Enterprise* mementos, scattering ships and medals everywhere, but he did not care. He was *justified.* "I will *not* give up the *Enterprise,"* he shrieked. "We've made too many compromises already, too many retreats! They invade our space and we fall back—they assimilate *entire worlds* and we fall back! Not again!" His voice grew shrill, began to break. "The line must be drawn here—*this* far and no further! I will make them *pay* for what they've done!"

The last he said with such force, such volume, such purely maniacal hate that he let go a gasping breath and drew back, startled into silence.

"You broke your ships," Lily said softly.

Picard glanced up. Her anger, too, had suddenly vanished, replaced now by somber, genuine compassion. She *had* been right, had come here to show him the insanity of his own consuming hatred—something that she, who had lost so much in the war and had so much reason to hate, must have known well.

He followed her gaze down to the deck, where *Enterprise* replicas and souvenirs lay scattered; then he turned and moved to the window, to stare out at the Earth and stars.

Had Lily been standing in his path when he hurled the rifle, it might have struck her instead. Might have hurt her, all because of his craving for revenge.

Just as he was now destroying his crew.

"See you around, Ahab," she said gently behind him; he heard her footsteps headed for the door.

Lily had known. Had known from the very beginning, when she first called him by that name in the minutes after their first encounter. Had it shown, even then, in his eyes?

Before she could reach the door, he recited, still staring out at the starlit darkness: "'He piled upon the whale's white hump the sum of all the rage and hate felt by his whole race. . . . If his chest had been a cannon, he would've shot his heart upon it.'"

With an ironic smile, he turned to see her gazing at him in puzzlement. "What?"

"Moby Dick," he replied.

She gave him a small, embarrassed grin. "Actually, I never read it."

"Ahab spent years hunting the white whale that crippled him," Picard explained. "A quest for vengeance. And in the end, the whale destroyed him—and his ship."

"I guess *that* Ahab didn't know when to quit."

For a long moment, he looked into her eyes . . . and found there trust.

Then he drew a breath of pure resolve and walked out onto the bridge. Immediately, Crusher and the others turned to him, their faces anxious, somber, concerned.

"Prepare to evacuate the *Enterprise,"* he said.

FOURTEEN

Picard sat in the captain's chair, on a bridge that had never before seemed so quiet, so still, despite the presence of others.

The order had been given. He spoke, knowing that at that very instant, most of the surviving crew members were now hurrying to escape pods "Computer. This is Captain Jean-Luc Picard. Begin autodestruct sequence. Authorization Picard one-one-zero-alpha."

Nearby, a junior officer worked swiftly at a control panel, typing in a response to the request ENTER DESTINA-TION COORDINATES. Immediately, a map of Earth appeared on the screen, which zoomed in on a mere pin dot of land in the South Pacific.

COORDINATES ACCEPTED. LANDING TARGET: GRAVETT ISLAND. AREA: TEN SQUARE KILOMETERS. POPULATION: ZERO.

Crusher, her face drawn and tense as she sat at the captain's right, continued the litany. "Computer, this is Commander Beverly Crusher. Confirm autodestruct sequence. Authorization: Crusher two-two-beta."

To the left, Worf, his voice as subdued as Picard had ever heard it: "This is Lieutenant Commander Worf. Confirm autodestruct sequence. Authorization: Worf three-three-gamma."

Instantly, the computer responded. "Command authorizations accepted. Awaiting final code to begin countdown."

"This is Captain Picard: destruct sequence one-A. Fifteen minutes. Silent countdown." He drew a breath, then felt his throat constrict painfully as he gave the final word: "Enable."

"Self-destruct in fourteen minutes, fifty-five seconds," the computer intoned matter-of-factly. "There will be no further audio warnings."

The three of them—Picard, Worf, Crusher— exchanged a solemn look. Picard rose and took a long, final look at his bridge.

"So much for the *Enterprise*-E," Crusher said, wistful.

Picard put a hand on his chair and gave a distracted nod, gazing out at the viewscreen image of the blue, slowly rotating Earth. "I barely knew her."

"Think they'll build an F?" she asked; he turned. The question was based on an unshakable optimism—that the Borg would indeed be defeated by this action, that they would never find a way to send reinforcements; that the future would indeed come to pass and would continue on without them. That thought—as perhaps she had known it would—eased his grief at this fresh loss.

Picard smiled at her with his eyes alone. "I have a feeling they'll keep building them until they run out of letters."

She nodded, then joined the calm group of bridge personnel, each awaiting a turn to crawl into the Jefferies tube hatch that led to the escape pods. Worf was among them, next in line and already crouching down, ready to climb through the hatch.

"Mr. Worf?" Picard called softly.

The Klingon straightened, waved the next person to take his place, then faced his captain. If he still harbored any resentment at Picard's attack upon his personal honor, his alert, open expression gave no sign.

Picard met his gaze directly. "I regret some of the things I said to you earlier."

"Some?" Worf cocked a brow in surprise, but one corner of his lips quirked upward, dimpling one cheek in a very un-Klingon-like display of humor.

Picard returned the smile and extended his hand; Worf immediately took it. "In case there's any doubt," the captain said, "you're the bravest man I've ever met." He paused to glance back at the image of Earth. "See you on Gravett Island."

The Klingon nodded, gave his captain's hand one last, firm shake, then moved quickly to the hatch and disappeared.

Picard followed, grabbing the hatch railings with his hands, stepping down onto the ladder rungs—then abruptly pulled his foot out and set it down again on the bridge deck. The lure of the *Enterprise* was too strong.

He turned back and began to move toward his chair, wanting to touch it one more time, to register the palpability of this reality—this ship, this other century to which he was born—before surrendering it to a limited, planet-bound life.

Abruptly, the whisper of the collective filled his skull.

Not now, not now—he tried mentally to push it from him, to break off all contact. They did not know of their imminent fate, and though he felt secure that the link was not mutual, he could afford no chances. Besides, now was the time for his own escape. He turned and moved quickly toward the open hatch.

But the cacophony would not ease; it filled his head with a thousand murmuring voices, all the same, all converging on one goal alone—the good of the collective. It rose, until it roared silently in his mind like thunder . . .

And from within that stormy chorus, a small, distinctive voice emerged—a voice individual, singular, pleading—and uttered a different message: *Captain.*

Picard gasped. "Data." And he *knew.* Knew, with the same mysterious instinct that had first warned him of the Borg's approach, that Data was himself, unassimilated. And about to be destroyed by his own captain's order . . .

As he tightened the old-fashioned restraints that held him fast to one of the copilot's couches, Will Riker glanced over at Geordi La Forge, who had finally figured out how the straps worked and had just settled back in the other copilot's seat across from him.

La Forge sensed the look and returned it with a small

grin. *Boring everyday business, hopping through space,* the grin said, *but today it feels a little different.*

Riker acknowledged with a wink and a nod, then busied himself with the old-fashioned control panel in front of him. History had always been one of his favorite subjects, especially the history of space travel—a good thing, since otherwise the dials and gauges and old-fashioned switches might have proven too difficult to master in so short a time.

But as Geordi had said, the *Phoenix* might look a little different, but all the basic concepts were the same.

Another rumble, this one of the metal blast door sliding shut, protecting Troi and the others inside the control room. Once Riker'd decided to violate the Prime Directive with Cochrane, it only made sense to do so in a big way—with himself and Geordi along to help out in case of emergency and Deanna in the control room to guide the trip. After all, the Borg's appearance had already altered the timeline somewhat—and Riker was not about to take any chances that some small deviation might trigger an unexpected glitch in the *Phoenix*'s maiden voyage.

As for Cochrane, the instant the blast door began to close, he immediately became a pilot—intent and efficient—and began flipping steel switches and calling out items on the checklist, swiveling his head to glance over his shoulder at the two assistants behind him.

"ATR setting?" he called to La Forge.

"Active."

"Main bus?"

"Ready," Riker replied.

"Initiate preignition sequence."

The cockpit shuddered slightly as the engines at the ship's base—sadly out of Riker's sight, making him wish this grandmother of all Earth-design warp ships were equipped with modern viewscreens—began spewing nitrogen gas.

Riker forced himself to calm and kept his gaze fastened on what to him were three-hundred-year-old displays.

Troi's voice filtered tinnily over the cockpit intercom. "Control to *Phoenix*—your internal readings look good. Final launch sequence checks are complete. You're at the thirty-second mark. Good luck."

Riker grinned wickedly, unable to resist, in his state of building exhilaration. "Thanks, *Deena.*"

He could hear her grimace in the silence that followed.

Finally, all last-minute checkdowns were completed; the tension in the cockpit suddenly intensified, prompting Riker to try to ease it. "Everyone ready to make a little history?"

"Always am," La Forge replied easily. But Cochrane half turned, displaying a nervously furrowed profile.

"I think I'm forgetting something. . . ."

Riker tried to lean forward in his couch, then remembered that he couldn't. "What?"

"I'm not sure," Cochrane replied uneasily, beginning to turn back to his own control panel. "It's probably nothing. . . ."

"Fifteen seconds," Troi intoned over the intercom, her voice deceptively calm and professional as Riker's own. "Begin ignition sequence."

A low rumble began at the ship's very base and

traveled upwards, growing in volume and intensity until the cockpit began to tremble.

"Oh, God!" Cochrane spun his head back over one shoulder. "Now I remember! Where *is* it?" Frantically, he began to pat down his pockets, searching.

The panic was contagious. "What? *What?*" La Forge demanded, over the engine's mounting thunder.

Meantime, Troi began the countdown: "Ten . . . nine . . . eight . . ."

"We can't lift off without it," Cochrane insisted.

Riker kept his own voice steady, even. "Okay, Geordi, let's abort—"

"Seven . . . six . . . five . . ."

"No! No—wait! I found it!" Exultant, Cochrane whipped an optical disc from a pocket, slipped it into a slot on the control panel, and hit a switch.

"Four . . . three . . . two . . . one."

The deafening roar of the engines blended with the equally skull-shattering blare of music—the same rock-and-roll tune, Riker realized, that Cochrane had played in the Crash & Burn for Troi. He glanced over to share a pained look with La Forge.

But Zefram Cochrane was grinning from ear to ear.

"Let's *rock.*"

Launch: the silo abruptly disappeared, replaced by an onrush of pale blue sky.

Riker settled back into his chair—or rather, was pushed back by the sudden intensification of gravity—and intentionally savored the rawness of primitive space flight: the unbelievable noise of the engines, the wild roar of the flaming ignition, the teeth-chattering vibration of the cockpit as the *Phoenix* hurtled heavenward on a column of fire and smoke. A sidewise glance at Geordi (for the increased g's made it impossible for Will to turn his head) showed that the engineer was also enjoying the novelty of it all. Impossible to experience such sensory overload and not feel adrenaline-charged, not be overwhelmed by the awesome transition from Earth to stars.

Zefram Cochrane, however, was overwhelmed by something far different than awe. From Riker's angle, he could see part of the scientist's profile and one side of his body. Cochrane's eyes were wide, bulging with pure terror; the hand Riker could see gripped the edge of the pilot's chair so tightly that each tendon and knuckle seemed on the verge of popping through the skin.

Of course, Riker realized, amazed at his own obtuseness. This was Zefram Cochrane's *first* spaceflight. To distract him, Riker called out, "Can you turn it down a little?"

Cochrane strained to lift his torso and arm, just managing to hit a control before the g-forces pushed him back against his seat. The small distraction seemed to ease some of his terror.

"There's a red light on the second intake valve," La Forge reported tersely.

Oddly, the comment seemed to relax Cochrane even more—or perhaps it was the fact that once again, he had work to do. "Ignore it," he said, almost casually. "We'll be fine." And after a beat: "Prepare for first-stage shutdown and separation on my mark. . . . Three . . . two . . . one . . . mark!"

Riker performed his assigned task, remembering the

simulations of the *Phoenix*'s launch sequence he'd seen many times in museums and history classes. Once again, he wished he could see the actual event itself: the first-stage booster dropping away, leaving three quarters of the craft spaceborne . . . and then the separation of the metal shields, allowing the primitive warp nacelles to extend themselves on either side of the fuselage.

The noise and vibration abruptly stopped, leaving glorious calm and silence as the *Phoenix* settled into Earth orbit.

Riker peered at his controls, grateful for the sudden ease of movement. "All right, let's bring the warp core on line."

Both La Forge and Cochrane set busily to work, but the latter glanced out the window and abruptly stopped, gazing open-mouthed at the sapphire-and-emerald Earth with an awe so deep it could not be hidden. Riker saw and gave Geordi a nudge; the two smiled and permitted Cochrane an undisturbed moment.

"Wow," Cochrane whispered, and looked back at his two copilots with a smile of unashamed delight.

Will grinned. "You ain't seen *nothing* yet."

Padd in hand, Picard moved down the empty evacuation corridor, passing the endless row of escape pods, either occupied with the hatches just beginning to lower or already sealed. Only two remained vacant.

He did not run—there was still time enough to move deliberately, and he had already spotted Lily jogging slowly toward him. She should, of course, have already been sealed safely in her own pod; she had been among the first evacuees, and he began to suspect that she had been waiting for him.

He met her in front of one of the remaining pods and handed her the padd before she could utter a word. She frowned down at it, then looked up at him, puzzled.

"If you see Commander Riker or any of my crew, give them this," Picard said.

"What is it?" She studied it curiously.

"Orders to find a quiet corner of North America—and stay out of history's way."

A brief but awkward silence ensued, during which Lily kept her gaze fastened overlong on the padd and Picard attempted to gather his thoughts, to decide whether anything more ought to be said.

It should not, of course; it would have been immature and foolish to give vent to feelings that could never, should never be acted upon. But for a brief instant, Picard permitted himself to envy the men of twenty-first-century Montana. Lily Sloane was a remarkable woman . . . as remarkable as all twenty-fourth-century history books proclaimed. After Cochrane's success, she would go on to receive her engineering doctorate, come up with amazing innovations on Cochrane's basic warp-drive design, and found one of the galaxy's finest educational establishments for those studying warp drive and space travel: the Sloane Institute.

But, Picard thought wryly, it had not been particularly easy trying to keep an eye on her—or to keep from calling her Dr. Sloane.

And the future Dr. Sloane packed a wicked punch.

"Well . . ." At last, Lily gazed up shyly. "Good luck."

"To both of us," Picard seconded, smiling. As she

climbed into her pod, he turned and headed back down the corridor.

"Hey!" she called, fumbling with the control panel until the hatch stopped lowering.

He turned.

"Your escape pod is *that* way." She pointed in the direction opposite the one he was heading.

"Oh. Yes. I was just going to check on some of the—"

"You're not leaving, are you?" Her voice grew husky, but there was still enough of the cynic in her to try to keep the sadness from showing in her expression. She did not quite succeed.

"No," Picard said honestly. "I'm not. When I was held captive aboard the Borg ship, my crew risked everything to save me. I have a friend who's still on *this* ship. I owe him the same."

Lily considered this and gave a slow, sad nod. "Go find your friend." She lingered an instant, no more, then pulled away decisively, entered the pod, and met his gaze steadily as he pushed the hatch control.

The pod sealed, and she was irretrievably, utterly gone.

He drew a steadying breath and made his way quickly to the master control panel on the wall, then launched the few remaining occupied pods. That done, Picard felt a sense of relief; he and Data were the only two crew members left on board.

But the relief was temporary, blotted out by the renewed sensation of knowing that compelled him to move calmly, deliberately, through his empty ship. No point in burrowing through the Jefferies tubes; no point in trying to keep his location secret. No point in arming himself with anything more than his own mind and body.

He halted in front of a large hatch that led to the engineering section, and there paused only briefly to gather himself before hitting a control on the bulkhead panel.

The hatch slid open; Picard stepped through, into a section of corridor defaced by the imposition of black Borgian machinery and glistening organic matter, very much the same thing he had seen inside the dead drone's gut.

Determined, he walked—and shook his head to try to clear it of the sudden distant whispers in his head; this time, they would not leave him, but gradually increased in volume as he continued his uneasy journey.

At the intersection of two corridors, a pair of drones suddenly appeared and blocked his path. Picard halted, stared hard into their blank, unfeeling faces, waited a tense moment for them to make the first move.

Had they known his intent, they would surely have killed him. Instead, they parted, stepping aside so that he might pass.

An invitation; he was expected. He walked, listening to the steadily growing babble of voices in his mind— yet try as he might, he could not find Data's among them.

At last he arrived at the closed double doors of Main Engineering, and there stopped. The sight evoked memories of the battle here: of the infected security guard pleading for help and Picard's horror at having to provide the only help possible—death; of the plaintive look on Data's face the instant before the Borg dragged him into their lair.

But there was more here than mere memory: there was knowledge, too. Knowledge that beyond those doors lay Data . . . and the Borg's heart, which he, Picard, was determined to pierce.

He drew a breath, steeling himself against the now overwhelming mental cacophony of the collective, and prepared to step through the doors. But before he stirred a muscle, the doors opened, and the incoherent chorus in his head abruptly stopped.

They were waiting for him.

He hesitated and glanced over his shoulder, reconsidering. This knowledge that had convinced him that Data was here and well, that had convinced him that, though he was alone and unarmed, he might still defeat the Borg—could he be sure that it had not been planted by them for some sinister reason, even though it had aided him in outwitting them in the past?

It mattered not, he decided at last. Data *was* here, and Picard felt no overriding compulsion anymore to seek revenge—only a desire to save his friend and his ship if at all possible.

He crossed the threshold, into the image from his dream.

Apathy: row after row of dull flesh-and-metal faces lined the vast chamber's walls, sleeping drones in their honeycomb cells. None stirred as he entered and gazed at his surroundings. It was even warmer here, the atmosphere so humid that beads of moisture collected on the drones, the machinery, even in the air itself to form thin wisps of mist. A droplet-bejeweled thicket of black cables and feeding tubes descended from the ceiling like thick jungle vines.

Apathy, yes, from the slumbering drones—but there was something more here, something passionate, emotional, driven . . . something with a heart that could be pierced: the one who had violated him so, the one whom, for all these years, he had yearned subconsciously to hurt.

Movement behind him. He froze, tried to ignore the sudden chill that seized him. An overwhelming second passed before he recovered enough to force himself slowly to turn; when he did, and saw her standing before him, he recoiled in shock.

"What's wrong, Locutus?" asked she—not in the passionless voice of the collective, but in a voice feminine, seductive, slightly mocking. "Don't you recognize me?"

He did. Memories bound for six years washed over him, forced the breath from his lungs in a purely physical shock. *On the Borg ship. Her face, sharply beautiful and pale above his, as she gazed down approvingly at Locutus's terrible birth . . .*

"Organic minds are such fragile things. How could you forget me so quickly?"

Face to face with her then as Locutus, Picard's mind trapped beneath the weight of the collective, beneath the Borg queen's will—yet straining to resist, all the same. Gazing into her insatiable vermeil eyes . . .

"We were very close, you and I. You can still hear our song."

Her hand and breath warm against Locutus's cheek. It was not Locutus she had wanted; he had known it even

224

then, but the memory had been kept from him all these years.

She had wanted Picard—but Picard, though mentally crushed and bound, unable even to lift a finger of what had become a Borg-human hybrid body, would not submit. Would not *return her desire.*

It was not the physical pleasure she had wanted; it was the control—the utter domination of flesh, mind, spirit. And she had grown bored with seizing it forcefully; she wished for him to offer it willingly.

He had resisted.

Picard staggered backward beneath the mental assault. "Yes," he said at last, the chill of fear transforming into bitterly cold anger. "I remember you. You were there . . . you were there the entire time. But—that ship and all the Borg on it were destroyed."

Her coy expression grew scornful. "You think in such three-dimensional terms." She turned her angular chin toward one shoulder. "How small you've become. Data understands me, don't you, Data?"

From one of the alcoves, Data stepped forth, his expression composed, entirely emotionless . . .

. . . And almost totally human, golden eyes now blue, brown hair tousled, face almost entirely covered by pink human flesh.

Picard's dismay at the resurfaced memories vanished, replaced by immediate concern for his friend. "What have you done to him?"

"Given him what he's always wanted. Flesh and blood."

"Let him go," he demanded. "He's not the one you want."

Her lips parted in the sly, slightly mocking smile from his dream. "Are you offering yourself to us?"

"Offering myself . . . that's it. I remember now."

His voice welled with sudden heat at the revelation, at the fierce surge of freedom and outrage it brought. "It wasn't enough to assimilate me; you wanted me to give myself freely to the Borg, to *you.*"

She seemed to sense that freedom, to be repelled by it; the corner of an alabaster lip curled in repugnance. "You flatter yourself. I have overseen the assimilation of countless millions. You were no different."

"You're *lying,*" Picard said, with bitter relief. "You wanted more than just another Borg drone. You wanted the best of both worlds, a human being with a mind of his own who could bridge the gulf between humanity and the Borg. You wanted a counterpart. An equal. But I resisted. I fought you."

The curled lip rose higher, baring hard, white teeth. "You can't begin to imagine the life you denied yourself."

Triumph rose within him. Whatever tragedy might follow, he at last had the satisfaction of knowing: *she* was his foe, not the mindless drones who served her. *She* was the Borg, the devourer of souls, and his resistance had *not* been futile—it had wounded her. And out of fear and pride, she had tried to keep this truth from him. *"That's* why you created Locutus—to ease the burden of your lonely existence. But it didn't work; I resisted. And in the end, you had to turn Locutus into just another drone."

A moment of silence passed, one in which the quick-silver gaze swept wistfully over the vast chamber of slumbering Borg, then again fixed itself upon Picard. "You cannot begin to imagine the life you denied yourself," she said, an unmistakable trace of sadness in her voice, her eyes. "Together . . . nothing could have stopped us."

He took a deliberate step toward her, fighting to suppress his revulsion. "It's not too late. Locutus can still be with you, just as you wanted him. An equal." He shot a sidewise glance at the unresponsive android-human hybrid. "Let Data go, and I will take my place at your side—willingly, without resistance."

She moved closer, her body almost touching his; she spoke, and he fought not to shudder at the feel of her warm, sterile breath upon his skin. "Such a noble creature—a quality we sometimes lack. We will add your distinctiveness to our own," she murmured. "Welcome home, Locutus. . . ."

She lifted a hand and stroked cool fingertips teasingly over his cheek; he forced himself not to flinch. Then, abruptly, she turned toward Data.

"You're free to go, Data."

The human android did not move.

"Data, *go,*" Picard commanded.

"I do not wish to go," Data replied simply.

The Borg queen smiled. "As you can see, I've already found an equal. Data—deactivate the self-destruct sequence."

Picard reacted with alarm, both at the android's refusal and the queen's knowledge. He took a desperate step toward Data; immediately, two drones stepped from the shadows behind him, each seizing an arm and holding him fast. "Data!" he shouted. "Don't do it! Listen to me!"

Undaunted, the android moved calmly to a computer console and pressed a series of controls with preternatural speed.

"Autodestruct sequence deactivated," the computer reported.

The queen directed a smile of purely malevolent triumph at Picard, though her words were still addressed to Data. "Now . . . enter the encryption codes and give me computer control."

Data complied, and as he worked, she stared into Picard's eyes with such infinite malice, infinite satisfaction, that the captain realized *He* had never truly been the one who sought revenge. It was *she,* and she had waited six long years for it.

At last, Data looked up from his console; simultaneously, the warp core began to pulse, and all consoles in engineering blinked to life. The near-human android moved to the queen's side and said, as the two Borg guards dragged Picard toward a surgical table: "He will make an excellent drone."

FIFTEEN

☆

Inside the *Phoenix*'s cockpit, Riker watched the chronometer while La Forge made a final report. The historic moment was almost upon them—and he wasn't about to let Cochrane miss it.

"Plasma injectors are online," Geordi said—words the engineer had uttered before on the *Enterprise* many a time, but this time his tone was not quite so casual. Even though Cochrane had forced his attention away from the radiant Earth, his sense of wonder at the beauty of space was infectious, so much so that Riker had to force his concentration back on his task.

"They should be out there right now," he told Cochrane and La Forge. "We need to break the warp barrier within the next five minutes if we're going to get their attention."

Geordi flicked a series of switches, then glanced down at a dial display. "Nacelles charged and ready."

Cochrane turned back, acknowledging this with a nod; then he caught Riker's gaze and held it with his own look of exhilaration.

"Let's do it," Riker said.

The thrill he felt at that instant was nothing compared to the next, when Cochrane turned back toward his controls, and—eyes passionately ablaze with determination, expression utterly composed—ordered, *"Engage."*

Riker immediately tensed, waiting for what would surely be an incredibly intense sensation of acceleration, then forced himself to relax. The ship did, indeed, accelerate, but this was not a starship; it would take a few minutes to attain warp speed.

"Warp field looks good," Geordi said, eyes focused on his instrument panel, his engineer's heart clearly far more thrilled by the readouts than the sight or sense of the ship accelerating. "Structural integrity holding. . . ."

Will switched on the speedometer and peered at the digital display. "Speed: twenty thousand kilometers per second."

Cochrane reached overhead for some switches, then happened to glance out the window. *"Jesus!"*

La Forge and Riker looked up in tandem; outside the window, the *Enterprise*-E, massive, sleek, and gleaming, sailed into view.

Riker grinned, pleased by the sight. The lack of communication with the ship had gnawed at him, made him worry that perhaps all aboard her had been harmed somehow by the Borg. Communications or not, she had made it here all the same, to offer up protection in case it was needed. "Relax, Doctor. They're just here to give us a send-off."

Six years later, the same horror repeated, the same images that had haunted Picard in dreams.

After Data's betrayal, the Borg had dragged the captain to a surgical table—but let their queen have the honor of slamming the human down upon it.

Once again, Picard stared up at her delicate white features, at the cold, metal-clouded eyes. The cruelty and hunger in them were depthless, unquenchable, but this time, he refused to tremble, to quail, to be afraid.

She would again steal his existence, his body, his mind—a fate to be profoundly despised—along with the realization that she had triumphed. He would again become her parrot, Locutus; and all of Earth and those upon it who dared dream would be obliterated, crushed.

But she had not succeeded utterly; she did not have his surrender, his agreement to become as she was—and in that, he found victory. And strength enough not to struggle or recoil when she lifted an instrument from the table, pressed a control, and watched a sharp, needle-thin probe emerge from its tip. Instead, he glared back at her, defiant.

"The *Phoenix* is coming into range," Data said, behind him and out of view. "I am bringing the phasers online."

She smiled, gloating, and leaned closer to her victim.

Footsteps beside her: Data. Picard glanced up as the android passed; Data's blue gaze met his—rather pointedly, the captain thought.

And then Data looked *up,* at a specific area on a distant bulkhead—again pointedly, yet so fleetingly that the queen gave him no notice.

Picard could not see that far wall; but though he had not had a long acquaintance with the *Enterprise*-E, he knew intimately every centimeter of the ship. And he knew precisely what was in front of that bulkhead and what Data had seen.

Masking his hope, he looked back up at the queen. If deliverance was to come to the *Phoenix* and the future, it would have to do so *now.* . . .

"Thirty seconds to warp threshold," Riker shouted over the roar, then clenched his teeth together hard in a vain effort to keep them from chattering. The cockpit was trembling so violently that Cochrane, who had begun to steer the ship with an old-fashioned stick rudder, was vibrating like a badly fritzed subspace image.

Riker looked back down at the speedometer display. "Approaching light speed . . ."

Light speed—such an outdated term; *warp one,* he had almost called it, but the standard would not be coined for almost another decade. Warp one, considered in the twenty-fourth century to be the speed of molasses.

Warp one had *never* seemed so fast.

"They're getting pretty close!" Geordi shouted beside him, and at his gesture, Will glanced out the window.

The *Enterprise* was indeed closer; if Riker hadn't known better, he might have thought she was giving chase.

If she was, there was little he could do about it now. The cabin began to shake so furiously that he found himself unable to focus his eyes, unable even to think.

From the pilot's seat, Cochrane bellowed, *"We're at critical velocity. . . ."*

Picard watched as Data moved in the direction of his mysterious glance to another console, on whose monitor was displayed the long, cylindrical capsule of the *Phoenix,* with her flanking warp nacelles—a primitive design, to be sure, but nonetheless strongly familiar. Replace the cigar-shaped capsule with a saucer, and voilà: a starship.

Ominously, the monitor image of Cochrane's ship was partly obscured by blinking red cross hairs. But Picard had not failed to notice that the console stood directly to one side of the plasma coolant tanks.

"Quantum torpedoes locked," Data said.

The Borg queen graced him with a savage smile, her delight in the moment distracting her from commencing surgery upon her latest victim. "Destroy them."

Picard drew in a breath as Data returned his attention to the monitor, lifted his android arm, and held the white-gold synthetic hand poised over the controls, on the verge of complying. But then he shot an odd glance back at the queen, turned, and took a step toward her— and the coolant tanks.

"Resistance," he said, with an irony Picard had never heard in him before, "is futile."

With blinding swiftness, he whirled and slammed his synthetic fist into one of the tanks.

Liquid gas spewed from the resulting puncture, carrying Data across the vast chamber in a roiling wave, sweeping into the nearest alcoves of sleeping drones.

At the same mad instant, the queen looked toward the ceiling, summoning three long black cables that snaked downward at her silent command.

Picard had prepared for this moment: at once, he freed himself and stood upon the table to avoid the lethal flood that washed past upon the deck. When the cables arrived, he threw himself at them, succeeded in grabbing one, and began a desperate scramble toward the ceiling—away from the slowly rising gas.

The queen caught one of the other cables and pulled herself up as well, half a leg's length from the swirling storm below. Then she shot an indignant glance at Picard and his cable and gave the tendril a silent command.

At once, the cable began to writhe, to lash, to whip about like an enraged serpent intent on breaking free. Its efforts loosened Picard's grip, causing him to slip slightly, closer to the swirling gas, and death . . .

. . . While in the nearby heavens, Zefram Cochrane was having the ride of his life.

"We're crossing the threshold . . . !"

Certainly, the madness had left him after the impressively painless "hypospray" Deanna had given him—as had the drunkenness, the terror, and the shakes. Despite what he had told Riker, he felt better physically than he had in ten years, but the ingrained pessimism of the postwar era had made it impossible for him to admit that, yes, he had hope; that, yes, while he *did* need and want the money, he also cared about the future and humanity and space travel.

He had spent so many years hurting over all he had lost—the people, the treasured possessions, the life he had known—and then so many years hurting for no reason at all, except a damned disease that had been curable for half a century, that admitting that he cared about something was unthinkable.

Lily and everyone else at the encampment shared the same belief, too: don't say you care about something— because then you will, and you'll wind up only losing it. Everything, everyone, was doomed to impermanence and decay.

Same with hope; same with love. Don't admit you feel them, and maybe you won't. After all, they lead only to disappointment and loss. In the war, six hundred million died; in the years-long aftermath, even more were lost, to disease, radiation sickness, famine, road gangs, suicide.

But now, war and despair were the farthest things from Cochrane's mind, for the *Phoenix* suddenly spread her wings.

The ship around him seemed to dissolve. He felt himself go hurtling forward, weightless, as if his entire body had been launched from a giant slingshot. The stars surrounding him suddenly blurred, then began to streak past at dizzying speed.

Zefram Cochrane let go a scream—of fear, of exhilaration, of the purest joy—and with it, released ten years' worth of grief and cynicism, pain and hopelessness.

"Whoooooooooooaaaaaa!"

* * *

Plasma coolant seething only inches beneath his boots, Picard struggled furiously against the thrashing cable—with no success. The cable had entwined itself so tightly around his arms, legs, torso that he could not climb, could not break free. Through some miracle, he managed to cling to it, but again his grip was loosened, and he slipped yet another inch downward toward the lethal gas.

On the cable beside him, the queen had managed to climb to his level; as he tried vainly to recoil from her, she reached forth with a delicate hand—capable, he knew, of crushing bone—and caught his leg.

He flailed, helpless, limbs too entangled to successfully kick back. She yanked downward; once more, his grip on the slick synthetic material faltered, and he lost another inch.

Again she pulled. This time when he slipped, the sole of his boot skimmed the gas and began to hiss as it melted away.

Again she reached—

A monstrous sight emerged from the roiling gas behind her: Data, the human flesh covering his face and arm grotesquely eaten away, revealing wiring and metal clamps strewn with half-liquefied blood vessels.

The android hurled himself at the queen, knocking her from the cable; together, they disappeared down into the swirling gas.

Picard's thrashing cable gave an abrupt twitch, then fell limp. Immediately, he scrambled up to the ceiling—and safety; only then did he dare look down.

Below, amid swirls of gas, lay the queen—the pale

flesh of her handsome face and hands bubbling as it slowly slid from her skeleton.

Inside the cockpit, the ride had smoothed out considerably, but the mood was still rapidly ascending.

"That should be enough. Throttle back; bring us out of warp," Riker told Cochrane, with as much professionalism as he could muster—which wasn't much, since he'd been grinning so hard his cheeks literally began to ache. They had done it, really done it, and from the look of elation on Cochrane's face, Will had no doubt that, within another hundred years or so, the statue of the great Zefram Cochrane would be standing next to the silo, precisely where it was supposed to be.

As for his momentary concern about the *Enterprise,* obviously, his secret fear that the Borg had somehow commandeered the ship had been foolish; if they had, the *Phoenix* would have already been reduced to space debris.

Cochrane sighed and worked his control panel; almost immediately, the ship dropped out of warp. The scientist paused to stare out the front viewshield, at the stars that were once again twinkling dots. In the far distance, a blue one shone more brightly than all the rest.

Cochrane nodded reverently at it. "Is that Earth?"

"That's it," La Forge answered, his voice equally quiet.

The scientist gave a slight shake of his head, marveling. "It's so . . . *small.*"

Riker leaned forward, still grinning, but no longer feeling the ache. "It's about to get a whole lot bigger. . . ."

* * *

Picard climbed carefully through the thick tangle of cables and conduits to the far side of the room and the third level of the engineering deck. Below, the gas had ceased its roiling and settled into a calm, soft blanket that covered the lower two decks, hiding the carnage there.

Swinging from one of the cables, he leapt onto the third-level grating, hurried to a wall panel, opened it, and struck a control. An enormous *whoosh* followed as the emergency ventilation system set to work; the captain at once moved to the edge of the deck and peered down.

In that brief instant, the powerful vents had already sucked away all but a few last wisps of plasma coolant, revealing a grisly—but relief-inspiring—sight: the stripped metal skeletons of Borg drones, most fallen from their alcoves as they slept, interior metal workings spilled everywhere.

Picard scrambled down the access ladders to the first level, wincing at the slight hiss as his boots met the deck. The sprawling metal carcasses were so numerous, the chamber so vast, that he spent some time looking through the black-and-gray sea before he recognized Data sitting among them.

All of the new human flesh on the android's face and right arm had been utterly stripped away, exposing the silvery android skeleton beneath; the synthetic flesh on his left arm, however, remained.

Picard hurried to him—but was stopped in mid-stride by a faint whisper . . . then two, then three, and more in his head. The voice of the collective: no longer thunderous, but slowly rising in volume, and doggedly persistent . . .

He froze, stricken, and glanced about the cavernous chamber for any sign of the queen, of surviving drones. At last, when he looked up, he saw to his horror several Borg convulsing on the upper level—unharmed by the gas, but apparently suffering from the harm done their queen.

And still, the voices whispered.

Locutus . . .

On instinct, he whirled and saw behind him she who was all: a blinking steel cranium atop a smooth metal spine. She writhed in frustrated anguish, struggling to lift herself, to rise, to conquer and control as she had done from the beginning of time. . . .

Her condition might have been seen as frighteningly pathetic—as indeed it was—but Picard wasted no time on such emotions. Instead, he summoned to his mind a million years of misery: a million planets and their lucky inhabitants consumed by fireballs, a billion planets and the not-so-fortunate natives assimilated, their wills consumed by the queen, their individual minds forced into endless purgatory.

Picard reached forth with his hands, and with a surge of adrenalized, inhuman strength, seized her slender metal spine and snapped it in two.

The cranium ceased blinking and glowed stark red for a long, agonizing minute . . . then abruptly darkened, and the queen fell still.

And within his skull, there was a silence so deep, so primal that he let go a silent sob, overwhelmed by the freedom. The collective at last was dead, all Borg within the entire chamber—including those writhing upon the third level—now nothing more than lifeless scraps of metal.

When at last he turned, he saw Data, sitting up now and apparently unharmed, though still unnerving in appearance.

"Are you all right?" Picard asked.

Apparently the emotion chip was active, for the android replied with remarkable good humor, "I would imagine I look worse than I feel." He gazed down at the corpse of the queen. "Strange. Part of me is sorry that she is dead."

"She was . . . unique," the captain allowed, though he shared the sentiment not at all.

"She brought me closer to humanity than I ever thought possible," Data confessed, and if ever a metal skull could convey a sense of shame, his did then. "And for a time, I was tempted by her offer."

Picard glanced up sharply, startled. "How long a time?"

"Zero point eight six seconds," said Data, and when the captain failed to repress a grin, added hastily, "For an android, that is nearly an eternity."

Still smiling, Picard helped him to his feet. "Try to put it behind you, Data."

The android hesitated, his golden eyes intense with curiosity. "Is that what you did, Captain, six years ago?"

The smile abruptly fled his face; he paused a moment, recalling the future that almost was not, because of his hate. "No . . ."

* * *

Captain's log, April 5, 2063: The voyage of the *Phoenix* was a success . . . again. The alien ship detected the warp signature . . . and is on its way to a rendezvous with history.

Braced by members of Picard's senior crew (who were, she sensed, also his closest friends), Lily stood beside Zefram, gripping his arm. Farther away, hidden by the darkness, Picard and the wise Dr. Crusher stood apart, taking care that their mere presence did not alter the line of history.

Lily—along with them all—gazed up at the sky, at the bright lights that shone through the night clouds, the lights that had drawn every townsperson here to the silo, the lights of a descending spacecraft.

A murmur passed through the crowd as the colossal ship—a good twenty times the size of the *Phoenix*—at last emerged from the clouds. To Lily, it looked rather like a huge pterodactyl spreading its great wings as it lowered itself, feet first, to the ground—a sleek, high-tech pterodactyl, of course, with wings suspiciously reminiscent of warp nacelles and landing lights aglitter like jewels. And the domed head in the center: that, she decided, would be the bridge.

Like us; they must think something like us. Or else we *think like* they *do.*

As it descended, landing gear emerged from its belly, and the "claws," which had been tucked under the nacelles, began to lower, merging with the gear to form a stable platform. With exceptional grace, it slowed almost to a stop, hovered a few feet above the earth, then settled down so delicately that the ground beneath Lily's feet never shuddered.

Lily watched, lips parting to release a soft and unashamed tearless sob, and remembered Picard's words: *If his chest had been a cannon, he would have shot his heart upon it. . . .*

As she had shot her heart now, but the emotion that filled it was not hatred, but pure joy. It was as if all the bitterness of the past ten years had been lanced, drained away; and now, her joy spilled out onto the community, onto Picard, whose help had permitted her to see this, onto Zefram, who, because of Dr. Crusher's blessed intervention, had never looked so strong, so sane . . .

Or so awed. As the alien ship's engines whined to a stop, she squeezed his arm and directed her bright, shining gaze upon him; he looked back at her, suddenly decades younger than the day they had met.

The ones known as Will and Geordi stepped forward and took Zef gently by the arm. "Doctor," Geordi said softly, "you're on."

Zef stared at them—perfectly sober, yet drunk with awe. "My God . . . they're really from another world?"

Will smiled in his easy manner. "And they're going to want to meet the man who flew that warp ship."

A whirr, a hiss; a hatch in one of the landing claws began slowly to open. Cochrane glanced deliberately toward the shadows where Picard invisibly watched . . . then took a deep breath and strode over into the blinding circle of light where the alien ship stood. There he waited, expression and eyes bright, nervous, until at last the hatch swung completely open.

Light spilled out, illuminating the night air; three hooded figures emerged, robed in elegant patterned brocades of charcoal, bronze, aubergine. *Human-sized,* Lily thought excitedly; two were slightly taller than Zef, one shorter.

One of the taller ones pulled back its hood—and at that instant, Lily ceased struggling against tears and permitted them to course unwiped down her cheeks.

It was a man. A handsome man, with a strong jaw, strong cheekbones, coal-black upswept eyebrows—all framed by a severe fringe of coal-black bangs. His skin was pale, but Lily could classify it neither as white, black, yellow, or brown; if the stark lighting did not deceive, his complexion had a faintly greenish cast.

But it was the ears that made her realize: *yes, this is a man; but it is most definitely* not *a human being.* They were unswept, pointed as a pixie's, yet they possessed a delicacy and naturalness that was becoming rather than ridiculous.

Behind him, the other aliens lowered their hoods as well, revealing another male with precisely the same coloring and haircut, and a striking woman with the same coloring and fringed bangs, but a waist-length jet braid entwined with jewels.

Slowly, regally, with remarkable and formal composure, the group's leader walked over to Cochrane and raised a hand, palm out. Zef mimicked the gesture, adding an uncertain smile and a little wave.

The alien indulged in neither. His expression pleasant but decidedly solemn, he kept the hand raised, then separated the thumb, index, and middle fingers from the ring, and little fingers to form two V's.

"Live long and prosper," he said, in flawless, unaccented English.

Zef worked frantically to emulate the gesture, but he finally gave up and instead smiled genuinely at the alien. "Um . . . thanks."

The alien tilted his head and cocked a black eyebrow at him. The exchange struck Lily as amusing; she smoothed away her evaporating tears with a palm as she repressed a chuckle.

From the nearby shadows, she heard Picard's voice: "I think it's time for us to make a discreet exit."

Beside her, Riker nodded and surreptitiously tapped the small insignia beneath his jacket. "Riker to *Enterprise*. Stand by to beam us up."

He, Dr. Crusher, and La Forge moved deeper into the shadows, out of view; Picard stepped to the radiance's edge and smiled at Lily, who walked up to him.

"I envy you . . . the world you're going to," she said warmly.

The corner of his lip quirked, and an amused look came over his face; she got the feeling he was thinking of revealing something, but then decided against it. "I envy *you*," he said, "taking these first steps into a new frontier."

"Might've been fun to take them together."

He said nothing for a time, merely looked at her intently as if to memorize each detail of her face. At last he said, very gently, "I'll miss you, Lily."

She smiled as he clasped her hands, and they gazed at

each other for a timeless moment. And then she forced herself to walk away, back into the blazing lights—but stayed near to the darkness to hear his voice.

"Picard to *Enterprise*. Energize . . ."

Then a strange, shimmering hum. They had gone, Lily knew, and she would never see any of them again; even so, she could not resist staring up into the night sky.

Aboard the *Enterprise*-E, now gratifyingly back to normal, Picard looked upon his bridge and his senior crew—Will, Geordi, Beverly, Deanna, Data—and the on-loan Worf—with newfound appreciation. He felt appreciation, too, for the future that awaited them, and all who had helped bring it to pass.

"Report," he said, with unalloyed pleasure.

"The moon's gravitational field obscured our warp signature," Worf responded. "The Vulcans did not detect us."

Picard gave a satisfied nod as he headed for his chair.

"I've reconfigured our warp field to match the chronometric readings of the Borg sphere," Geordi was explaining at his console.

"Recreate the vortex, Commander," Picard ordered.

"Aye, sir." La Forge set to work.

"All decks report ready," Riker confirmed.

Data half turned from his station, most of his face still silver, gleaming android. "Helm standing by."

"Lay in a course for the twenty-fourth century, Mr. Data." The captain hesitated, gratefully studying his bridge crew for a moment. "Something tells me our future will be there waiting for us."

"Course laid in, sir," Data reported.

Picard permitted himself a small sigh, and the faintest ghost of a smile. "Make it so."

And in the unseasonably warm Montana night, Lily Sloane stood just outside the Crash & Burn, staring up at the sky. There she saw what she'd been waiting for: not the horrifying bolts of laserfire streaking earthward, but a flash of rainbow light and a tiny star sailing inside it, then abruptly vanishing into the future.

She smiled and took a step back to peer inside the tent, where Zef was standing near the jukebox, waving his arms and talking a light-year a minute; seated at the bar, the ones who called themselves Vulcans listened with polite, reserved expressions. Nice people, apparently, but a bit uptight; they refused Zef's offer of drinks, and she had yet to see them smile.

As for Zef, he was far too excited to touch the glass he'd poured for himself. Excited, but utterly lucid—Dr. Crusher had taken a timeline liberty and permanently cured his brain-chemistry disorder with a single injection.

Zef suddenly reached out and, grinning broadly, hit a control on the jukebox; at the instant hard-driving rock music filled the air, each Vulcan lifted his or her right eyebrow, then listened with perfectly detached scientific curiosity. Lily could not help but laugh delightedly, along with the other settlers who had silently crept up, hoping to catch a glimpse of the aliens.

The *Phoenix* had risen at last, and she was never coming down. . . .

A First Look at
Star Trek® First Contact™

A special report by Judith Reeves-Stevens and Garfield Reeves-Stevens, authors of *The Art of Star Trek and Star Trek Phase II: The Lost Series*

Thirty years after its creation, there are still secrets to be learned in the *Star Trek* universe, unknown stories to be told, sights to be seen that no one has ever seen before. *Star Trek: First Contact,* the newest installment of the most successful science-fiction franchise of all time, is living proof. True to its title, and to the spirit of *Star Trek,* this action-packed movie is full of firsts—a testament to the limitless possibilities of the creative arena originally imagined by Gene Roddenberry more than three decades ago.

Surprisingly, one of the seeds for this new movie dates back almost as far as *Star Trek*'s creation, to "Metamorphosis," an episode of the Original Series written by Gene L. Coon. It was here that Captain Kirk, Mr. Spock, and Dr. McCoy met Zefram Cochrane, the reclusive genius who invented humanity's first warp drive. At the time of the episode, Cochrane was more

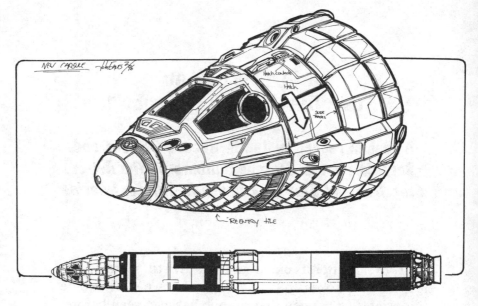

An early concept sketch of Cochrane's warp-powered space vehicle, owing more to the science of the twentieth century than to that of the twenty-third or twenty-fourth.

Artist: John Eaves

than two hundred years old and had been kept alive by a mysterious alien known as the Companion. Nothing was revealed about the circumstances in which Cochrane had come to discover the principles of faster-than-light warp propulsion. Nor was any mention made of the events that immediately followed his first warp flight.

But now, as the saying goes, the official story can be told.

No one was more surprised that it *could* be told than Ronald D. Moore. Moore shares screenplay credit for

First Contact with Brannon Braga and story credit with Braga and producer Rick Berman. Moore and Braga both began their television writing careers on *Star Trek: The Next Generation.* Today, Moore is a producer on *Star Trek: Deep Space Nine,* and Braga is a producer on *Star Trek: Voyager.*

Thinking back on the genesis of the *First Contact* story, Moore explains, "It's a funny universe, *Star Trek,* because it hangs together far better than it ever should in truth. I mean, we do try to maintain continuity, but given the thirty-year history of the show, and the countless episodes, and the movies, it's amazing that any of it makes sense. And yet it does."

Moore knows that continuity is an important part of *Star Trek*'s ongoing appeal. "Making it a believable universe," he says, "has always been important to the people who worked on the series, right from the very beginning. That was Gene Roddenberry's vision from the start—that this franchise had to be believable. You *had* to believe these people were on a starship. You *had* to believe that it all made sense. You're in such a fantastical environment, you *had* to try and hang onto reality, and so the more the backstory made sense, the more you accepted it all."

But Cochrane's story was not the starting point for *First Contact*—at least not at first. Instead, two other story elements began the process.

At the initial story meeting held by Rick Berman, Brannon Braga, and Ron Moore, Berman said he wanted the new movie to be a time-travel story. Why? Rick Berman explains: "All of the *Star Trek* films and episodes I have been most impressed with—*Star Trek*

IV: The Voyage Home, "Yesterday's Enterprise," "City on the Edge of Forever," and I could give you half a dozen more—have all been stories that deal with time travel. In a way, *Star Trek Generations* dealt with time travel. Nick Meyer's wonderful movie, *Time After Time,* dealt with time travel. The paradoxes that occur in writing, as well as in the reality of what the characters are doing and what the consequences are, have always been fascinating to me. I don't think I've ever had as much fun as being involved with "Yesterday's Enterprise," and having to tackle all the logical, paradoxical problems that we would run into and figure out ways to solve them."

For their part, Moore and Braga wanted to tell a story about *The Next Generation*'s most popular alien threat, the Borg, and it was quickly decided that the new movie would combine the two.

For everyone involved with the production, the chance to bring the Borg to the movie screen was an opportunity for a real *Star Trek* first. As Rick Berman says, "This is our chance to see the Borg the way we've always wanted to do them."

The Borg—half-humanoid, half-cybernetic aliens who share a group mind—originally appeared in the second-season, *The Next Generation* episode "Q Who?", written by Maurice Hurley. They returned in several episodes, most notably the two-part "Best of Both Worlds," considered by most *The Next Generation* fans to be among the best of the series.

But for all the Borg's popularity and previous appearances, Rick Berman says, "We have never had the time for the R&D necessary to make the Borg what we always

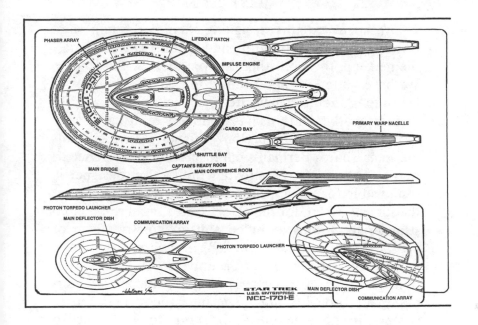

Sleeker, faster, more muscular . . . the first new *Starship Enterprise* in almost a decade.

Artist: John Eaves

wanted them to be like. Nor did we ever have the money. The money and the time have always stood in the way of turning out the Borg the way we've always envisioned them. But this film has allowed us to do that at last."

With a budget more than ten times that of a single episode of *The Next Generation,* and months of preproduction time to design this new incarnation of the Borg instead of the typical television schedule of a week or two, the Borg of *First Contact* promise to be a breathtaking new addition to the *Star Trek* universe.

251

"We spent months designing them," Berman says. "And then months building and refining the costumes, the makeup, their prosthetics, even the way they move. We have gotten an opportunity to take the group who are among the most favorite *Star Trek* villains and do them properly. And this has been very exciting for us."

First Contact's production designer, Herman Zimmerman, shares Berman's enthusiasm at this chance to re-present the Borg. A movie's production designer is responsible for the appearance of everything we see on the screen, except for the actors, and Zimmerman is no stranger to guiding a skilled and imaginative team of artists, designers, and technicians in creating fascinating new visions of the *Star Trek* universe. As production designer of *The Next Generation*'s first season, Zimmerman, had brought *Star Trek* into the twenty-fourth century. In the same role on the third *Star Trek* series to be made, he had conceptualized the distinctive and visually compelling Cardassian esthetic of Space Station Deep Space 9. And he brought all his skills to bear on the new look for the Borg.

"The Borg ship is basically the same cube that was seen on the television series," Zimmerman says, "but with considerably more detail. When it was done in the series, it was done on a crash program, and it was quite successful and very effective for the television screen. But when you blow up something made for television to the size of a cinemascope screen in a theater, you need a great deal more detail. The screen is thirty feet high instead of nineteen inches diagonal, and that makes a big difference in what your lens will see. So the Borg are more detailed. There's a lot of mechanical fussiness. We used a lot of different optical tricks and lighting tricks to create the look of the Borg for this picture. We've used fiberoptics in the walls and black light, and we've used strobe lights, and smoke. . . ." Zimmerman smiles as he spreads his arms to encompass all of a production designer's tricks of the trade. "You name it, we'll try it."

With both the Borg and time travel in the mix, the question for Berman, Moore, and Braga, became how to blend the two story elements. From the very first story meeting, Moore recalls, they knew the Borg would go back in time. That raised questions: Where are they going to go? And what's the time period the Borg will seek out and why?

"So we started talking about the places and times that had been done on screen or had not been done on screen," Moore recounts. "Certain things we just crossed off, because they would be too hokey. We could go to the Roman Empire, which would be cool in a lot of ways. But Picard in a toga?" Moore chuckles. "You don't want to do that. Put him in a spacesuit."

Other periods the writers and producer discussed included the American Civil War, and even World War II. But in the end, they decided all those periods had been seen too often in other time-travel stories.

Eventually, though, at Berman's suggestion, they began exploring a period of Earth's history that hadn't been overexposed, and from which, had the Borg been present, humanity might never have progressed to form the United Federation of Planets.

No, we haven't come back to the age of Zefram Cochrane yet. This first time period of choice was the Italian Renaissance.

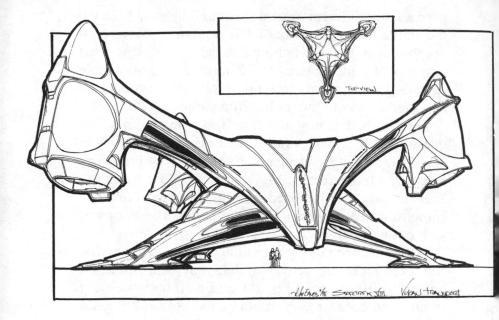

Concept drawing for a twenty-first-century Vulcan landing vehicle. Note the triangular design, reminiscent of late-twentieth-century reports of unidentified flying objects.

Artist: John Eaves

"It was a time of intellectual awakening," Moore says excitedly. "It was a time of Earth coming out of a dark age, of the loosening up of intellectualism, and the fact that people were starting to become freer in expression and all forms of the arts and scientific inquiry. And it seemed like a time that if the Borg went back to it and interfered with it, the Earth might never get out of that dark age."

In an initial outline of that story—tentatively titled *Star Trek: Renaissance*—Picard and his crew know where and when the Borg have gone in Earth's history and go looking for them. When they arrive at a small village at the time of the Renaissance, they hear tales of strange creatures or evil men taking over other villages in the surrounding area. "Then," Moore continues, "we begin to realize that these horrific monsters of the time were the Borg. We track them down to a castle near the village where a nobleman runs a feudal society. We suspect the Borg are working in there, but no one can get in. So Data becomes our spy by impersonating an artist's apprentice."

Ultimately, Moore says, "Data became friends with Leonardo da Vinci, who, at the time, was working for the nobleman as a military engineer." Moore says that Data's friendship with the great inventor would have resulted in da Vinci's arriving at one of his great insights, and then adding a drawing of Data to his notebooks.

But, Data aside, the main action of this film would have taken place in the castle's dungeon. "It was going to be the Borg hive," Moore says, "which was going to be pretty nifty. Our people would be running around with swords and lances and spears to fight the Borg in another time period."

Eventually, though, Berman, Moore, and Braga realized that setting a *Star Trek* adventure in a small Italian village resulted more in a history lesson than an action-adventure film, and they began searching for another time period.

It was then that lightning struck and they realized that by going back into *The Next Generation*'s past, they didn't necessarily have to go back into the *present day's* past—they could go into our future. And what event in our future is, perhaps, the mot important event of *Star Trek*'s past?

There are two answers to that question: Cochrane's first warp flight, and humanity's first contact with aliens.

In thirty years of *Star Trek* story-telling, neither one of these pivotal events had ever been described in a filmed episode or motion picture—though it had been established in a fourth-season *The Next Generation* episode, also called "First Contact," that another world's first warp flight was the triggering mechanism by which the Federation made contact with a new race and revealed the existence of an interstellar civilization.

In other words, according to *Star Trek*'s own rules, Cochrane's first warp flight and humanity's first contact with aliens might be two events that were inextricably linked.

Moore is still surprised by how perfectly all these disparate elements suddenly meshed. "This was a section of *Star Trek* history that was left vague—purposefully vague, I'm sure—for many years. Gene had always said way back in the *Original Series* that there was a third world war at some point. And that somehow out of that came warp drive, came first contact with aliens, and came the Federation.

"It was embroidered a little bit over the years, but we were surprised when we went back and were looking at *Star Trek* history to see that we hadn't really loaded ourselves with a lot of detailed backstory.

"In 'Metamorphosis,' Cochrane's age was fortunately vague enough, and we looked through Mike and Denise Okuda's *Star Trek Chronology,* and all the dates came

256

Finding the perfect angle on the bridge of the new *Enterprise*.

together very nicely. Warp drive and first contact could have taken place simultaneously, which made everything possible."

At last, Berman, Braga, and Moore had a *Star Trek* focus for their story. Best of all, it still matched the themes they had been working with in their first pass at the movie, set in the Italian Renaissance. Now their movie would be set in a new period of rebirth for humanity.

"That's exactly the analogy we drew," Moore says in confirmation, "coming out of a dark age. A time when

257

there was hopelessness, and the people couldn't look to the future because they could barely look ahead to tomorrow.

"And then, within that really downtrodden, dark society, suddenly Cochrane made some things happen. That was exactly the notion of the time period we wanted."

Berman enthusiastically agrees. "We're going back to the mid-, postapocalyptic, twenty-first century, and we're getting a glimpse of life on this planet at one of its darkest times. We are going to learn to some degree how and why this dark trench in Earth's history turned around in a very short time to the wondrous world of *Star Trek*—the wondrous world of the United Federation of Planets and space exploration. We're going to be present when that turnaround begins to occur and, at the same time, see how Captain Picard and company were a very integral part of it. Which is something that I think for fans and nonfans alike is going to be a lot of fun. And," he adds, showing his understanding of the message of optimism that is at the heart of *Star Trek*'s ongoing appeal, "I am hopeful it will be somewhat inspirational in the way we depict it."

With the broad framework of the *First Contact* story in place, Berman, Moore, and Braga then had another question to face: What is going to be the tone and the style of the movie? Part of the reason for *Star Trek*'s success over the years is its ability to contain many different types of stories, from the light comedy of *The Voyage Home,* to the grim conflict of "The Best of Both Worlds." Which style would *First Contact* take as its own?

Once again, the direction came from Rick Berman.

He remembers saying to Braga and Moore, "Let's do a story where Jean-Luc Picard can stop brooding and can start being more of an action hero."

The writers agreed at once.

Berman explains that while Patrick Stewart's Jean-Luc Picard has always been considered an action hero by those behind the scenes of *Star Trek* productions, "the character tends to be a little more introspective than others. I think it went too far in *Star Trek Generations* in that the death of his brother and his nephew caused him great emotional pain, and he spent the film

Jonathan Frakes doing double duty as actor and director. For once, the first officer can give orders to the captain.

working his way through that. It was time to not have our character brooding anymore. It was time to have our captain actively involved in a very heroic as well as a very fun adventure, and I think we have managed to pull that off." However, before anyone worries that *Star Trek* is taking a turn toward mindless action, Berman quickly adds, "There are elements of this film where Picard's emotional core is challenged. It's not as if he's become a two-dimensional figure at all."

When it comes to the style and tone of a movie, perhaps no member of the creative team is more important than the director. Once again, *First Contact* scores another first, marking the feature-film directing debut of Jonathan Frakes, known to *Star Trek* fans as *The Next Generation*'s Will Riker.

Frakes is not a newcomer to the director's chair. He directed eight episodes of *The Next Generation* and has continued his association with *Star Trek* by directing additional episodes of *Deep Space Nine* and *Voyager,* as well as the Simon & Schuster interactive CD-ROM, *Star Trek Klingon.*

Though the complexities—and the budget—of a motion picture are far greater than those of a single-hour episode, Frakes is comfortable with the transition from the nineteen-inch screen to the thirty-foot-tall one.

"It's the same universe," he says with a smile. Focusing on the differing technical demands of making a widescreen motion picture, Frakes observes, "The frame aspect is different, which changes the staging and the framing of a shot. But it allows you more latitude, literally and figuratively. And it's been a really great challenge, and great fun, to learn that part of it."

Frakes is even more enthusiastic about the other side of filmmaking—the personal one. He has found no awkwardness in taking on a role both in front of and behind the camera, directing fellow actors he has worked with for almost a decade.

"We have done so many episodes together with that relationship," he explains, "that there was really not a problem. I was looking forward to it. I think, frankly, we all were. We not only know and respect each other as people, but as actors. And we all know the characters and the characters' relationships, so there's a lot of stuff that can go unsaid and that we can remind each other of in shorthand.

"With any luck, that ease and history will come across on the screen, especially with Patrick, who is the star of the movie. My relationship with him, I hope, is allowing him to give the 'freest' performance I've ever seen. He's fabulous."

For Frakes, relationships are what make *The Next Generation* stand out. "It's very relationship driven," he says, "which is what Gene always claimed was essential."

As to the tone Frakes is trying to impart to the movie, his answer is as direct as a Borg's call to surrender: "I hope to bring the fun back to *Star Trek*. I think the best of *Star Trek* over the thirty years has always been when it's had some wry, ironic humor. Not as obvious as a wink or a poke in the ribs, but certainly not taking itself so seriously that the audience can't enjoy the sweep of it. It helps frame the serious moments when you do that."

Frakes's ambition doesn't end with just that, though. With a touch of humor himself, he adds, "I think this is going to be the best movie, obviously. I was a big fan of *The Voyage Home,* and I loved the humor in that one. Especially the sequences in San Francisco. It was wonderful. Tongue deeply embedded in the cheek. And the camaraderie of the original cast, we have our version of it in this company. I think it's palpable on the screen for *First Contact.* I think it was true of the series. And I think it was one of the reasons why the series was so successful. Because either by luck or design, back when the series began, the producers put together a cast that worked."

Frakes's goal to bring the fun back to *Star Trek* was in complete agreement with the goals of Berman, Braga, and Moore, who had set the initial tone for the film with their story and script.

Moore says that from the beginning they intended to "do a little more razzle-dazzle and a little more action-adventure than had been done in a while." Just as Frakes looked to *The Voyage Home* as a *Star Trek* film with humor, the writers also looked to an earlier film as their benchmark.

"I think," Moore says, *"The Wrath of Khan* was the last, true, let's-go-out-and-kick-some-butt-for-a-few-hours movie. *First Contact* is certainly the most action-packed one since then. Maybe even more."

That universal desire to bring a new level of action to a *Star Trek* film brought Frakes his greatest challenge as a director, because all-out action is not usually part of a television production.

"You don't have the time," he says. "They write the scope, but you don't have time to shoot it." *First Contact* is a total change of pace. Frakes says his

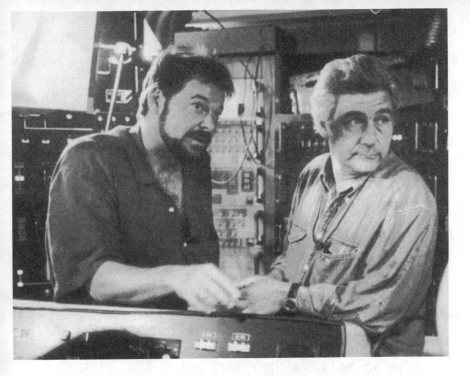

Though *First Contact* marks his feature film–directing debut, Jonathan Frakes is no stranger to that task in the *Star Trek* universe. He has directed eight episodes of *Star Trek: The Next Generation*, as well as episodes of *Star Trek: Deep Space Nine* and *Star Trek: Voyager*.

objective upon getting the assignment to direct *First Contact* was "to surround myself with department heads who had made a lot of movies so that I—making my first one—would be able to enlist the help of all those other people." He smiles with good-humored relief. "Fortunately, it worked out that way."

Indeed, the talented, behind-the-scenes people Frakes names are creative forces to be reckoned with. Among them are Terry Frazee, the special-effects wizard who worked not only on *Generations,* but on 1996's box-office blockbuster, *Eraser*; film editor Jack Wheeler, noted for his work with the legendary director John

Frankenheimer; Academy Award–winning makeup artist and long-time *Star Trek* alien expert Michael Westmore; director of photography Matthew Leonetti; stunt coordinator Ron Rondell; and first assistant director Jerry Fleck. "I'm very fortunate," Frakes says emphatically. "It's big to have all these guys around, and the budget to do it. The budget is a big part of it. And then," he adds with another grin, "staying on the budget is another big part of it." But the bottom line, Frakes says, is that Paramount wants an action film, too, so that's what he and Rick Berman, and all the other members of the production team are going to deliver.

As Frakes says, "I know from going to a lot of conventions that the audiences have always wanted more action in *Star Trek*. They love it. They eat it up. And this one's got no shortage."

When asked about what elevates this *Star Trek* film above all others in terms of action different members of the team name different favorite sequences as evidence—the opening space battle, the shoot-out in Cochrane's missile silo, even the scene where the Borg invade a Dixon Hill holodeck scenario. But without exception, the one action set piece that *everyone* points to as the one that will bring down the house—*and* bring the audience back to see the film for a second and third time—is the space battle on the outer hull of the *Enterprise.*

True, in the very first *Star Trek* film, there was a brief scene in which Kirk and some of his crew stepped out onto the saucer of the original *Enterprise.* But that was in the protected environment of V'Ger, with no spacesuits necessary.

Two of *Star Trek: First Contact*'s firsts—a new Borg on the spectacular, almost-full-size deflector-dish set.

For *First Contact,* what the writers described was a no-holds-barred hand-to-hand battle between the crew of the *Enterprise* and the Borg, in the vacuum of space, on the outside of Starfleet's most powerful starship.

It's hard to choose which group is more excited at the prospects of this sequence—the people who are making it or the people who are eagerly looking forward to seeing it on the screen.

Ron Moore describes his and Berman's and Braga's intentions for this scene. "What we're hoping for is that the battle on the outside of the hull is what's going to bring the audience back to this one. It was something we wanted early on. We wanted to do the battle on the outside of the hull, put the crew in spacesuits, go outside with magnetized boots, and fight the Borg."

In this case, what the writers imagined, the production team took to heart. For the first time, a substantial section of a starship's exterior has been built on a Paramount sound stage—the *Enterprise*'s deflector dish.

"The set is enormous," Moore says with appreciation. "It's like a James Bond set."

The set is only part of the equation for this sequence, though. An important part of every *Star Trek* film, or any science-fiction and/or action film, is the visual effects that bring the writers' and director's imaginative visions to life.

First Contact is no exception. And returning to deliver the state-of-the-art visual effects for which they are renowned is Industrial Light & Magic.

Even Rick Berman, who has been in the forefront of *Star Trek*'s visual effects production for almost ten years, is impressed by what ILM has provided for this film. "We have some remarkable shots in here that are very new. The advances in CGI [computer-generated imagery] in motion picture film have continued since we got involved with *Star Trek Generations*. You can't see an action film now, whether it's *Independence Day* or *Twister* or whatever, that is not taking full advantage of computer work. And we have continued to do the same, sticking with ILM because they did very well by us the last time."

Indeed, for *Generations,* ILM provided the first entirely computer-generated starships for a *Star Trek* film, with such high quality that few people could tell the difference between the shots done with models and those done completely by computer.

Berman goes on to explain that "ILM has developed a good relationship with *Star Trek,* and certainly with Paramount, and as a result, we have continued to try to push the envelope and get visual effects in this film that are going to be spectacular."

Ironically, for the past ten years, the *Star Trek* television productions have been the industry leaders in terms of the quality of visual effects produced for the small screen. Every science-fiction series that has been developed over the past decade has had to at least match the look of *Star Trek*'s effects or risk being perceived as behind the times. Now, Berman acknowledges, *Star Trek* films face the same challenge in the realm of movies.

"We're living in a world now where we have much tougher competition in visual effects," he says. "You see the heavily visual-effects films that are out today—and these are films that in my opinion are nothing but visual effects—but it's still hard to compete with them because the visual effects are so remarkable and so much money is being spent on them.

"For *First Contact,* we need to find ways to at least stand up to these films. I think in terms of the story and the plot and the performances, we are in a position where we're going to outshine all of these films. But in terms of the visual effects, the time and money involved is a little bit more limited. So we had to come up with clever ways to achieve some of our effects, by putting the money where it would count. And I think we have done that. *First Contact* certainly has more visual effects than *Generations.*"

Herman Zimmerman is equally pleased with ILM's state-of-the-art contributions to *First Contact.* In fact, the movie's opening shot is technically similar to one imagined by William Shatner for the opening shot of *Star Trek V: The Final Frontier.* Shatner, who directed that film, hoped to include an "infinite zoom," in which the camera would open on the Earth in space, then push in closer and closer until it ended up in close-up on Captain Kirk climbing up the side of a mountain. But ten years ago, the technical demands of that sequence were beyond the budget of the film, and the shot was dropped.

But now, for *First Contact,* ILM will create the same camera movement in reverse, starting in extreme close up on Patrick Stewart's eye, and then, as Zimmerman describes it, "pulling back to reveal his face, then his uniform, and then that he's in a Borg regenerative alcove. Then the pullback continues to show that he's standing next to a dozen other alcoves, and then in a tier of twelve hundred, and then in a hive of one hundred and fifty thousand, and then outside into a Borg ship, and then outside the ship into space. It will be one of the longest pullbacks ever done."

For the eagerly anticipated hull battle, ILM will once again seamlessly combine its computer magic with live-action footage. On the stunning deflector dish set, actors in spacesuits, suspended by "flying rigs" to simulate microgravity, will be pulled away from the dish as if they have been blasted into space. But after only a few feet of travel, the live-action actor will be replaced with a computer-generated double that will be able to tumble and fall away in a much more realistic manner, in a way that would be time-consuming and dangerous to attempt with real stunt people on a live stage.

And, Ron Moore adds as he describes this sequence, in addition to all the action, "we'll have the Earth hanging out there and casting light on the hull, and it's going to be pretty groovy."

Zefram Cochrane's warp vessel, poised on the brink of its historic flight.

However, despite the first look at untold parts of *Star Trek*'s history, the enthusiasm and respect for *Star Trek* of its first-time director, and the emphasis on catapulting the *Next Generation* crew into their first, flat-out action adventure, perhaps no single element of *First Contact* is more eagerly awaited than the unveiling of the first new *Enterprise* in almost a decade—the NCC-1701-E.

As production designer, Herman Zimmerman led the creative effort to update what Gene Roddenberry always felt was as much a character in *Star Trek* as any of her flesh-and-blood crew. The key illustrator for the E was noted *Star Trek* artist John Eaves, who has also been responsible for many distinctive elements of *Star Trek* productions, past and present.

With thirty years' of tradition behind the basic design of the *Enterprise*'s various forms, Herman Zimmerman admits the task was, at first, daunting.

"This is the second time I've had the opportunity to start with a blank sheet of paper on a *Star Trek* project," he explains. *"Deep Space Nine* was essentially built from the ground up. And once again, with the destruction of the *Enterprise*-D in the *Generations* film, we had the opportunity to redesign the *Enterprise.*

"We had no prior concepts to limit us, except the tradition of the *Enterprise* that we've seen for nearly thirty years. What we came up with was an *Enterprise* that owes as much to the original Matt Jefferies design as it does to Andy Probert's design for the *Enterprise*-D.

"We followed the established conceptual ideas for the *Enterprise*-D more in the interior space, in the ready room, the observation lounge, and the bridge. But the

Star Trek's makeup master, Michael Westmore, with a few of his latest creations—in Rick Berman's words: "The Borg as we've always envisioned them."

exterior of the ship is sleeker, more aerodynamic. That's not a word that is important in space, but it was always important to Gene Roddenberry. More 'for esthetics than for the necessity of streamlining."

The initial stimulus for this latest version of the *Starship Enterprise* came, as do all things in the world of movies, from the script. "We described the new *Enterprise* in some detail," Ron Moore says. "We said we want a sleeker look, with more of a muscular, almost warship kind of a look to it."

Zimmerman and his team were up to the challenge. "It's a ship that's not as comfortable in the sense of being equipped to handle families for long periods of time in space," he says. "It's basically a ship that is intended to—as much as anything else—be able to fight the Borg."

Choosing his words carefully, Zimmerman goes on to say, "We never couched the starships of the Federation as warships. Instead, they are 'research vessels with heavy armaments.' And we had to develop some new weapons in our minds to equip this ship properly for that service.

"I think the thing that will strike the *Star Trek* fan about the ship is that it's in the same vein as other starships we're familiar with, but it's more beautiful, more esthetically balanced, if you would. It's got all the same basic elements: two warp engines and a saucer section, which may need to separate at some time. That's not in any of our plans for the near future, but it's always a possibility."

The final design of the *Enterprise*-E, as shown in these pages and in *First Contact,* was the result of an ongoing

Though *First Contact* is the first all—*The Next Generation* feature, it contains several crossovers from both current *Star Trek* series, including Worf on *Deep Space Nine*'s *Starship Defiant*.

collaborative process. "We just did a number of sketches," Zimmerman explains, "and kept winnowing the sketches down, saying, 'This looks good, this doesn't. This works, that doesn't work. Let's raise the nacelles, let's lower them, let's make them smaller.' Basically, we took all the elements that we're all familiar with and tried to make the best-looking and fastest-looking ship that we could come up with."

One aspect of the *Enterprise*-E's design process was also a first for Zimmerman. Not only must the ship's design fulfill all the needs of the script and the expectations of the production team and the audience, but it had also to accommodate the demands of the unprecedented hull battle.

Zimmerman admits that after building the full-scale deflector dish on the sound stage, "We did have to make some modifications to the exterior of the model." To simplify ILM's work in matching the full-size set and the live actors to the model of the *Enterprise*, long, raised edges were added to the sides of the dish, cutting down on the amount of background that had to be digitally replaced.

But, Zimmerman points out, "Our biggest challenge with the deflector dish set was its size. We had to compromise. The set we built on stage is about fifteen percent smaller than it would be in actual size, if we were building the *Enterprise* for real." Fortunately, Zimmerman is confident that the size discrepancy will not be apparent in the final film, thanks to the judicious use of wide-angle camera lenses, which will make the set photograph much larger than it actually is.

Untold history, all-out action, and a brand-new starship . . . they're still just the tip of the iceberg of the *Star Trek* firsts in *First Contact*.

There's the matter of the film's uplifting climax, when we are witness to the historic first contact between humans and our first alien visitors, the Vulcans. The familiar-looking triangular scoutship in which they arrive bears an interesting resemblance to reports of triangular-shaped UFOs from the late twentieth century.

Then there're the crossover elements, especially meaningful in *Star Trek*'s 30th anniversary year. *Star Trek*'s favorite Klingon takes leave from *Deep Space Nine* to rejoin his former crewmates on the bridge of the new *Enterprise*. But watch for a crossover from *Voyager* as well. In fact, with Zefram Cochrane's character having been established in the *Original Series, First Contact* combines elements from all four *Star Trek* series. Another first.

The defining moment of *Star Trek*—Zefram Cochrane's, and Earth's, first contact with Vulcans.

Though studios in general, and Paramount in particular, follow the good business practice of never counting their Hortas before they're hatched, even months before *First Contact*'s release, the excitement the movie is generating on and off the lot is genuine. And at the end of principal photography, each set from the new *Starship Enterprise* was carefully disassembled and packed for storage at a special—and secret—*Star Trek* warehouse, to await the day the next *Star Trek* film begins production.

Though the movie has many secrets, the fact that there will be more *Star Trek* movies in the years to come is not one of them.

While final details will never be confirmed until the day of an official announcement, unofficially, Rick Berman says, "I think there's no doubt that the studio is interested in continuing with the production of *Star Trek* movies, and we'll be here to make them."

In other words, the best thing about *Star Trek: First Contact* is that it won't be the last.